Four Weddings and a Festival

Annie Robertson

ORION

An Orion paperback

First published in Great Britain in 2019
by Orion Books
an imprint of The Orion Publishing Group Ltd
Carmelite House, 50 Victoria Embankment
London EC4Y 0DZ

An Hachette UK Company

1 3 5 7 9 10 8 6 4 2

A CIP catalogue record for this book is
available from the British Library.

ISBN 978 1 4091 8999 2

Typeset by Input Data Services Ltd, Somerset

Printed and bound in Great Britain by Clays Ltd, Elcograf S.p.A.

MIX
Paper from
responsible sources
FSC® C104740

www.orionbooks.co.uk

For Mum & Dad, my guiding lights

I

Wednesday 25 April

If I were a character in the opening titles of a Richard Curtis film, I probably wouldn't be standing here with my hand inside a chicken. I'd be dashing around in my shabby chic Notting Hill mews house, throwing on some fabulous attire, sprinting to a wedding or getting ready for my dream job. Only I don't live in a London mews because, last I looked, I'd need several million in my account and I'm lucky if there's several hundred in there at any one time.

No, as luck would have it, I rent a house in Notting Hill's poor distant neighbour Acton, with my blissfully loved-up flatmate, who, I admit, does have a whiff of a Richard Curtis-esque 'roomie' about her. Lizzie isn't quite as revolting in her habits as the Welsh bloke from *Notting Hill*, or quite so irreverent as Scarlett from *Four Weddings*, but she certainly is untidy and exceptionally scatty. But she also happens to be one of the nicest people I've ever met, and I'm not quite sure how I'll cope when she gets married next month and finally moves in with her adorable fiancé, Jack.

'Hiya, Bea,' she calls, closing the front door of our small terraced house.

'In the kitchen!'

Lizzie appears in the doorway, holding a handful of post in one hand and a cake box in the other. Her bicycle helmet is still perched on her head, her blonde pixie hair poking out through the holes. I have serious reservations about Lizzie cycling in London; she can barely walk down the pavement without colliding into a lamppost. She's always been that way; she used to fall off the balance-beam at school with predictable and spectacular regularity.

'Bad day at work?' She gestures to the mountain of vegetables yet to be prepped for the overly ambitious dinner I'm attempting to cook for the girls. Lizzie knows that a spot of cooking is my ultimate wind-down, even if I'm not very good at it.

'Sir Hugo was in one of his moods.'

'What was it this time?' she asks, putting down the cake box and absently flicking through the post – mainly wedding RSVPs.

'The usual – things not being done that he "*absolutely remembers*" giving instructions to be carried out.'

'But I'm assuming that as his PA you made everything shipshape with a sprinkling of your Anne Hathaway magic?'

I laugh drily. If only my work life were quite as rosy as Lizzie perceives it to be. 'How was your day?'

'The usual madness.' She casts the RSVPs aside and hangs her helmet on the edge of the radiator. 'I've a new patient who thinks everyone in the room is a penguin. We spent three hours making papier-mâché fish.'

'As you do.' I hand her a potato peeler, wishing that my days were as creative and worthwhile as Lizzie's. She had her mind focused solely on becoming an art therapist since a Year Ten careers day. It's possibly the only thing Lizzie's mind has ever been focused on, apart from Jack and having babies – oh, and maybe dog agility, which was her big obsession when she was twelve. I, on the other hand, had the grand plan of becoming a famous jewellery designer, but when I realised that wasn't going to pay the bills I wound up working as an assistant to the principal of the art college Lizzie and I went to – my first job of many in the unplanned route to becoming a career PA. I long for the creative freedom Lizzie has at work, though probably not the penguin-seeing patients, and maybe a smidge less of the nine-to-five; I always fancied a more nomadic existence, unlike the one my mother had, tied to the house and her kid. 'You do remember that Hannah and Kat are coming around at seven thirty for dinner? Apparently, Kat has news.'

She doesn't say as much but it's clear from her widened eyes that she's forgotten.

'I'll have a quick shower and then I'm all yours!' she says, leaving me to peel the potatoes, and to contemplate what Kat might be going to tell us.

By the time the doorbell rings, the veggies are prepped, the chicken is in the oven, I'm out of my work clothes and Lizzie is just about decent in her pyjama bottoms though she's yet to find the corresponding top.

'I hope for your sake this is one of the girls and not

Simon,' I say, going to the door. Admittedly, it wouldn't be the first time my boyfriend has seen Lizzie without her top on. She's constantly in a state of undress, trying to figure out if an item of clothing is clean but hanging somewhere in the house other than her wardrobe, or dirty but still possibly wearable if only she could find it under the bed, over the banister or on top of the microwave.

'Simon isn't interested in my breasts – yours are far superior.' I can hear her in the front room tossing the sofa cushions about looking for her top.

With a roll of my eyes, I open the front door. 'Hi Hannah, how are you?'

'Starving!' She stoops her tall frame over my short one, giving me a light, sweaty hug then undoes her laces before placing the trainers neatly beside the front door.

'Food's almost ready, unlike Lizzie.'

'What's she lost this time?'

Lizzie pops into the hallway, triumphantly holding her top aloft. 'Found it!'

I shake my head, laughing, wondering what I'll do without her. Who will make me smile when I've had a tough day? Who will bring me breakfast in bed on a Saturday morning, or drive me crazy by trying and failing to dry several weeks' worth of laundry all at once in the tumble dryer? I should be doing something about it, advertise for someone new or put out some feelers, but I can't bring myself to. No one could ever match Lizzie.

'Why can't I have a flatmate who walks around topless?' asks Hannah, scrunching her long dark hair with a towel then wrapping it round her neck to keep warm after the eight-mile run from her work in Lincoln's Inn.

'You'll have one soon enough,' I say, leading her through into the kitchen to check on the food and to put the tartlets and salad she's brought into the fridge.

'Remy isn't really one for nudity.'

'Really? That surprises me.' Given that she's a diminutive French yoga instructor, Hannah's fiancée strikes me as exactly the sort who would parade around in the all-together at any given opportunity. 'Do Grandma and Grandpa Jones know about Remy yet?'

Hannah shakes her head.

'Do they still think she's a man?' asks Lizzie, pulling on her top in the hall.

'Yup!' I say, with a chuckle.

'Hannah, you have to tell them!'

'I know, and I will, I just haven't found the right moment.'

'I can't believe you've managed to keep your sexuality from them this long, it's not as if it's ever been a secret from anyone else.' Hannah never really came out, she just always liked girls and was never afraid of that, other than when it came to telling her grandparents.

'Remind me again why you didn't tell them at the time?' I ask, recalling the moment Hannah told them about her engagement on Skype. The connection wasn't great and they misheard 'she' for 'he', and Hannah, for some reason, chose not to correct them. At the time it was funny, now it's just kind of weird.

'Because it would have broken their hearts.'

5

'Do you really think so?' I ask. 'They never struck me as being narrow-minded.'

'Maybe not, but they're super traditional. Don't you remember, when I went to law school, they imagined my life away? They saw me marrying a *male* lawyer, giving up my career, and never wanting for anything ever again.'

'Right, but surely they'll see that you provide for yourself now, and that your love for Remy is more important than any plan they might have had for you?'

'Bea's right,' says Lizzie, now fully clothed. 'And besides, aren't they paying for the wedding?'

'Don't remind me.'

'Clock's ticking,' I say, opening the oven. 'Only two months until the big day. You need to tell them soon.'

Hannah pinches a sizzling-hot roast potato from the tray and then does the fast breathing of someone who's just put something scorching in their mouth.

'And besides, people who move to Australia in their seventies aren't the sort who would care about gay marriage.'

Hannah half chokes on the potato. 'They moved because of my grandmother's arthritis, not because they planned to surf in their old age. My grandparents aren't the laid-back type.'

I shrug uncertainly. I only have a dim recollection of her grandparents from when we stayed at their house once when we were about eleven, they let us watch *Four Weddings and a Funeral* even though it was a fifteen rating. They seemed pretty laid-back to me. That was

6

the first time we saw the film, and we fell head over heels with it, watching it over and over, each of us falling for a different character. Lizzie wanted to marry Tom, Kat drooled over Charles, Hannah was infatuated with Fi, and I always had a soft spot for David, Charlie's deaf brother. And then one night, when we were about thirteen, Lizzie made us swear a solemn oath that we'd all get married in one summer, to live out the fantasy of our own Four Weddings. Naïve as we were and fuelled by Coke and Doritos, we dutifully put our hands on hers and swore our allegiance to the plan. Thankfully, we've all grown up a bit since then.

'Do you know what Kat's news is?' I ask Hannah.

'I've no idea.'

'She hasn't said anything at all?'

'Not a peep.'

'Wow,' I say, thinking how unlike Kat it is to keep a secret. 'It must be something really big!'

We're spinning around to Kylie and setting the table in the dining room when Kat eventually arrives.

'Sorry I'm late, traffic was a nightmare.' She takes off her coat to reveal her white physio tunic, which shows off her super-toned upper arms. I've always been a bit envious of Kat's effortlessly athletic physique – one slackers like me can only dream of having. She tightens her ponytail then empties a big bag of crisps into the bowl on the table.

'It's fine, dinner's a bit behind anyway,' I say, studying her to see if there's anything to suggest what might be up. Kat and I have been best friends since primary school so if any of us is going to notice something different about her it's me. I study her face for signs – if she were sick then I'd see it in her green eyes, which always take on a grey hue when she's under the weather; changing jobs, I'd see it in her neck and shoulders, and moving house wouldn't be a big deal for Kat so it can't be that. I'm stumped.

'What?' she asks, self-consciously touching her nose and mouth to make sure she hasn't got anything gross on either. It's then I realise I'm not the only one staring at her. All three of us have narrowed our eyes, scrutinising her for clues as to what the news might be.

'Nothing,' Hannah and I say in unison, trying to hide our curiosity by busying ourselves with laying the table.

'Lizzie?' Kat asks, knowing that Liz will definitely blab.

'They're trying to figure out what your "big news" is.'

Kat smiles wryly, and pops a crisp into her mouth. 'You can have one guess each.'

We pause our table preparations. Hannah, ever the analyst, looks her up and down before saying, 'You're moving to New Zealand.'

It's not such a long shot; Kat's wanted to spend time in New Zealand practising physiotherapy since her geography teacher, Mr Carter, whom she had a massive crush on, taught her about its hot springs and bubbling mud pools. She's always been one for adventures – a gap year in Thailand, physio placements in America and

South Africa, and holidays twice a year. I never seem to have the money to do the same, even though I'd love to, and it doesn't help that Simon's idea of a big adventure is a long weekend in Cornwall. But I hope desperately Hannah isn't correct. The prospect of losing both my flatmate and my best friend at the same time would be too much to bear.

'Nope!' she says. I let out a sigh of relief.

'You've been given a promotion,' says Lizzie.

Kat laughs. 'Not likely!'

'True,' says Hannah.

'Oi!' says Kat, casting Hannah pretend daggers, and reaching for another crisp.

It's then that I see it — the light catches her hand, revealing the unmistakable sparkle of a diamond.

'Henry asked you to marry him,' I say, hoping that my voice doesn't convey the sinking feeling in my stomach that all three of my closest friends are now settling down. I don't understand how it is that they're all so established in what they do and in their relationships. I'm still floundering, uncertain about the whole idea of marriage, and looking for the thing that enables me to have the life I've always dreamt of — a creative job, and the chance to travel the world.

Hannah and Lizzie's eyes dart expectantly between Kat and me, waiting for her to confirm one way or another. The pause feels unbearably long, and then, suddenly, Kat's face breaks into an enormous smile and she squeals, holding up her hand for us all to see the ring.

'Oh my God,' Lizzie shrieks, rushing over to hug her.

'Congratulations, Kat,' says Hannah, hugging her too. 'Such great news. Have you settled on a date?'

'We thought sooner rather than later, so we've decided on September.'

'September?' says Hannah. 'How can you possibly arrange a wedding in less than five months?'

'Because Kat isn't as OCD as you,' says Lizzie, baiting her mercilessly.

'Hah–bloody–ha!' says Hannah, screwing her face up at Lizzie

I'm still standing, rooted to the floor in shock, when Kat turns to me. My response is too late to pull off genuine excitement, and I can't conceal the look of astonishment on my face; I fail to know how to react, and I'm angry with myself for spoiling my best friend's moment.

Kat crosses to me. 'Don't worry, Bea. Henry may be my husband but you'll always be my best friend.'

Immediately I can feel tears welling, and I pull her close.

'I'm happy for you,' I whisper, through my snuffles.

She pulls away to scrutinise my face.

'I am, I promise!' I laugh, emotionally. 'It's just a bit of a shock.'

Kat laughs too. 'Imagine how shocked I was! I'm not sure I ever expected Henry to be *the one*.'

'But he is?'

Even though I'm not really a believer in 'the one', I still want to be certain my dearest friend has made the right decision and hasn't just been caught up in the moment. When Lizzie introduced them two years ago at a drunken Christmas do at the hospital where both Lizzie and Henry work, it never occurred to me that the slightly bombastic, South African psychiatrist would turn out to be the person with whom Kat would spend the rest of her life. He's all nit-picky and contrary, and she's so laissez-faire. I can't pretend to understand the attraction.

'He is,' she says, the certainty in her eyes radiating out. 'Even if he is madder than most of his patients!'

'Well, I can't argue with that!' I say, laughing through my tears.

We embrace again, me holding her until I'm certain she can feel the happiness I was unable to express in words.

'Oh my God,' says Lizzie, her eyes lighting up. I recognise the look, it's the one that appears when she's cooking up some crazy plan or other. She claps her hands excitedly and in that moment I know exactly where her mind has wandered. 'Do you remember when we were thirteen . . .?'

Yup, I think. *She's going there.*

'And we made the pact for all of us to marry in the same summer . . .?'

She can't really think any of us will get on board with this as grown, responsible adults.

'Oh yeah!' says Kat, her eyes dancing up with delight.

'And three of us are engaged, which means . . .' Hannah turns to me.

Have they lost their minds? We're thirty, not thirteen.

'If Simon proposes, it could be *four* weddings in one summer!' squeals Lizzie.

I smear away the last of my tears, laughing at their craziness.

'Oh my goodness, what an amazing thought!' shrieks Kat. She reaches out a hand to me, squeezing my arm. 'Bea you're so going to be next. We have to get Simon to hurry up and propose so that we can have our Four Weddings!'

'Guys, let's not get carried away,' I say, noticing an alarmingly acrid smell coming from the kitchen. Leaving the girls for a moment, I open the oven door and am greeted by a waft of smoke and a shrivelled, charred chicken. *I'm so not cut out for domestic bliss.*

As I attempt to rescue the chicken, I try to imagine my wedding to Simon – really visualise it, with him in a grey morning suit and his mother in a hideous hat, wiping an elegant tear from her eye, and the girls grinning at me as I proceed down the aisle in a ludicrous meringue of a dress – but I can't. It isn't a real image; it's a parody of a Richard Curtis wedding. In fact, I can't imagine marrying Simon at all.

'You okay?' Hannah is leaning against the doorway, watching me with concern.

Hannah is the only one who has any inkling about my doubts about Simon. Kat has been so caught up with Henry recently that there hasn't been an opportunity to chat, and Lizzie is in her own loved-up little world. Hannah knows that I've begun to question whether part of the reason I've been hanging on to Simon is because of his slightly Hugh Grant-ish charm. Because recently Si's old-world appeal has begun to wear a bit thin, and, if I'm perfectly honest, the spark we used to have has fizzled to a companionable glow. I've kept telling myself that's just what happens in long-term relationships – that it's better than falling in and out of love with unsuitable men, chasing 'the one', like my mum did.

'I'm fine,' I say, shaking off my doubts. 'Better than the chicken, anyway.' I hand her the salad to put on the table. 'Come on, let's eat!'

With the starter in place and everyone seated, Lizzie raises her glass. 'A toast,' she says. 'To Kat and Henry.'

'To Kat and Henry,' we chorus, clinking our glasses together.

'And to Simon proposing,' says Kat, with a glint in her eye. 'And our Four Weddings Summer!'

'Our Four Weddings Summer!' I say with everyone else, though my mind is swimming with the prospect of Simon jumping on board the plan and proposing. How would I ever turn him down without breaking his heart, and bursting my friends' Four Weddings bubble in the process?

2

It's mid-morning, and despite having drunk a litre of water and an unspeakably revolting 'revitaliser shot' from the local juice bar, my head is still foggy from last night. After the initial shock of Kat's news, the evening turned out to be fun enough, with the girls plotting and scheming as we sewed bunting for Lizzie's wedding. We ate the 'caramelised' chicken, drank a couple of bottles of wine, and were all tucked up in bed before midnight. And yet still I woke this morning feeling as if a team of microscopic road workers had set to work on me overnight – one with a pneumatic drill in my left temple, a second having stripped the surface of my tongue and replaced it with gravel, and a third pouring hot tar over my eyes.

'You all right, Bea?' asks Bev, catching me staring out of the window to Berkeley Square below.

'Huh?' I say, unable to break my gaze. I've been focused on the same bloke on a bench drinking a coffee for ages.

'You seem a bit . . . away with the fairies.'

I turn my gaze towards her, at her desk opposite mine. 'Do I?'

She nods. 'Something the matter?'

Bev, Sir Hugo's diary secretary, is a little older than me, a mum of two teenage girls. Sometimes I wonder if she thinks of me as her third.

I exhale long and loud and tell her about the 'Four Weddings' plan, trying to sound breezy about Kat's engagement – but my scepticism is plainly written on my face.

'Are you feeling left behind?'

'It's not that, exactly. I . . .'

I'd like to tell her that, unlike the girls, I don't dream of settling down, that after a whole night of discussing the Four Weddings plan I'm terrified that neither marriage nor Simon is right for me, and that I've been quietly thinking of ways to break up gently with Simon ever since I went to bed last night. But I can't tell her that because Simon is Sir Hugo's son and also the vice-president of the company, so it's not exactly appropriate. I'm about to fudge some vague response about the prospect of feeling lonely without Kat and Lizzie in my day-to-day life when Sir Hugo steps out of his office.

'Bea, did you get hold of the Matisse curator?' Sir Hugo's voice is disconcertingly large, as is he. You don't get to be a world leader in public relations by being a shrinking violet.

Despite my brain fog I know that Hugo hasn't asked me to contact any curator but, rather than tell him so and bear the brunt of his temper, I instead think on my feet. 'He's out of the country. His assistant has left him a message to call me.'

'Fine. Anything else I need to know?'

'I found the film for the windows to protect your artwork.' *This* is the job he asked me to do this morning, which he's confused with the curator.

'Very good. Talk to Lady Annabel about having the work done at the house,' he says, and returns to his office.

'I'm sure once the waters have settled everything will be clearer,' says Bev.

'I hope so,' I say, absently sketching an earring on my notebook. Doodling jewellery designs always takes my mind off things. When I was a kid and my parents were getting divorced I used to escape into my imagination by drawing sparkling necklaces for princesses, with shiny sequins stuck on as jewels, and elaborate rings made from tin foil and bits of wool that princes would give to their one true love. I was safe in that place, secure in my imagination, free of bickering parents and slamming doors. The design I'm creating now is a dangling feather of coloured beads and I momentarily stop worrying about how to break up with Simon, and instead I'm transported back to that same safe place of endless stories and imagination.

'What's this?' asks a voice, sometime later, when I'm fully absorbed in my drawing. It takes me a moment to re-join the external world of the office and Simon, who is standing at my shoulder.

'Nothing!' I rapidly close the book and swing my chair round to face him. His fresh face looks particularly boyish today.

He kisses me square on the mouth, something I've

always wished he wouldn't do at work. When we first started dating and he'd kiss me in the office, I was embarrassed that people might think I was taking liberties because I was seeing the boss's son. Four years on it still makes me cringe. 'It didn't look like nothing.'

'Well, it was.' I've no idea why I'm hiding it from him – it's not as if he'd care about me skiving for five minutes – but I don't want him just to dismiss it as a 'pretty doodle'.

For a second he looks at me, perplexed, then shakes away whatever thought he was having. Simon rarely dwells on anything for long, at the beginning of our relationship the girls used to tease me by referring to him as Simple Simon, I hate to say it but it kind of suits him.

'What's going on?' I ask, swinging in my chair.

'I just popped by to see how you're doing. Everything okay?'

'Sure,' I shrug, trying to block the thoughts which are now screaming – *he isn't right for you, break it off, stop stringing him along* – because the last thing I want is for him to see it in my eyes before I've spoken to him. 'Why wouldn't it be?'

Again he looks at me, foxed by my clipped manner. He narrows his eyes. 'You're remembering our date tonight?'

'Thursday night. Same as every week.'

'Rules, seven thirty?'

'Absolutely.'

'I can't wait,' he says, smiling at me with a tenderness that is like a dagger to my heart.

'Me too,' I say, and a part of me means it. For all I don't want to marry him, and for all I wish Simon were a little more spontaneous and exciting, there's no mistaking the fact that he's a really good guy, someone I've spent four years of my life with, someone I know absolutely adores me. Someone I really, really don't want to hurt.

He kisses me lovingly on the lips and for once I don't hurry him away. It's as if I'm trying to store the feeling in my memory bank, stashing it away for a rainy day.

'You know it's better you let him go now rather than later,' says Bev, once Simon is in his father's office.

I shoot her a look that says, *I've no idea what you're talking about.*

'It will hurt him more in the long run if you try to hide it than if you're up front and honest now.'

'Is it really that obvious?' I ask, knowing she's right, knowing it's best I tell him tonight.

''Fraid so,' says Bev, with a motherliness that makes me want to burst into tears.

The moment I see Simon waiting for me outside the restaurant, I feel twice as horrible about my plan to break up with him. My day was completely unproductive, given all I could think about was how to let him down without breaking his heart.

'Early, as ever,' I say, trying to sound light.

I can't remember an occasion when Simon arrived after me. Tardiness isn't a concept he's familiar with, which always makes me feel a little bit guilty if I'm late. Not that he would ever want me to feel bad; it's part of his gentleman's approach to life, that a lady should never be left standing on her own. When we first met it was one of the things that I found charming about him, but now I find it a little jarring, slightly out of touch with the world.

'You look beautiful,' he says, kissing me lightly on the lips.

'And you look very dapper.'

Not helpful, Bea. But it's true, he does look dapper, Simon is always well turned-out. During the week he wears a three-piece suit and at weekends jeans and a sharp shirt with brogues. He only ever wears cashmere sweaters and his socks never have holes in them. Many women would die for a man who prides himself on his appearance but the trouble is I'd prefer someone who'd just throw on an old pair of jeans and a rugby shirt, so that I might be able to relax too.

'Shall we go in?' he asks, opening the door for me, oblivious to what I'm about to tell him.

Rules is Simon's favourite restaurant. It's traditional and old-fashioned but also incredibly warm with its brilliant red banquettes, crisp white linen and walls covered in original drawings, paintings and cartoons. Over the years, food has been the glue to our relationship. Both of us could dine out every night of the week with three courses at each sitting without ever tiring, and Rules never leaves you feeling hungry.

'Let's have a splurge,' he says, when we're sitting at a cosy table for two near the back. He rubs his hands together, his eyes shining at the thought of it.

My stomach churns nervously.

'In celebration of us!' He reaches over to take my hand and my heart fills with guilt.

I remove my hand from his under the pretext of picking up the menu. 'What are you going to have?'

'Always the broth, then steak and kidney pudding, and the steamed syrup sponge for dessert.'

'So a nice light option then!'

He laughs, watching me tenderly; I glance away.

'What will you have?'

Despite my turning stomach I still feel like eating. 'Pear and walnut salad, lamb shoulder, and pistachio and blackberry tart.'

'Delightful, just like you.'

I fiddle with the glassware, thinking about how to plant the seed of us breaking up. But just as I'm about to say something the waiter arrives, and the moment is lost.

'How was your day?' Simon asks once the order has been taken.

'Unproductive.'

'Why so?'

'I've been sort of . . . distracted.'

'Anything I can help with?' he asks, which is just like him, caring to the last.

Tell him, Bea, tell him you want to break up. 'Kat and Henry are engaged,' I say, unintentionally. *That's not telling him!*

I wonder if he hasn't quite heard me because it takes him a moment to respond. He looks a little crestfallen, deflated even, as if he's been robbed of Kat, which makes no sense at all.

'Well, that's wonderful news,' he says, throwing back a glass of water as if it were something stronger. 'We should toast to their happiness.'

He beckons the waiter and requests two glasses of champagne.

'But that's not all that was distracting me,' I continue. *Come on, Bea. You can do it.* 'They're getting married in September.' *Again, so not telling him.*

'Splendid, though I can see that would be distract-ing – lots to help organise and not much time.' There's something about his tone that isn't quite right, but I can't figure out what it is.

'Right, and then Lizzie reminded us of a pact we made when we were teenagers that we'd all get married in one summer.' I roll my eyes heavily in a *worst idea ever* sort of way, praying he won't pounce on the idea.

'Good Lord, what a prospect! Would there have to be a funeral too?' We laugh, Simon heartedly, me slightly sadly. I'm reminded of how many laughs we've had over the years, because from time to time Simon really does make me chuckle, and I'm sorry at the prospect of giving that up. 'Now I think about it, my grandfather's been looking a bit peaky recently!'

For all his good humour there's something about it in this moment that sounds like a deflection, as if he's as shaken by the prospect of four weddings as I am. It's a bit of a relief when the food arrives and we've something else to talk about.

'The broth is sensational,' says Simon, somewhat over-zealously.

'Mmm, the salad is too.'

There's a pause between us; I can hear him slurping. 'You can always bank on Rules,' he says.

'Yes,' I say, wondering what he's thinking.

Usually at dinner Simon is swooning over me and doing his best to ensure there are no lulls in conversation but currently he only has eyes for his food. It's as if he's trying to eat and get out as quick as is humanly possible. And then it hits me: perhaps Simon doesn't want to marry *me*. Perhaps all these months that I've been sensing things aren't right between us, he's been feeling the same way. Perhaps he's also having doubts about our future.

'I told the girls not to get their hopes up, about the four weddings thing,' I say, tentatively testing my theory.

'Yes, good plan.' He barely looks up from his plate.

'Because I'm not sure we're on that page yet, right?' I say, carefully.

'Absolutely, couldn't agree more,' he says, brisk in his delivery.

So that's that. He feels the same way I do. But probably best not to break up tonight, let it happen when the moment's right, when we're both ready.

Although it's what I want, it's still a shock, and I feel an even deeper pang of sadness for all we'd be losing. Four years is a long time to spend with someone, learning all their little foibles (Simon always has to wear socks in bed even in a heatwave) and seeing them through highs and lows. Lady Annabel had breast cancer last year, which floored the whole family. I hope, at the very least, we'll be able to remain friends.

After we've worked our way uncomfortably through the main course and our plates have been cleared, the waiter appears and asks theatrically if we're ready for dessert.

Simon clears his throat and says, rather grandly, like his father, 'Actually there's been a change of plan. We'll have to renege on dessert this time.'

Really, when did we ever pass on pudding?

'Very good, sir.'

'May we have our coats?'

'Of course.'

As the waiter helps me with my jacket, Simon says, 'Why don't you wait outside while I settle up?'

'Sure,' I reply, thankful for the chance to catch a breath of fresh air, even if I am disappointed to miss out on a sweet.

I'm contemplating Simon's feelings about us when I catch sight of him through the restaurant window. He's engaged in a discussion with the waiter, which seems more animated than one would expect for a simple bill transaction. Perhaps there's a problem with the card – or, more probably, the realisation that it's time to call things off between us has sent him into a bit of a spin. It's not ideal, but I'm relieved we'll be parting on mutual terms, rather than one of us being left heartbroken.

3

It's just like Lizzie to choose to have her hen night *with* her fiancé – I swear it's as if one would die without the other. It's a miracle they've survived the last year, they've barely seen each other with Jack off touring the country and recording his band's album in some farm-house in Dorset. In fairness, she had planned a girls' only night but when the band, Carburetor, landed a gig at the Roundhouse there was no way on this earth she was going to miss it.

'Isn't this the greatest night ever? I'm so proud of him,' she says, between sucking on a whisky and Coke, Lizzie's tipple of choice. In our final years at school Lizzie used to fill a hipflask with whisky from her father's drinks cabinet then sneak out to the barn where we'd mix it with Coke and drink it from mugs behind the hay bales. Hannah was always really nervous about getting caught, Kat couldn't care less, and I giggled myself silly. Nothing much has changed.

'It is pretty cool,' I say, taking in the incredible venue with its cast-iron columns supporting the domed roof.

It's early evening and the doors aren't yet open. The band are doing their sound check, Jack tweaking his drum kit. Lizzie and I are sitting in the balcony with our feet on the backs of the chairs in front.

She examines the 'Access All Areas' pass hanging round her neck and beams. 'Can you be a groupie if you're engaged to one of the band?'

'Not sure. Maybe as wife-to-be you're considered crew. The rest of us get to be the groupies.'

I wave to Kat who has just arrived.

'Look at you, Mrs Jack-to-be,' she says, hugging Lizzie. She takes in the venue and the band up onstage. 'This really is your nirvana, isn't it?'

'The only thing closer would be if I were marrying Kurt Cobain himself!'

Kat laughs and rubs Lizzie's arm affectionately, probably thinking, as I am, about Lizzie's Kurt Cobain obsession as a teenager. 'I think Jack has a kind of Kurt Cobain look about him.'

'Do you really? I've thought it myself, but—'

Lizzie's train of thought is broken by Jack jumping off the stage, his tall, lean figure winding up to the balcony.

'Hi,' he says, stooping to lovingly kiss Lizzie. She strokes his beard and gazes into his light blue eyes as if they've been apart for weeks, and sweeps his scruffy blond hair back off his face.

'How's it going down there?' I ask, when they've stopped mooning. 'Everything coming together?'

'Yeah, Bea, it's all good,' he says, sounding as he always does – as if he's smoked a dozen spliffs.

'Simon mentioned you're having your stag do next weekend.'

25

'It's gonna be great,' he says, bobbing his head, happy to let a long pause hang in the air.

'I can't really imagine Simon in a beer bath!' I say.

'You have to take photos,' says Kat. 'The idea of Henry up to his waist in beer is too good to be true.'

Jack, Simon and Henry's friendship is an unlikely one. Simon as old-fashioned and straight as you get, Henry always a ball of fiery energy and Jack, as laid-back a person as I've ever known. But, one way or another, because of us girls, they've forged an alliance of their own. The prospect of them all hanging out with Jack's band mates at a 'beer spa' cracks me up – or it would, if my stomach didn't clench with guilt every time I think about Simon.

'Well, I'd better get back to it. Coming?' he asks Lizzie, reaching for her hand.

They head off together, their arms wrapped tightly around each other as they walk.

'They really are love's young dream,' says Kat.

'Sickening, isn't it?'

'I've never known two people more in love.'

I turn to her. 'Not even you and Henry?'

Kat chuckles. 'I think it's fair to say we aren't so de-monstrative as Lizzie and Jack.'

'I'm not sure there's any couple out there as outwardly affectionate as those two.' Jack and Lizzie have their arms locked round each other's waists, walking around the stage, Jack pointing out all the technical stuff. 'It's as if they're one person.'

'Like you and Simon.'

Kat's comment stops me short, the reality of the demise of our relationship suddenly hitting home.

'Bea?' she asks, when I don't respond.

I stare straight ahead at the stage. 'I think we're about to break up.'

'Yeah, right!'

'I'm serious,' I say, turning towards her, my eyes confirming it's true.

She looks at me as if I've lost my mind. 'Simon adores you, almost as much as Lizzie adores Jack!'

'That's what I thought, but when I told him the other night about how Lizzie had cooked up the idea of a Four Weddings summer . . .' I tail off, lost in the memory of telling him.

'And?'

'And he couldn't get out of the restaurant fast enough.'

Kat furrows her brow. 'That doesn't sound like him. I thought he'd have jumped at the chance of proposing.'

'Apparently not!'

'How does that feel?'

I pause, not wanting to betray Simon by telling Kat I had planned to break up with him first. 'Honestly?'

'Honestly.'

'I feel a bit relieved.'

This time it's Kat's turn to stop short, trying to make sense of what I've just told her. Simon and I have been dating the longest out of all of us – we met when I started working for Sir Hugo – he's become part of the group. It wouldn't be just my loss, it would be theirs too.

'I just assumed, after all this time, that's the direction you were headed in.'

'Right,' I nod. 'Maybe I did too, or maybe I hadn't given it much thought, but when Lizzie mentioned the Four Weddings idea I just saw it, clear as day. Simon and marriage aren't for me.'

Kat laughs. 'Are you the Charles of this group?'

I laugh too. 'Do you remember how much of a crush you had on Hugh Grant in *Four Weddings*?'

'I'd still swap Henry for Hugh, any day of the week!'

'I believe it! Though funnily enough I don't think Lizzie would swap Jack for Kurt, even if he wasn't dead.'

Kat glances over to the two of them now sitting on the edge of the stage, Lizzie's head on Jack's shoulder. 'You know, you don't have to marry Simon. You could do what Charles and Carrie did and agree not to marry.'

'I'm pretty confident that wouldn't sit comfortably with Simon; he's more the traditional, marrying type.'

'Yes, I suppose it would mean him giving up on his dream of a wedding at St Paul's Cathedral.'

'With the reception at the palace!'

Kat laughs for a moment until it becomes clear that I'm not laughing, that I'm actually feeling quite low about it all.

'Do you really feel it's right for both of you – to end it?'

'It breaks my heart to say it but, yes. As much as I respect him, as much as I hope we can remain friends, the thing that should be there, isn't.'

'What thing?'

'You know,' I say, surprised that she's asking. Her expression is blank. 'The spark. The chemistry. The thing that no one else sees but you.'

'Right, of course,' says Kat, nodding quietly. 'So, what are you going to do about it?'

'Hope he ends things first?'

Our conversation is cut short by the arrival of Hannah and Remy, who blends in perfectly in her asymmetric linen tunic and leggings, her hair in a bun with spiky ends, unlike Hannah, who couldn't look more out of place if she tried. She's got her stiff lawyer suit on and her hair is scraped tightly off her face. Lizzie runs up to greet them.

'How are you?' she asks, kissing Remy twice on her flawless cheeks but Remy goes for a third and they end up kissing on the lips. Lizzie turns crimson.

'Dreadful,' says Hannah.

'What's up?' I ask.

'It is nothing,' says Remy, in her thick French accent. She reaches for Hannah's hand, her dark eyes looking lovingly at her fiancée. 'Hannah worries too much.'

'She's good at that!' I say, remembering how much time Hannah spent chewing her nails over exams.

'If my grandparents still not knowing about you,' Hannah says to Remy, 'and the wedding photographer pulling out at the last moment is your idea of nothing, then it's nothing!'

'You can have our photographer's number, he's amazing,' says Lizzie, brightly. 'He knows one of your yoga clients,' she says to Remy. 'That's how I got his details, when I was at one of your classes. He's really brilliant, just sometimes a little hard to pin down.'

'I'll take anyone at this stage,' says Hannah. 'Who wants a drink?'

Lizzie's hand shoots straight up in the air. 'Definitely me!'

With a laugh I say, 'I could use one too.'

I feel my phone vibrate in my pocket as Hannah and Remy head off to the bar. It's Simon.

Any chance you could pop round later? There's something we need to talk about.

'What's up? asks Kat. My face must give away my feeling of trepidation.

'Looks like he's going to be the one to break up with me,' I say, handing my phone to her.

She puts an arm around me and pulls me in. 'Guess it's time you faced the music.'

I ducked out early from the hen night, telling Lizzie I was too exhausted to be much fun, but that I'd see her at home. She was so absorbed in the set that it was easy not to tell her about Simon, which I knew would spoil her night more than me leaving early.

The air is surprisingly warm for April when I leave Victoria Station. It transports me back to an evening three summers ago when Simon and I had been to a concert at Kenwood House after which we'd sauntered back to his place from the Tube. My feet were aching from a new pair of shoes and rather than have me go barefoot Simon had given me a piggyback. We were tipsy and full of giggles and in love. It was one of those evenings where the world seemed perfect in every way. As I cross the road towards Eaton Square I wonder how all of that slipped away without us noticing.

By the time I turn onto his cobbled street, where he lives with his siblings in the mews at the back of his father's house, I've bolstered myself for what is to come.

'Better that it's mutual,' I say to myself before ringing the bell.

Sophie, his eighteen-year-old sister, answers.

'Hi, Bea!'

'Hi, Sophie.' As she lets me in it hits me that I won't just be losing Simon but his siblings too, who've welcomed me into their home these last few years without protest. I've seen Sophie transform from a gawky teenager into a beautiful woman, and Ed change from a lazy student to a busy professional. 'How are you?'

'Good. I'm good,' she says.

Why does she sound nervous? Has Simon told her what's about to happen?

'Let me take your coat.'

'I'll keep it on.'

'Don't be silly!' she says, removing it for me. I figure she's trying to make me feel better about the inevitable. 'Simon's upstairs.'

As I climb the stairs I'm aware that Sophie's watching me from below. I give her a little wave and she dashes away with a giggle.

Weird.

At the top of the stairs I call out for Simon.

'In my bedroom,' he calls back.

I take a deep breath, steadying myself for what is to come. I adopt a solemn demeanour. But what I see when I enter the room changes everything.

'I was worried you wouldn't come,' he says.

There's a long pause as I fully take in the scene, my eyes widening in horror. His room is festooned with candles and more roses than I've ever seen in my life. Then Simon removes a small box from his pocket and starts to awkwardly get down on bended knee.

'Oh fuck!' I whisper.

'Beatrice Jennifer Henshaw,' he says, his voice grave and sincere. 'Will you marry me?'

My mind should be a whirl of activity and my emotions running riot but they're not, it's almost as if both have stopped working all together. All I can do is stare.

After what must have been thirty seconds at least, Simon says, 'Will you?'

His words give me a jump start and I feel my heart begin to race.

'I . . .'

'Yes?' he asks, eagerly.

'I thought you were breaking up with me,' I blurt.

His puppyish expression falters.

'Why would you think that?' he asks, still down on one knee. I crouch down beside him in a kind of awkward squat.

'The other night at Rules, when I mentioned Lizzie's

Four Weddings plan, you pretty much bolted from the restaurant.'

It surprises me when he laughs, relaxing enough to sit rather than kneel.

'That's because I was going to propose during dessert. I had it all planned out, the waiter was going to bring champagne and a cake after I'd popped the question. But when you mentioned Lizzie's plan I thought you'd think I was asking because of that, not because I've been thinking since last summer about proposing to the girl I love.'

Oh God, that makes perfect sense. How could I have got it so wrong?

'And afterwards, when you were paying the bill, you had to explain to the waiter what had happened?'

'He was quite animated about it all, and sorry that things hadn't worked out.'

I laugh dismally. 'I thought you were in a flap because you'd realised you were having doubts about us.'

He turns to me, his eyes burning with sincerity. 'I could never have doubts about us; you mean everything to me.'

I inhale sharply. *How the hell do I back out of this one?*

Just then there's a knock at the door.

'What is it?' Simon calls.

'What did she say? Can I come in?' Sophie's face pops round the door. She is beside herself with excitement and I feel horrible when the penny drops and her smile fades.

'Maybe give us a little more time,' I say, trying to

sound encouraging, even though I know it's only providing false hope.

'Okay,' she whispers, sneaking away.

'I guess "us" isn't just us,' I say. *Which makes this ten times harder.*

'Sophie and Ed adore you too, as do Mum and Dad.'

It's then I realise that if I say no to Simon, work will become unbelievably difficult. How could I possibly face Sir Hugo, who's always been so kind to me, after turning down his son? And how could I continue to work with Si after breaking his heart?

'But my siblings shouldn't influence your decision. All that really matters is you and me.'

I've no idea how to make this easy on him.

'The trouble is,' I say, taking his hand. 'I'm just not sure I'm the marrying sort.'

Simon laughs, as if I'm joking.

'I'm serious. My dad left us when I was five. I didn't have a positive male role model. I grew up seeing my mother doing everything on her own, and coping just fine without a husband.'

'But think how much easier it would have been for her if she'd had the support of a good husband. And I'd be a good husband to you, Bea. You wouldn't want for anything.'

I look into his eyes, which are brimming with sincerity. I can't deny it, there is a part of me that thinks it would be easy to say yes. Because if anyone would be a good husband, it's Simon. His parents would help us buy a house; we'd throw dinner parties for his university

34

friends; we'd end up with a brood of angel-faced children and a clutch of spaniels, even better behaved than the kids. But then a little voice at the back of my head reminds me about my dream of being a jewellery designer and not being tied to one place.

'I know that, I do,' I say, squeezing his hand.

'But?' he asks, sensing the inevitable.

'But I don't think it's the life I want. I want more than stability, I want a creative life, a life of freedom, one that doesn't involve dressing for society dinners and writing endless thank you cards.'

He looks at the ring in the box that he's still clasping.

Go easy, Bea.

'I'm so sorry, Simon, but I think the answer is no.'

In our four years together I've never seen Simon cry, not even when his mother was diagnosed with breast cancer, but now his eyes flood with tears.

God, this is horrible.

'I'm so very sorry.' My words are barely audible. 'But I think it's right, for both of us.'

Perhaps. Or maybe I'm making the worst decision of my life.

4

There were endless things to say after Simon and I broke-up, but we decided not to drag it all out there and then, agreeing it was best we both slept on it and talked things through when the time felt right. My plan was to take the Tube straight home but in the end I found myself walking through the park towards Notting Hill, which made me think of all the times I forced Simon to watch the movie with me, and how he always pretended to enjoy it just as much as the first time we watched it together. And then, one way or another, I kept on walking towards Holland Park, Shepherd's Bush and then Acton. By the time I arrived back at the house my feet were aching, which somehow made the pain in my heart more tolerable.

Lizzie was asleep when I got in, and up and out before me, so I didn't have the chance to tell her what had happened, though even if she had been around I'm not sure I would have mentioned it, taking time to process the decision on my own first felt the right thing to do.

This morning I tidied the house from top to bottom – Lizzie's wedding paraphernalia has started to take over the place – only stopping to check my phone. Whenever it pinged or rang I immediately checked to see if it was Simon, but he didn't call, choosing, like me I guess, to lick his wounds alone. But there was only really one person I needed to talk to: my mother's aunt, Great-Aunt Jane. As soon as I rang to ask if I could come over in the evening, she instantly knew that something was wrong – but rather than tell her then and there, I told her we'd discuss it tonight.

After that I filled my afternoon by sketching necklaces in front of Richard Curtis films, an old copy of the *National Geographic* on the sofa open at an article about traditional Native American weaving and beadwork. Before I knew it, time had got away with me, and I needed to get ready to go out.

'What's happened?' asks Aunt Jane, opening the door to her pied-à-terre in Chelsea. Aunt Jane's never been one for small talk.

'Simon proposed,' I say, taking off my coat, which she hangs in the tiny entrance hall, every inch of which is covered in artwork and artefacts from all over the world. I've known this flat since I was very young, when Aunt Jane was still working full-time at her auction house in Lots Road, but I still find things that surprise me.

'And?'

'I said no.'

'Good decision!' she says, bluntly, and I laugh. 'He was far too conventional for you.'

There's no one in the world I trust more to get straight

to the point than Aunt Jane. When we were teenagers, and Mum was at work, the girls and I used to pile round to her house in Chippenham – her old family home that she'd inherited from her mother, and which she referred to as 'her retirement project'. Not that Aunt Jane ever fully retired. Even now, in her seventies, she's still got a hand in the business. In the kitchen, round an old oak table, she'd offer us candid advice and the best hot chocolate known to man, I'm convinced she used to put a dash of rum in it, even when we were only thirteen. Aunt Jane may be my great-aunt but for years she's been like a surrogate aunt to the others.

I follow her tall figure through to her elegant living room, an homage to everything mid-twentieth century, where she immediately pours me a large gin and tonic.

'It's true. He's very nice and very rich but all the money in the world can't make up for a lack of zing.'

She gestures for me to relax on the sofa while she heads into the galley kitchen for some nibbles. A cool spring breeze blows gently through the window, bringing with it the smell of the first cut grass of the season from the public garden beyond. As I wait for Aunt Jane a photo catches my eye on her 1950s record-player cabinet. It's of Hannah, Kat, Lizzie and me, sitting on her sofa, back when we were fifteen or sixteen. I guess it was taken during a school holiday when Aunt Jane used to let us crash there for days on end. We loved the fact she allowed us to sit out in the garden until all hours of the morning, chatting about films and music and what our futures might hold, and forgetting for a while about exams and body image and boys.

'Where did you find that photo?' I call through to the kitchen.

Aunt Jane returns with a tray of nibbles, a small floral apron wrapped round her long, belted skirt.

'Isn't it super?' she says, placing the tray on the table and rolling up the sleeves of her cream blouse. 'I was having a clear out and found it in a box. You all look so youthful, so untouched by the world.'

'At the time we felt we knew it all.'

She laughs, lightly, her emerald eyes dancing. 'Do you remember when Lizzie thought she was pregnant because she'd sat on a toilet seat with the lid up?'

'Oh yeah! That was out there, even by her standards.'

'There was always some drama unfolding.'

'I guess some things never change,' I say, distantly, my mind wandering to Simon.

Aunt Jane sits down beside me offering me an olive on a cocktail stick. 'You've done the right thing, Bea.'

'Then why do I feel so awful?'

'Because you've a good heart, and the last thing you want is for someone you care deeply for to be hurting.'

'Maybe,' I say, biting the olive from its stick. 'I wonder what Mum would have to say.'

'I expect she'd tell you you've made a mistake, but then, how much should you trust the advice of a woman who's notoriously bad at finding husbands?'

'Aunt Jane! You can't say that,' I say, smiling.

'Why not? It's the truth, isn't it?'

I shake my head with a laugh.

My mother married my father after a whirlwind romance when she was only twenty-one. The marriage came crashing down seven years later when she discovered he'd been seeing another woman from almost the moment she became pregnant with me. She was forced to sell up the nice family house, move into a two-up two-down on an estate, and take a job at Tesco's, which I guess is what happens when you get married before you've figured out what to do with your life. Just after I left home she married someone else, moving to Majorca to be with him; turned out he was a cheating scumbag too. He left her after a couple of years for someone else, but she got to keep their villa and some cash, so at least something good came of it. Now she lives with her dogs in the sunshine, occasionally dating holidaying Brits, but mostly she keeps herself to herself.

'If Simon walked through that door right now and proposed for a second time, would you say yes?'

'No.' It surprises me just how quickly I reply.

'So, there's your answer.'

'You're right, I know you're right,' I say, leaning in to examine the olives. 'It's just super confusing with everyone around me getting married. Even Kat's engaged. Did I tell you?' Aunt Jane shakes her head. 'Apparently, Henry is "the one" after all.'

'You don't sound convinced.'

I inhale, thinking while I munch on an olive. 'Maybe it's more I'm unconvinced about the idea of "the one",'

I say, parking my uncertainty about Kat and Henry. 'Do you believe in the one?'

Aunt Jane shrugs lightly, as if it's not something she's given much thought to. 'Maybe there was someone once, but that was many moons ago.'

This comes as a surprise to me; in all the time I've known Aunt Jane, I've never known her date anyone or heard mention of someone from her past. She's always seemed perfectly content on her own, happy to be 'a confirmed spinster'.

'Who was he?' I ask.

'Never mind that, it was a long time ago and I'm very happy on my own,' she says, making it clear that she's finished talking about the matter. 'When you were thirteen,' she says, patting the back of my hand, 'you came to me and asked if you should kiss a boy because all the other girls had. I give you the same advice now as I gave you then.'

'Which was?'

'Don't feel pressured into something you don't want, and certainly not because everyone else is doing it.'

'You're right,' I say, putting my cocktail stick down on a neat little napkin. 'I've always felt marriage was about timing. When two people have found what they want, and make a logical decision to do those things together, it's more likely to work out. Simon's never really questioned what he wants, it's a given that one day he'll inherit his father's company, but I . . .'

'What do you want, Beatrice?'

'Do you know what I really want?' I ask, finding the

courage to say it out loud. 'I want to concentrate on designing jewellery again. I want to use all the time I used to spend with Simon on creating a new collection, something that's entirely my own.'

Aunt Jane gives me a sharp look of approval. 'I think that's a wonderful idea. You've always had a good eye, and for as long as I can remember jewellery has been your passion. Do you remember that when you were a little girl the first thing you'd reach for when you came to visit me was my jewellery box.'

Images of Aunt Jane's jewellery box come flooding back to me. It was an old wicker sewing basket in burgundy and cream, and inside were rolls of velvet, boxes of every shape and size, and endless strings of beads. I used to sit for hours trying on her diamond rings, signet rings and watch chains she'd inherited. Never once did she rush me or tell me something was too precious to play with; she knew that box opened up so many stories for me – from dazzlingly rich women, flapper girls, and wealthy criminals in suits and spats. That box transported me to different times and places, and stories old and new. It was like stepping into a time–travelling machine in the safety of Aunt Jane's home.

'I do remember. Even then I think that's what I dreamt of doing, but these last few years that's somehow been forgotten. Maybe now is the time to say, "to hell with men" and start realising my dream of becoming a jewellery designer.'

'That's the spirit.'

'After all, you had your career as an auctioneer, and your life has always been rich and varied.'

'You're absolutely right,' says Aunt Jane, clutching my hand supportively, but I can't help wondering if I notice just a hint of 'what if' in her eyes.

LIZZIE & JACK

*Together with their families
invite you to join them in
a celebration of their love*

Houghton Farm, Wiltshire

Saturday, 12 May

5

It feels really weird to be back in Lizzie's childhood bedroom, preparing for her wedding. Hardly anything has
changed since we were twelve years old and we were
invited over for the first time to meet the new family
puppy, Daisy the springer spaniel. I can remember so
clearly Mum driving me up their lane and me telling her
to turn around when I saw the farmhouse for the first
time; I thought we'd come to the wrong place. Compared to our boxy village home on the estate with only
a patch of grass bound by six-foot-high fencing, Lizzie's
home looked like a castle. Even Aunt Jane's house was
nothing compared to this.

'I can't believe you still have all your trophies,'
I say, glancing at Lizzie's dog-handling prizes. 'Dog
agility was all you could talk about when we first met
at school.'

'It was my first love.'

'You were such a geek, Liz,' says Hannah.

'*I* was a geek?' says Lizzie, mock-outraged, looking
at Hannah in the mirror of the small dressing table. The
hairdresser positions a headband of wild roses on her,
tweaking her elfin-like hair around it. 'You were the

one who cried when you found out school didn't teach Latin and Greek.'

'I *still* think they were helpful for the law degree—'

'Hannah, you really are a dweeb,' says Kat, battling with a pair of low denier tights.

'We can't all be sports captain and snog most of our brother's mates by the time we're fifteen,' says Hannah, retaliating.

'You did snog a lot of boys,' I say, browsing Lizzie's CD collection. The album titles bring back memories of all the nights here in Lizzie's room. Saturday nights spent giggling over boys and listening to Radiohead, Coldplay and Keane, not forgetting Nirvana.

'Better that than obsessing about one guy and never having the guts to talk to him,' says Kat, teasing me.

I put down a picture of the four of us, aged seventeen, at our first music festival, plastic pint glasses raised to the camera. We'd just played a game of Truth or Dare with a bunch of guys we'd met that involved far too much exposure of body parts. 'Ah, Stephen Finnigan, how many hours I spent dreaming of you. I wonder what became of him.'

'He's a fishmonger,' says Lizzie.

'Urgh,' I squirm. 'Close shave!'

'I think almost all the guests have arrived,' says Hannah, glancing out of the window to the large garden below. The purple blooms of the wisteria tickle the edge of the windowsill. I join her.

'Can you see Jack?' Lizzie asks.

Hannah scans the garden, from the gravel drive to the

lawn beyond, which has been laid with simple wooden chairs facing a wedding arch of branches festooned with apple blossom. And further still, fields stretch into the distance full of grazing sheep and bleating lambs. It's absurdly idyllic.

'Actually, I'm not sure Jack's here . . .' says Hannah.

For a split-second Lizzie believes he isn't there, until she catches me hitting Hannah, playfully, for winding her up.

'Don't!' Lizzie clutches her chest. 'You know I can think of nothing worse than Jack getting cold feet. I miss him *so* much.'

'Two things,' says Hannah. 'One, Jack would never drop out of marrying you, and two, you saw him less than twenty-four hours ago!'

'I know,' says Lizzie, pitifully. 'It feels like a lifetime.'

'You've survived much longer without him,' I say. 'Think of all those weeks when he was stuck in the studio last autumn, and all the weeks at the start of the year touring the country with the band.'

'Don't remind me,' she says, pathetically. Living with Lizzie this last year has been like living with a love-sick puppy. 'Having a rock star boyfriend does have its troubles.'

Hannah and I are laughing at Lizzie when Kat mutters, 'Shit!' Her big toe has pushed through her tights, and she wriggles it ruefully.

'Would you like me to help with the next pair?' I ask. Watching Kat struggling with her tights puts me right back to when we were about eight years old. I always wanted to play dressing up, using my mum's heels and jewellery, but even then, Kat shunned the idea.

I've been dressed in my white eyelet bridesmaid dress for a good twenty minutes, as has Hannah, but Kat is still in her bra and pants. Lizzie chose the same fabric for all the dresses but each of us has a different style. Mine's cut above the knee with a V-neck and capped sleeve, Hannah's is mid-length and off-the-shoulder, and Kat's is a mini with fitted bodice and A-line skirt. Hannah and I love our dresses, while Kat is wearing hers under duress – but then Kat wears any dress under duress.

'Has Bea's date arrived yet?' Kat asks Hannah, as I ball up the tights and inch them over her toes.

I shake my head despairingly, remembering the moment I'd returned home from Aunt Jane's and told Lizzie about breaking up with Simon. After talking it through for what must have been over an hour, she told me, 'I know just the guy to take your mind off him.'

'Liz!' I cried, incredulous at her ceaseless desire to see everyone paired up. 'I've just ended a relationship of four years; I'm not going to jump into another one. I need a break from men.'

'Don't be silly – you'll love Dave. He's Jack's cousin, you know who I mean, he's been out with the guys before, rugby, cricket, stuff like that.' When she mentioned it, I did have a vague recollection of Simon talking about Jack's cousin, Dave. 'I've only met him a few times but he seems great. Jack and I have never been able to figure out why he's single!'

I went to bed that night and completely forgot about her plan, until the girls came round the next evening, Lizzie having invited them over to cheer me up.

When I told them about the break-up over dinner, a silence engulfed the flat as if I'd just told them I was off to join the Cirque du Soleil.

'But I'm setting her up with Dave, Jack's cousin, at the wedding,' said Lizzie, as if that changed everything.

'Such a good idea,' said Kat, vaguely. She still looked dumbstruck that I'd actually ended it with Simon.

'And if you don't like him,' said Hannah, 'I know Remy is desperate to set up a friend of hers.'

'A different date at each wedding,' said Lizzie, thrilled to bits.

I could think of nothing worse.

'What does he look like?' Hannah asks now, searching the guests below.

'He's looks a lot like Jack, just taller and with less facial hair,' says Lizzie.

'Then I *think* the answer is yes.'

I resist the urge to look, my thoughts turning to Simon. When we've seen each other at work I've found it painfully awkward, despite Simon's efforts to be professional, and I've avoided all social situations where he might be there. He should really be here, seeing Lizzie getting married, but he emailed to say he felt it best he didn't come, 'to let you enjoy Lizzie's big day without upset'. It's so like him, to put me first, it makes me wonder why I let him go, particularly today when everyone else is paired up and I'm being set up with Dave.

'Maybe Jack's cousin will turn out to be our wedding number four!' Lizzie teases.

'Guys, let's not jump the gun,' says Hannah, seeing the look of unease on my face.

'You know it's only a bit of harmless fun,' says Lizzie, stepping into her vintage lace dress, which hugs every curve of her body perfectly. For all I don't hanker after a wedding, there is something really special about seeing Lizzie preparing for hers – something that makes me wonder if I might like to do the same one day, in spite of all my doubts. 'We don't really expect him to fill Simon's shoes, it's too soon for that.'

'How's he doing anyway?' asks Hannah, stepping over to help Lizzie with the tiny mother-of-pearl buttons which run up the back of her gown.

I scrunch up my nose, uncertainly. 'Hard to say. We haven't really spoken, though we said we would. He hasn't let his emotions show at work but I think underneath he's a mess. Bev thinks he's gutted but . . . I don't know.'

'What did Sir Hugo have to say about it all?' asks Hannah.

'He didn't. He's either forgotten or Simon hasn't told him. You know how they are, stiff upper lip and all that.'

'And how are you doing?' Kat asks, successfully pulling up her tights. Nobody's said as much, and everyone's been really supportive, but I can tell none of them really gets why I broke it off with Si. I'm pretty sure they all think I made a mistake.

I inhale deeply, gathering myself. After all, it's Lizzie's

day, not mine. 'I'm okay. I've decided to pursue an old love of mine.'

For a moment the three of them look at me with wrinkled brows and puzzled expressions.

'I thought I might try and find Stephen Finnigan on Facebook.'

'You're kidding?' says Kat, the other two stunned into silence.

I shrug, allowing them to think for a moment that I'm serious. 'Of course I'm kidding!' I say, laughing, and eventually they do too, once the penny's dropped. 'I've signed up for a jewellery refresher course, that's all.'

'For a moment I thought you were serious about Fishy Stephen Finnigan!' says Lizzie, feigning fluster.

'Never in a million years.' Other than Simon and Neil, the guy I dated at art college for a couple of years, there hasn't been anyone really significant, and certainly not my old schoolgirl crush.

'That's really exciting, Bea, good for you,' says Hannah.

'It's about time you got back to the thing you're best at,' says Kat. 'I always thought you were capable of making a living from jewellery. Remember when you set up a friendship bracelet stall for Young Enterprise and you made a killing?'

'Oh yeah, I'd forgotten about that. Those bracelets were cute.'

'Didn't you customise them to have names?' asks Kat. 'I think I did.'

'But those bracelets were nothing compared to your

A-level art project,' says Lizzie. 'Those Aztec-inspired necklaces were sensational.'

'They were pretty good,' I say, thinking back to all the times I sat up through the night perfecting them.

'And the Peruvian collection you did for college finals was knock-out. You're right to go back to it. You could really make a go of it, if you want to.'

'Thanks guys,' I say, encouraged by their comments. If nothing else it gives me some impetus to move forwards. 'But moving on, let's talk about you. Look at how beautiful you are. You're just like Carey Mulligan.'

'Oh Bea.' Lizzie's eyes brim with tears at the mention of her style icon. 'Do you mean it?'

I reach out to adjust a small flower in her hair that has drooped. 'I've never seen you look prettier. Now hurry up, you can't be too late; it's time for you and Jack to be married.'

Lizzie didn't want her bridesmaids walking down the aisle in front of her, so we left her with her parents in the house and took our places at the front of the congregation in the garden.

'She's almost ready,' I whisper to Jack, giving his arm a rub and offering a supportive smile. He smiles back, anxiously, playing with his tie and cufflinks, like a man – well, who's about to get married.

'Have you met Dave yet?' Jack asks, indicating to his cousin, who is sitting behind him. I recognise him from the photos of Jack's stag do that I couldn't avoid on Facebook.

'No,' I say, extending my hand. 'Nice to meet you. I'm Bea.'

Dave jumps up to greet me, eagerly pumping my hand. He's extraordinarily tall and thin, with a crop of strawberry-blond hair. A sort of Stephen Merchant meets Shaggy from Scooby Doo. I can tell instantly that there's no chemistry, but I feel I have to make an effort, for Lizzie's sake. 'Hi Bea,' he says, his eyes wide, head bobbing and smiling inanely. 'Pleasure's all mine. Would you like to join me?' The West Country accent alone is enough to make me want to run for the hills.

'I think I'm to sit on Lizzie's side of the aisle.' I gesture to where Kat and Hannah have taken their places with Henry and Remy. Hannah waves me over indicating that there are two seats available. I dart my eyes at her to suggest I'd rather Dave remained where he is, but she either doesn't notice or, more likely, does notice but decides it will be more fun this way, and beckons us both over.

'Everybody, this is Dave,' I say, as we take our seats.

'Hardly an improvement on Simon,' mutters Aunt Jane, who's sitting in the row behind. She's wearing a blue wide-brimmed hat with ostrich feathers that must have been mouldering in her cupboard since the late eighties.

I lean over the bench to kiss her twice on the cheeks. 'He's Jack's cousin; be nice.'

'You know me, Beatrice – I say things as I see them.'

'Jane,' says the older gentleman next to her in a reprimanding tone. He's nattily dressed in a pale linen suit

55

and sporting a cravat; I can't remember meeting him before.

'Well, look at him. He might have at least brushed his hair.'

It's clear that she isn't going to introduce her guest so I offer out my hand. 'I'm Bea, Jane's great-niece.'

'Tom,' he says, shaking my hand, his soft, ageing blue eyes smiling at me.

I'm about to ask how he knows Aunt Jane when she interjects briskly with, 'How are you getting on without Simon?'

'I'm okay. Keeping busy.'

Aunt Jane is explaining my break-up to Tom, when Lizzie's mother arrives, walking quickly down the aisle, followed by the arrival of Lizzie on her father's arm.

'Is she wearing *wellington boots*?' whispers Aunt Jane, catching sight of Lizzie's brand-new, white Hunter wellies.

I stifle a giggle and shush her. 'It's all part of the rustic feel.'

Mark, Carburetor's guitarist, stands and begins his acoustic rendition of Wet Wet Wet's 'Love is All Around Us'.

'Such a perfect choice,' says Kat, dabbing her eye with the hanky she's retrieved from Henry's top pocket.

'It couldn't have been anything else.'

We clutch each other's hand tightly as Lizzie strolls down the aisle, her eyes fixed on no one but Jack.

'Welcome to the marriage of Lizzie and Jack,' says the minister, the three of them standing under the wedding arch. When a gust of wind blows over the garden, apple blossom scatters over Lizzie and Jack and for a moment it's as if they're in their own miniature snow globe. 'To love is to come from the paths of our past and to move forward, hand in hand, along the road of our future, ready to risk, dream, and dare.'

It's such a lovely sentiment – I half expect to feel a twinge of loneliness, but instead I find myself believing with all certainty that I did make the right decision in breaking up with Simon, and that someone is out there for me who's prepared to dream and dare.

The service is short and intimate: the vows are written by Lizzie and Jack, with no awkward singing – much to my relief – and only a handful of readings. Just as the two of them are about to exchange rings a cloud covers the sun, and I shiver, pulling my cotton shrug a little closer.

'It isn't a sign,' says the minister, causing a ripple of laughter. But just as the service finishes and Jack is kissing Lizzie, rain bursts from the sky.

'It's raining!' cries Kat.

'Unlike Carrie, I had noticed!' I call back, delighted at the turn of events, joining most of the other guests in seeking shelter.

'Take my jacket,' says Tom, gallantly taking off his blazer and placing it round Aunt Jane, which she accepts, slightly grudgingly. Dave offers to do the same for me, but I decline.

'Come on, let's get you to the barn,' I say to Aunt Jane.

'The barn!' she says. 'Are we all to be animals for the

afternoon, running around with our snouts in the hay?'

'No!' I pull my shrug closer, aware that Dave is sneaking not-very-subtle glances at my increasingly transparent white dress. 'The reception is in the barn, it's all set up. You'll see. Come on!'

Aunt Jane, unamused, purposely takes her time. Poor Tom's shirt is already soaked through.

'Here, let me help,' says a voice from behind. I turn to find a good-looking American, holding out an umbrella.

'Thank you,' I say, my eyes locked on his olive skin, amber eyes, and dark choppy hair that's begging to have someone's hands run through it. Dave stands next to him like a pound mutt next to a Crufts champion.

He flashes a smile that almost floors me then takes off, a lens camera in hand, chasing after the guests, snapping the fun and excitement of the rain shower.

And then, just as quick as it began, the rain stops, and in its place a huge double rainbow arches over the farm.

'My, my,' says Aunt Jane, a mischievous smile forming on her lips, her eyes glinting. 'Have we just found the pot of gold at the end of the rainbow?'

6

'Who is that?' I ask Hannah, once I've safely deposited Aunt Jane on a dry bench under the wisteria and Tom is fetching her a glass of champagne.

'Oh, that's Leo,' she says.

'Leo?'

'The wedding photographer. He's very nice, in a Californian kind of way. Lizzie managed to talk him into doing our wedding too.'

'Good to know.'

Hannah eyes me suspiciously.

'I know how much you were worried about your photographer dropping out,' I fumble, hoping she won't figure out my alternative interest in Leo. 'It's great you've found a replacement.'

'Uh-huh.' She drinks her champagne, one eye still on me.

We watch Leo take Lizzie and Jack to the far corner of the garden, the sheep grazing behind them, where he begins directing them for their photos.

'She should have worn Carrie's Bo-Peep dress!' says Hannah.

The thought of Lizzie in a corset and bonnet makes

me laugh. 'Before today I couldn't have imagined them being any more loved-up but they seemed to have entered a whole new stratosphere.'

'They put the rest of us to shame.'

'Who do?' asks Remy, joining us. She looks adorable in a tiny tuxedo.

'Lizzie and Jack,' says Hannah.

'You think?' Remy reaches out her hand then pulls Hannah towards the bottom of the garden, where she starts chatting to Leo. I envy her ability to talk to him so effortlessly. I'd probably end up talking gobbledygook with a mouth so dry my lips would stick to my teeth. *Stop it, Bea. Just because you're back at Lizzie's childhood home doesn't mean you have to behave like a teenager.*

'They look happy,' says Dave, joining me and handing me a glass of champagne.

'Yes, they do.' I use the pretence of looking towards Lizzie and Jack to continue watching Leo.

'I admire anyone who gets married. It can't be easy.'

'Maybe when you find the right person,' I say, vaguely.

'Yes.' Dave bobs his head. It's as if it isn't on quite tight enough. 'Tricky business, though. Finding that person.'

'I reckon it's mostly timing.'

'Do you?'

'Sure, you know, it's about two people knowing what they want and being prepared to commit. Don't you think?'

'I wouldn't know,' he says, with a nervous laugh.

'I know it's not very romantic but it applies to everyone I know who's married or engaged.'

'And what about you? Are you ready to commit?'

'Hardly,' I say, downing my champagne. The waiter passes with a tray and I grab another. 'I'm not sure I want another relationship.'

Hopefully that makes it clear I'm not interested.

Dave looks into his glass and, realising it is empty, quickly excuses himself.

'You weren't being cruel, were you?' asks Kat, a moment later, stepping into Dave's place.

'Only to be kind.'

Kat offers a gentle but reproachful look. 'Henry did say he's not very worldly. I think cricket and ale is about all he knows.'

'Not to worry,' I say, laughing it off. 'I'm not on the market anyway.'

We sip our champagne quietly for a moment, watching Hannah and Remy in front of Leo's camera, their faces lit up, Remy on Hannah's back.

'They're really working it today,' I say.

'Hannah needed Remy in her life. She's softened her.'

'I agree.'

Before she met Remy, Hannah would never have dreamt of giving her girlfriend a piggyback, let alone have a photographer take a picture of her doing so.

'Does her grandmother know about Remy yet?' Kat asks.

'Nope!'

'Good job she can't see this PDA!' Remy, still on Hannah's back, has stretched round to kiss her. I snap a shot on my phone.

'I can't believe how much more relaxed Hannah is since they met,' Kat says wistfully.

'What do you think Henry does for you?' I ask.

'Good question!' She glances over to where he is talking to Jack's brother. 'What do *you* think he does for me?'

Kat and Henry are one of those couples who enjoy bantering and bickering with each other, riling each other. I've never quite understood it – Kat's normally so laid-back and conflict-averse – but I've given up trying to fathom it so I fudge a response. 'He complements your easy-going approach to life – he gees you up a bit, and embraces your tomboyish spirit.'

'I can't dispute that! I could never have a Jack and Lizzie relationship – all that mooning. It looks exhausting. But what do you want from a relationship, Bea? I know Simon wasn't the most exciting of boyfriends but he was kind, really kind. It's hard to top that.'

My eyes move towards Leo, who is squatting, the small of his back exposed, shooting another couple from the ground.

'Bea?'

'Yes?' I ask, still absorbed in Leo.

'What was it that you felt was missing with Simon?'

'A bit of freedom, or spontaneity, I suppose,' I say, still staring.

'You don't think he was capable of giving you more space?'

I pause, uncertain of the answer, moving my eyes away from Leo. 'What do you think?'

Kat shrugs. 'I think freedom is in the mind.'

'I might need more champagne to make sense of that!' I laugh it off as Henry walks over, looking suave in light tweed. With his dark hair and eyes, and impeccable posture, he looks like a romantic suitor from *Downton Abbey*.

'Kat,' he says briskly in his clipped South African accent when he's a few feet away. 'It's time we had our photograph taken.' He makes it sound more like a command than something they might do for fun.

'Got to go,' she says, Henry's hand is outstretched for her though he's still standing some distance away. And then with a wink and a glance towards Leo she adds, 'Go get Dave. You don't want to miss your opportunity with the photographer.'

'Who's next?' calls Leo, after Kat and Henry have posed, side by side, his hand behind her back. Before I can do anything about it, Dave is waving enthusiastically at Leo.

Oh God, please don't let him think Dave is my boyfriend.

Leo ushers us forward to beneath the large oak tree, where Dave takes my hand in his, which is clammy. Out of politeness, and trying my best to make an effort for Lizzie, I hold it; I've never felt so wooden.

'This is fun,' says Dave, keenly.

'Nice and relaxed now,' says Leo, his eye pressed against the camera.

Sweet Lord in heaven, how does he make that zoom lens look so erotic?

'And smile.'

Never have I produced a more contorted smile.

'I'll bet that was a good one!' says Dave.

Leo flicks through the shots, his perfectly formed biceps flexing beneath his polo shirt. I dread to think how the photos look.

'Maybe just a few more.'

Act natural, he doesn't know you think he's the hottest thing you've seen since Matthew McConaughey's strip scene in Magic Mike.

'Perfect,' he says, after a couple more attempts. He indicates that we can go. Dave bounds off in search of canapés.

'Thank you. Sorry if we made your job difficult,' I say, wincing inwardly at my terrible attempt at a flirtatious tone.

'Don't worry. Not everyone's photogenic,' he says, positioning the next couple.

Well, that's bloody charming! My face burns with embarrassment, but he's already looking down the lens, framing his next shot, clearly oblivious to my existence. *Lucky for me I'm done with men for the foreseeable future.*

'Are we really having the wedding breakfast in the cow shed?' asks Aunt Jane as we saunter in past the potato crates, stacked artistically at the entrance and cascading with loose petaled flowers in delicate shades. Tom and Dave follow on behind.

'It's really fashionable, plus it's a free venue. Weddings are expensive these days.' I stop at the seating plan, which is written on brown paper and tacked to an easel made out of old pallets. Lizzie has put Tom next to me on one side and Dave on the other.

'So long as they don't expect me to eat cattle feed!'

Even Aunt Jane's look softens when she enters the barn and sees for herself just how romantic it feels. Our home-made bunting in muted colours hangs from the rafters, the circular tables are dressed with white cloths, gleaming glass and shining silverware, and there are the first of the summer flowers and dancing candles everywhere.

'This is us,' I say, showing Aunt Jane and Tom to their seats, which are prettily decorated with a hessian sash holding a trio of wild flowers.

'How will we keep warm?'

'There are blankets and muffs available,' says Hannah, arriving with Remy. Lizzie has sweetly put us all together, rather than split us up.

'Taken from the stable block, I suppose!' continues Aunt Jane.

Tom pulls out Aunt Jane's seat. It's clear from the glint in his eye that he is amused by her scathing commentary.

'And what do you make of all of this?' she asks him.

'I think it's very sensible. Spending less on the wedding means saving more for the future.'

'Well,' she bristles, 'isn't it just like you to see the positive.'

There's something in the way Aunt Jane speaks to Tom, the sparky banter between them, that makes me think they've known each other for a long time, and I wonder how they met, and why I haven't heard of him before.

I pull out my seat and make myself comfortable between Tom on my right and Dave on my left. Dave reaches for the bottle of champagne, uncorks it, almost taking out someone's eye on the next table in the process.

'All rise for the bride and groom,' calls the best man.

I reach out my hand to Lizzie as she and Jack weave their way through their guests towards the long top table at the far end.

'I've never seen her look so happy,' I say.

'Nor Jack,' says Dave. 'I envy what they've got.'

'You'll find it one day.'

'He may not,' whispers Aunt Jane, with an impish giggle.

'I can't believe this will be us soon,' says Hannah, receiving an asparagus tartlet from the servers who were out almost as soon as Lizzie and Jack sat down.

'*I* can't believe you haven't told your grandparents yet,' says Kat.

'Hannah hasn't told her grandparents that I am a girl. They think I am a boy,' says Remy, for the sake of Dave, Henry, Jane and Tom. She laughs at how ridiculous it is. Dave almost spits out his champagne.

'Why ever not?' asks Aunt Jane.

'It wasn't my intention,' says Hannah, a touch defensively. 'But they assumed Remy was a man's name and I didn't correct them, and now too much time has passed . . .'

'What difference does it make whether she's male or female?'

For all Aunt Jane's snobbery, she could never be accused of being prejudiced.

'It would make a lot of difference to my grandparents.'

'But why should it matter what they think?'

Hannah looks at her plate. 'Because they're paying for the wedding.'

Aunt Jane releases a guffaw of delight, relishing Hannah's moral dilemma. 'So, it's keep schtum and get married, or tell all and risk everything?'

'That's about it, in a nutshell.'

'Well, it's perfectly simple, my dear. You must tell.'

Hannah casts Aunt Jane a questioning glance.

'The lie of not telling is unforgivable, for both them and for you. It would be better not to marry than to marry on a lie.'

'I'm not sure I agree,' says Henry, wading into the conversation.

'What do you mean?' Kat asks him, fiddling with her knife.

'Hannah hasn't lied. If her grandparents have misinterpreted the facts, that isn't her fault.'

Kat narrows her eyes. 'But she's had several opportunities to put them straight.'

'People hear what they want. Maybe they've *chosen* to believe Remy is a man.'

'That's bullshit!' says Kat, attacking her asparagus with her knife.

'I just think sometimes it's kinder to keep people in the dark. Why cause unnecessary fuss?'

An awkward lull hangs over the table until Remy, seemingly oblivious to Kat's irritation, pipes up with, 'How are your wedding plans?'

'Fine, you know, all the big things like the venue are booked, I'll figure out the smaller things nearer the time.'

'Kat would get married in her parents' front room,' says Henry, chuckling. 'It's what I love about her – my no-frills gal.' He pulls her tight and kisses her head. 'I'm putting a wager on her walking down the aisle in sweat pants!'

'Why not?' Aunt Jane says with a dry laugh. 'After all, this bride wore wellington boots!'

Aunt Jane excuses herself between courses, muttering about the lack of facilities. 'Am I to relieve myself behind the hay bales?'

'How do you know Aunt Jane?' I ask Tom as we're served spring lamb, crushed potatoes and French beans.

'From our days working at an auction house, probably long before you were born.'

So they have known each other a long time, as colleagues . . . or something more?

'And you've kept in touch over the years?'

'Life took us in different directions, but recently we got back in touch,' he says, a little cryptically.

'And you're just friends?'

'Oh yes,' he says. '*Definitely* just friends. She thought

68

she might need one today, a companion, in the midst of all this young love.' He casts his eyes around to see if she's in earshot. 'And we might seem like old codgers now, but I knew your Aunt Jane in her miniskirt and motorbike days.'

'Pardon me?' I falter. I had no idea Aunt Jane used to have a motorbike though, when I think about it, it doesn't seem so surprising. Very little surprises me when it comes to Aunt Jane.

'Your aunt Jane, when we met, she had a motorbike. She used to ride it to work.'

'In a miniskirt?'

'Surprising, isn't it?' he says, his eyes twinkling, his fly-away white hair standing on end as if in excitement.

'What is?' asks Jane, returning.

'Nothing!' I say and Tom winks at me, leaving me to wonder what else I don't know about Aunt Jane.

A peal of metal being tapped gently on glass cuts through the hubbub of conversation and the room falls silent.

'Ladies and gentlemen, may I have your attention?' says Lizzie's father. 'It gives me great pride to be standing here today . . .'

A sort of veil comes over my senses, not because Lizzie's father's speech isn't interesting, but because I've become aware of Leo, working the room with his camera. His movement around the barn, confident yet unobtrusive, is mesmerising. From the way he squats his lean body effortlessly, to the way he rests one foot on a chair, using his knee as a prop, to how he sidles past guests, brushing himself against them without a hint of self-consciousness.

'He's quite the sight,' whispers Aunt Jane, when she catches me staring.

'Mmm,' I whisper back, trying to hide my interest but feeling my cheeks flush. 'Though typically American, and rude.'

'Check out the picture I got earlier of you and Remy kissing. I'll send it to you,' I say to Hannah, my bowl of Eton Mess scraped clean in front of me. Her phone beeps and she smiles when she brings up the photo.

'It's pretty great,' she says, handing her phone to Remy, who in turn hands it to Aunt Jane and it's passed round the table until it finally reaches Henry.

'Wouldn't it be funny if I accidentally sent it to your grandparents?' says Henry, slightly slurring his words.

'Don't you dare!' barks Hannah.

'Just bringing up her name . . . Grace, Graham, Grandma Aus—'

'I mean it, Henry – don't!'

Kat shakes her head. 'He won't.'

'Henry, hand it back – joke's over,' I say.

He waggles it at me, like a child taunting another kid with a toy. He can be such a prig. I swear, sometimes I really don't see what Kat sees in him.

Furious, Hannah jumps up and tries to grab her phone and in doing so knocks it out of his hand and onto the table.

'Oh-oh!' says Henry, bursting into fits of drunken giggles, his eyes wide.

'What?' asks Hannah. She isn't laughing.

'I think you just hit send.'

'You're fucking joking me!' All colour drains from her cheeks. 'Pass it to me. Now!'

Henry picks it up and relinquishes the phone.

Collectively we hold our breath as Hannah checks it, beads of sweat breaking on her brow.

'You shit,' she says, glaring at Henry. 'It sent!'

7

'Everyone huddle round,' calls Lizzie, from where she's standing on the back of a trailer, attached to one of her father's tractors. 'Time for the bouquet toss.'

A throng of women hurtle themselves towards the front of the crowd of guests who've gathered to say farewell to Lizzie and Jack. I hang back awkwardly, embarrassed at how eager they all look, and catch sight of Leo standing to one side, no doubt hoping to capture the flowers in flight and the response of the excited recipient.

'Three, two, one,' says Lizzie, throwing the bouquet with such force that it travels past the hopefuls at the front and hurtles towards us drifters at the back.

'Get it, Bea!' shouts Kat, as it tumbles towards me as if in slow motion, the white ribbons flaying in the night sky like the tentacles of some monster from the deep.

I make no attempt to grab it and it falls with a thud at my feet.

As I'm looking at it, forlorn on the gravel, someone picks it up and then, in the next instant, Dave is there.

Fuckety fuck.

'It's yours,' he says, handing it to me with what I think is meant to be a suave grin.

Really, no thanks.

'Who got it?' cries Lizzie, jumping up and down on the back of the trailer to catch a glimpse.

Before I can stop him, Dave has pushed the bouquet into my hand and held it aloft. Lizzie coos in delight and the guests are clapping and fawning at Dave and me.

Can this be any more mortifying?

'Over here!' says a voice.

And yes, in fact it can.

Leo has his lens in my face and Dave immediately puts his arm enthusiastically around me, pulling me close. For one awful moment I think he's going to kiss me. Thankfully, Leo is quick to move on – probably because I'm so 'unphotogenic'.

'I'm just going to say goodbye to Lizzie. Why don't you go to the bar?' I say to Dave, extricating myself from his clasp, and thrusting the bouquet at Kat.

Shortly after we've said our farewells, Lizzie and Jack wave goodbye from the back of the trailer, both of them sitting on thrones made of hay, and trundle off into the night. It's the picture-perfect end to their magical day.

'Where's Henry?' I ask Kat, who's still holding the bouquet, which looks oddly incongruous in her hand.

'Passed out on a hay bale.'

'It was a good wedding,' I say, slipping off my shoes and hopping gingerly over the gravel to the lawn.

'Bar the bit when Henry dropped Hannah in it.'

'Yup, not his finest moment.'

'Where is she anyway?'

'Skyping her grandparents.'

73

'Ouch.'

'Aunt Jane's right, though, it is better to be honest. Henry may have done her a favour.'

'Sure,' says Kat, sounding unconvinced. 'Has Aunt Jane gone home?'

'She called it a night when the barn dance began.'

'Who could blame her? Your man Dave gave Gareth from *Four Weddings* a run for his money on the most ludicrous dancing.'

'First of all, Dave is not my man, and second, you're right, for a moment I thought he'd started having a fit!'

Kat laughs at the thought of it. 'I might call it a night too. What about you?'

'I've a Dave to get rid of first.'

'And someone else to hook?' She directs her eyes towards Leo.

'Wa-aay out of my league.'

And unspeakably rude, if mightily gorgeous.

'You mean the way Carrie was out of Charles's league?'

She has a point. 'I might go off in search of Hannah first, see how she's getting on.'

Far less stressful.

I'm heading in the general direction of where I last saw Hannah, behind the portaloos, when Dave stumbles towards me.

'Bea,' he slurs, three sheets to the wind. He eyes me like a teenage boy at a school disco, calculating whether or not to make a move. 'Beautiful Bea.'

Dare to kiss me and I'll knee you in the balls.

Barely able to focus he says, 'How's about it – fancy coming back to the hotel?'

'Tempting,' I say, backing away from his ale-soaked breath. 'But Lizzie's parents have made me up a bed in the house, so I don't think—'

'Bea, Bea, Bea, Bea, Bea.'

'Yes?' I ask when he fails to say anything more.

'Why would someone as beautiful as you not want a ree-lay-tion—' He hiccups, loudly. '—ship. It's such a waste.'

How the hell do I get rid of this? I think, and then it comes to me.

'I tell you what, you get on the bus back to the hotel and I'll head along once I've made sure Lizzie and Jack's gifts are in order. I promised I'd make sure they're safely away at the end of the night.'

He frowns at me, swallowing back a burp. 'But how will you get there?'

'Taxi – bridesmaid's perk.' Miraculously this seems to placate him. 'Wait for me in the bar. I won't be long behind you.'

He smiles coyly. 'The moment I saw you I knew you liked me.'

I shoot him an insincere smile and he walks away backwards, tumbles, gets up and, without embarrassment, climbs onto the bus.

'Thank Christ for that,' I mutter, when the bus door is safely closed, and he's gone.

It takes me a minute or two to locate Hannah and when I do it's clear from the intense look of concentration on

75

her face and the finger jammed in her ear that now is not a great time.

'Plan B,' I say, and head to the hot dog and doughnut van, which Lizzie and Jack hired for late-night munchies. 'Four sugar doughnuts, please.'

'Hungry?' For a moment I think it's the doughnut guy asking, but then I realise that Leo is leaning against the van.

Four doughnuts, Bea, really? Great impression to make.

'I thought I might share them.'

Yeah right.

'With your boyfriend?' He looks around for Dave.

'Oh, that wasn't my boyfriend. That was Dave.'

'Dave?'

'My wedding date. The groom's cousin.'

'Gotcha.'

I offer him a doughnut, which he accepts.

'I thought the chemistry was off but hey, when it comes to you English, it's not always easy to tell.'

'Right,' I say, pleasantly surprised that he should have given the chemistry between Dave and I any thought at all, particularly given his previous comment. 'I'm Bea, Lizzie's flatmate – or I *was* Lizzie's flatmate.' I extend my hand, wishing I'd had more to drink to lessen my nerves.

'Nice to meet you, Bea. I'm Leo,' he says, taking my hand. Tingles of excitement rush through my fingers and up my arm causing hundreds of tiny goosebumps, and I pull my shrug closer round my shoulders.

'Another doughnut?' I ask, offering the box.

As we eat, I look out over the lawn at the late-night

76

stragglers chatting merrily, and the fairy lights suspended in the trees. Country music drifts over from the barn as I search for an opener. 'How does an American photographer find himself in rural Wiltshire?'

He smiles lazily, wiping sugar from his supple hands and mouth. 'I like to move around, see new things, meet new people. Last week I was in Morocco, doing a wedding there.'

'Sounds pretty idyllic.'

The sort of life I'd like to have.

He sits down at the top of the lawn, his legs bent up in front of him. I shoo away a thought of me straddling him. 'What is it you do?'

'I work as a PA.' I sit down beside him, a little tentatively, wishing I had more of his easy-going spirit. Then the *unphotogenic* comment flashes through my mind again, and I stiffen slightly. 'But I've realised that what I'd really like is to be a jewellery designer.'

'What's stopping you?' he asks, holding my gaze.

'Time,' I say. '*And* money.'

'You don't have someone who could help you out?'

I push away an unhelpful thought of how Simon would have offered to help, if I'd asked. ''Fraid not.'

Picking absently at a blade of grass Leo says knowingly, 'The things worth having are worth striving for.'

'Did you have to graft to become a photographer?'

A wry smile forms at the corner of his mouth. 'Let's just say it wasn't straightforward.'

'But it was worth it, in the end?'

He shrugs. 'One wedding blurs into another.'

'Tell me about it!'

He looks at me quizzically, as if this isn't the response he's used to hearing.

'My three closest friends are all marrying this summer. It feels like one long bunting-sewing session.'

'And you and Dave?' he says, a cheeky glint in his amber eyes.

'Actually, I just turned down a proposal, but *not* from Dave.'

'He wasn't the one?'

I laugh wearily. 'My father did a good job of making me question if *the one* really exists.'

Gazing up at the stars he lies back, placing his hands behind his head. 'Sounds like we might have something in common.'

'What did yours do?' I feel a bit prim sitting poker straight beside him but it feels too bold to lie down next to him.

'Took off when I was seven, leaving my mom to raise me and my brothers alone.'

'Mine left when I was five. Kind of spoils the idea of marriage, right?'

'Right,' he says, scanning the night sky. 'But then again, if he'd stuck around, I might not have been so motivated to make it on my own. I couldn't sponge off my mom for ever.'

'Did you always want to be a photographer?'

He nods. 'I liked the idea of being able to work anywhere, being able to see the stars from different parts of the world. You see Orion's Belt up there?'

'Which one is it?' I ask, scanning the night sky.

'Put your head here.' He pats the ground beside him and, slightly awkwardly, I shimmy in beside him.

'There,' he says, pointing upwards. 'The one with three stars in a row.'

When I still don't see what he sees he takes my hand in his and holds it up, pointing into the dark. I try really hard to act natural but my heart is racing ten to the dozen.

'I see it.'

He lays our hands down, brushing his fingers over mine.

'In the Namib Desert you feel as if you could reach up and touch it.'

He's rubbing his thumb against my hand and has turned his gaze to me. Self-conscious, I continue to stare at the stars. And when I should be thinking about Leo my mind is instead awash with Simon. *What would he feel if he knew I was lying here looking at the stars with another man?*

'What are you thinking?' he asks.

I turn and our eyes lock. Before I can stop myself I blurt, 'I can't remember what it feels like to kiss someone new.'

'Let me remind you,' he says, leaning in.

I swear my heart almost catapults out of my chest when his lips press against mine, still dusted with sugar.

When we eventually come up for air, Leo grins at me, verging on cockily, and says, 'So, how did it feel?'

Oh, just one of the best kisses of my life.

My lips are tingling so much I'm not convinced they'll

work. 'Good to know I've still got it when I need it,' I manage.

He smiles coyly. 'Weddings do that.'

'Do what?'

'Remind people they've still got it.'

What the heck does that mean?

'Well,' he says, sitting up and stretching. 'Time I packed up. I've a wedding in Truro tomorrow. Long drive in front of me.'

Is that it? I sit up woozily, still reeling from the kiss, but Leo is already on his feet, and whatever moment we shared seems to have vanished.

I smooth out the creases in my dress. 'Well, I guess I'll see you at Hannah's wedding next month.'

'Right,' he says, making the connection. 'Guess I'll see you there.'

And without any further ado, not even a peck on the cheek, he's off, leaving me on the grass, my mind in turmoil.

8

'Tidy house equals tidy mind,' I say to myself the following week, folding the last of my long-sleeve tees and placing it in the drawer with the others. I've arranged them by colour, stacked on their sides, and have done the same for all my other tops too. Marie Kondo would be proud, but so far it hasn't done anything to help the muddle in my head that's been there since I kissed Leo. And it certainly hasn't sparked joy!

'I wish you were here, Liz. You'd know how to cheer me up.'

Lizzie would sit me on the sofa and put on *Notting Hill*, allowing me to watch the 'there's something wrong with this yoghurt' scene over and over without complaint or judgement. Then she'd make me a stack of pancakes as big as my head and smother them in maple syrup, cream and blueberries. And, after all that, she'd tell me everything that's great about me and reassure me that breaking up with Simon was the right thing to do (even if she doesn't fully believe it), that kissing Leo wasn't a betrayal, and that when I see him at Hannah's wedding he'll want to kiss me all over again, which I should do without regret, because I'm still young and should be having fun, not fretting about everything.

Because the truth is I haven't been able to stop wondering what Leo meant when he said, weddings 'remind people they've still got it'. Was he trying to tell me he has a different girl at every wedding, that I was just another nameless conquest? I feel sort of foolish about it all, and worse, disloyal to Simon, because how would I feel if Simon was kissing someone else after only a few weeks?

'You'd tell me to stop making a big deal of things, Lizzie.' I throw one of her bras, which I found in my undies drawer, into the cardboard box in the hallway, already overflowing with the stuff she's forgotten to take with her. 'You'd also remind me I've a potential flatmate coming round in five minutes and to hurry myself up.'

But who could be better than Lizzie? I trudge downstairs, carrying the cardboard box. I had begrudgingly put an advert on SpareRoom last week for someone to rent Lizzie's old room, but I'd rather pay double than have the wrong person.

I pop the box down and cast my eye about the place. There's no laundry on the radiators, jackets on the floor or bike parts on the stairs. Whether I like it or not, Lizzie has gone, and so too has Simon.

'You're on your own, Bea.' I swallow back a surge of emotion and, as I do, I hear the sound of the latch on the garden gate.

I open the front door to find a woman younger than me, her hair in a ponytail, wearing a bulky sweatshirt and carrying a large holdall.

'Hi – you must be Eva. I'm Bea,' I say, reaching out my hand.

'Hi, Bea,' she says, in almost a whisper.

'Come in.'

We stand together in the hallway, the space feeling a little tight with her cumbersome belongings. 'Feel free to pop your bag down,' I say, when she shows no indication of letting go of it. But she doesn't, instead she clings to it even tighter. *What's in there?* 'Let me show you round and then we can have a chat, get to know each other a bit,' I continue, hoping to lessen her unease.

I lead her through to the kitchen and dining room, which she gives a cursory inspection.

'All pretty self-explanatory,' I say, showing her the washer/dryer in the under-stairs cupboard before taking her to the living room, where I've beadwork out on the coffee table. 'The front room gets great light in the evenings, and it's big, as you can see.'

'Is the bedroom at the front or back of the house?' she asks, as we head upstairs.

'The back.'

'Good,' she responds, quickly, and I find myself wondering what seedy plans she has for it.

'This is it.' The room is unrecognisable without Lizzie's belongings piled here, there and everywhere. As it is, it's no more than a box with a bed, a wardrobe and a small table with a few boxes of jewellery supplies stacked on it. It looks as empty as I feel without Liz. 'It's the smaller of the two but still a good size. Plenty of room for all your things, I imagine.'

83

She pays little attention to any of the room other than to check that the curtains close fully, which strikes me as a little odd but, each to their own and all that.

'And this is the bathroom.' I open the door. She barely looks in. 'Can I get you a cuppa?'

'Oh, that's okay,' she says, beginning to sway a little, now making *me* the nervous one. She also has a look in her eye that makes me think she'd prefer to leave, so it comes as a surprise when she says, 'I'll take the room, if you'll have me.'

'Okay,' I say, inching past her to go downstairs. 'I just thought it might be good to get to know each other a little, before we make a decision. You may not like me,' I joke, awkwardly. *And, more to the point, I really may not like you.*

'I can tell we'd be fine. When do you think you can let me know?' There's a note of desperation in her voice.

'I've a couple of other people to see. Maybe the end of the week?'

'Oh, right,' she says, disappointed.

'Important that we're both sure, I think.' I'm just about to open the door when a sound comes from her that I can't place, a sort of muffled whimper. 'Are you okay?'

'Sure,' she says, beginning to sway again, this time a little faster. 'I'd best be off.'

'If you're sure,' I say, but as I reach for the lock a huge cry sounds from beneath her sweatshirt. 'Eva?'

After a moment's contemplation she drops her bag to the floor and lifts up her top.

Strapped to her chest in a papoose is a tiny baby dressed in pink.

'How old is she?' I ask, dumbfounded. Then it all falls into place. Of course – the bag is full of baby paraphernalia, and she needs a quiet room at the back of the house with blackout blinds for the kid to sleep.

'Three weeks.'

There's a painful silence as I look at Eva, Eva looks at the baby, and the baby gazes blearily at me. My tiny house – slightly mouldy bathroom and all – is certainly not the place for a new mother and three-week-old baby, but I do feel bad to turn her away.

'What's her name?'

'Whitney.'

I stroke her silky hair. 'She's very beautiful.'

'And no trouble. You'd barely know she was here.'

Other than when I'm woken three times a night. 'I'm sure you're right. Let me think about it.'

I open the door to let her out, finding Kat and Hannah on the doorstep, poised to knock. Eva shuffles past them. 'I'll let you know!' I call.

'Who was that?' Kat asks, after Eva has gone, and they're inside.

'Someone who probably won't be taking Lizzie's room.'

'How come?'

'She has a three-week-old baby under that sweatshirt.'

'Shit.' It's fair to say Kat doesn't have a maternal bone in her body. She sees the look on my face and slips an arm through mine. 'Don't worry, the perfect person will turn up.'

85

'Perhaps,' I say, really not convinced.

'Wow, look at this place! I've never seen it so tidy,' says Hannah, as we enter the living room.

'It may be the only upside of losing Lizzie,' I say, dejectedly, wishing she were here with us.

Kat reaches out to hug me and I hold her close, far tighter than normal, my loneliness surging back.

'You okay?' she asks, holding me at arms' length and scrutinising my face.

I breathe in deeply and release it slowly, determined not to give in to my emotions. On the upside, Eva and her baby did put my own problems into perspective. I may be feeling a bit lonely, but at least I'm not lonely *and* looking for a flat with a newborn baby.

'We brought pancake batter!' says Hannah, holding up a poly-bag, and that does it, I burst into tears. Aunt Jane used to make us pancakes when the shit really hit the fan, like when Kat failed her GCSE science prelims and her parents vowed not to let her out of the house unless she went to science 'clinic', which meant no after-school sports for months and Kat having to drop out of hockey scratch. They might as well have locked her up in prison for all life meant to Kat without sports. Since that time, all ails have been sorted over pancakes.

'I'll do sofa and DVD, you do pancakes,' says Kat to Hannah, ushering me towards the sofa. 'Sit down, put your feet up, I'll get the Valium.'

'Valium' is how Lizzie referred to *Notting Hill* and despite my low spirits I find myself laughing through the tears.

'Careful, you'll get snot bubbles!' When we were at primary school everyone tried to dodge sitting next to a boy named Luke Mathews, aka Snot Bubbles due to his uncanny ability to blow large bubbles of mucus when concentrating. It's been a gross-out topic of ours ever since.

Kat sits down beside me and wraps a throw around the two of us. It takes me back to when we were teenagers, doing the same thing on Friday nights.

'Hugh will cheer you up, he never fails.'

We've got to the birthday party scene by the time Hannah comes through with the pancakes, dripping in syrup.

'I'm not sure they're up to Lizzie's standard, but I've done my best,' she says, sneaking under the blanket.

The three of us eat quietly, absorbed in the film.

'Well, if nothing else, I won't have to eat for another week,' I say, finishing my pancakes.

Kat pats her belly. 'They were a bit leaden.'

'Where's Lizzie when you need her?' says Hannah.

'Probably drinking a herbal infusion in a yurt somewhere?'

'Who goes on a detox honeymoon anyway?'

'Lizzie and Jack!' we say in unison.

'For a musician and an artist they're so un-rock 'n' roll,' I say.

'The wedding was beautiful though,' says Kat. 'Even if sparks didn't fly between you and Dave.'

I have to stop myself from spitting out my coffee. 'Tell me neither of you thought Dave had genuine potential.'

'All Lizzie's fault,' says Hannah, holding up her hands.

'Oh sure, blame the one who isn't here!'

'He was a bit of a dork' says Kat.

'A bit? It was like being on a date with Tom from *Four Weddings*! Thinking about it, no wonder Lizzie thought he was a catch . . .'

'Wait till you see who Remy and I have lined up for you.'

I roll my head back on the sofa. 'No! Not another one. I've told you, I'm sworn off men.'

'Trust me, this one's good. This one's good enough to make even me consider turning! This one definitely has wedding number four potential!'

You mean like Leo? The thought catches me off-guard.

'I'm sorry if Henry spoiled the reception a bit by being a berk,' says Kat.

'It's fine,' says Hannah. 'He was drunk. People do weird shit when they're drunk.'

'Henry does weird shit even when he's not drunk,' mutters Kat.

'What did you say to your grandparents?' I ask.

'I fudged it a bit, agreed with them when they said how "slight of build" *he* was.'

'You didn't tell them?' I ask, amazed at how a successful lawyer can have so much trouble telling the truth to her grandparents.

'I couldn't. I didn't know how.'

'You know they're going to find out eventually. Won't the rift be even deeper then?'

'At least I'll have Remy by my side, as my wife.'

'I take it they're not coming to the wedding?'

'It's too far. Grandpa isn't well enough to fly, which, though I feel terrible saying it, is a relief.'

'And everything else is in place?'

'Yup, I double-checked with the photographer yesterday and he's on board so we're all set.'

'Oh yeah,' says Kat, teasingly. 'The wedding photographer! What was his name again?'

'Leo,' says Hannah, matter-of-factly before realising where Kat is going with this.

'Le-o, lovely Le-e-e-o.' Kat sings his name to Day-O.

I hit her with a cushion. 'Sworn off men, remember!'

'Methinks the lady protests too much,' says Hannah, prodding me playfully in the ribs.

'Methinks the lady's colour gives the game away,' says Kat, putting her finger to my cheek with a 'sizzle' sound. I bat her away, but she's right, I'm blushing. I know that Leo was just flirting with whichever single wedding guest came his way – even an unphotogenic one – and that I should stop thinking about that kiss. I just don't know how . . .

HANNAH & REMY

*Invite you to celebrate their
marriage at Burgh House,
Hampstead*

Saturday 16 June

*Ceremony at 2pm
Carriages at midnight*

9

'This is my kind of bridesmaid's dress,' says Kat, admiring her little black trouser suit in the standing mirror of the hotel suite.

'I'm glad you like it.' Hannah places a white rose in the buttonhole of Kat's lapel. 'Remy wasn't sure at first but when I told her she could have free rein on her bridesmaids dresses she was happy.'

'Are we the groomsmen or the bridesmaids?' Lizzie asks, joining them to look at her own reflection. Her face scrunches up uncertainly.

Hannah chortles. 'You're whatever you want to be!'

I put my arms around the three of them, our image reflected back at us. 'We look like the cast of *Pulp Fiction* meets *Charlie's Angels*.'

'But way cooler,' says Lizzie, using two fingers as a pistol and pretending to blow smoke off the barrel.

'It certainly couldn't be any more different from your wedding, Liz.' I flump on to a sofa and help myself to a pastry, happy that all of us are together again. Since Lizzie and Jack got back from their honeymoon, the four of us have only managed to get together once and that was just for a meal out midweek.

'How is married life?' asks Kat, also reaching for a Danish.

Lizzie's face lights up, and despite the fact we've barely seen her, and I still miss her like crazy, I couldn't be happier for her. She crashes into an armchair as if the bliss of it all has completely worn her out. 'It's heaven. I love him even more than ever. The other day, I was totally exhausted after work and I really didn't feel like cooking. When I got home, I found he'd prepared a gorgeous vegan curry – I swear, sometimes I think we're one person.'

'You guys are sickening!' says Kat. 'Don't you ever argue or annoy one another?'

Lizzie shrugs and twists her lips, searching for something negative to say. 'He's been offered a tour; I'm not overly chuffed about the idea of him being away for so long.'

'You'll be fine,' says Kat. 'You've been through it before.'

'I guess,' says Lizzie, hugging a cushion.

'How are your wedding plans coming along?' asks Hannah, reclining on the sofa opposite mine. It's impossible to believe she's about to get married in just over an hour. I've never seen her so relaxed.

'Not bad,' says Kat, reaching for some grapes. 'The hotel's taking care of most of it, everything from the flowers to the DJ. And Bea and I chose the dress.'

'You went dress shopping without me?' asks Lizzie, her little face crestfallen.

Hannah pulls an 'oh-shit, now you're in trouble' face.

'Oh Lizzie,' I say, knowing how much she would have loved to have been there. 'It wasn't really planned, more me dragging Kat round Oxford Street two Saturdays ago when I realised her wedding was three months away and she didn't have a dress.'

'You bought your wedding dress on Oxford Street?' Lizzie looks utterly horrified; she would have taken Kat round every vintage shop in the city.

Kat laughs. 'Liz, I know it's impossible for you to believe, but not everyone enjoys looking at wedding magazines and haunting bridal boutiques.'

'You did almost come to blows with Kat when we went shopping for your dress,' I remind her.

'Which time are you referring to?' asks Kat, putting her hands to her throat as if to strangle herself. 'The first time or the hundred-and-twentieth time?'

'Ha-bloody-hah!' says Lizzie, pretending to shoot Kat. 'Did you find something that isn't made out of sweat-shirt fabric?'

'Yes we did, thank you very much!'

'It's *so* Kat,' I say, smiling at the thought of it. 'After almost seven hours of her refusing to try anything we eventually found the one.'

Lizzie's jaw hits the floor. 'You only tried on one dress?'

'One is all I need.'

'Do you think Henry will like it?' Hannah asks.

'Henry's probably more interested in what's under-neath the dress,' says Kat.

'Sounds about right,' mutters Lizzie.

It's such an uncharacteristic comment that all three of us turn to her, even she looks a bit surprised.

'What does that mean?' asks Hannah.

'I don't know why I said that.' She laughs awkwardly, hugging her knees. 'Sorry, Kat.'

'Don't be,' she says, unfazed. 'I doubt very much he'll be able to describe the dress the day after the wedding, but the lingerie will stick in his mind for ever. That's just his way.'

'He'll remember the dress, of course he will,' says Lizzie. Kat doesn't notice but there's something in Lizzie's voice which makes me think she isn't saying something. And when I cast her a questioning glance she is quick to divert her eyes, purposefully ignoring me.

'Who is Bea's date today?' Kat asks Hannah.

'Oh my god, the ultimate "dish"!' Hannah can never resist a *Four Weddings* reference. 'Remy has outdone herself.'

'Even hotter than the wedding photographer?' Kat teases.

'I'm telling you, even I had to admit he was attractive.'

'What do you mean, the wedding photographer?' asks Lizzie.

Hannah looks at her aghast. 'You mean you don't know?'

'Know what?'

'Guys . . .' I say, but I know it's pointless. Even though Kat and Hannah don't know that I kissed Leo, they've still managed to pick up on my crush and have been teasing me mercilessly about it for the last month.

'Bea has a thing for Leo,' says Hannah.

'Le-o!' sings Kat, because that's what she does every time he's mentioned.

'Leo? As in Leo, the wedding photographer?'

'I really don't,' I say, my cheeks reddening. I wish they'd drop it. This entire week has been torture just thinking about how it will be when we see each other at the wedding, with me wondering if I really was just one of many. The last thing I need is for the girls to be watching my every move around him.

'But he's lovely,' says Lizzie. 'Why wouldn't you fancy him?'

'For the last time, I'm not interested!'

'It could be fun to have someone new. Simon is bringing a date today.'

'Is he?' The news knocks me, though I try hard not to let it show. Even though it's sort of a relief to know he's moving on, that I'm not the only one to have dabbled, it does take the wind out of my sails. 'Good for him!'

'It would be okay for you to have someone too.'

'I just want to focus on me for a bit.' *So why have I kept thinking about Leo for the last month?* 'I'm taking another course, to help me build the idea of a small jewellery business.'

'That's great, Bea,' says Hannah. 'Good for you.'

'It is good,' says Kat. 'But it might be even better with a gorgeous American photographer by your side!'

Thankfully, I'm saved any further humiliation by a knock at the door.

'Come in!' calls Hannah.

'Coo-ee,' her mother calls back. She's wearing a very traditional mother-of-the-bride outfit in duck-egg blue; Carole Middleton would be proud. 'We have a surprise!'

Hannah's parents stand either side of the hotel door, their hands positioned as if displaying a prize on a game show.

'What is it?' asks Hannah.

I guess we're all wondering the same because we sit up from our lounging positions to look.

'Twenty-four hours on an aeroplane, it better be worth it,' comes a voice from the hall. Hannah's face quickly takes on the appearance of stone.

'Surprise!' shouts her mum.

'Grandma, Grandpa,' she stammers, getting to her feet, her eyes wide and unblinking. 'You came!'

'They're going to object, I know it,' says Hannah, standing in the foyer of Burgh House, her entire body tight with anxiety. 'How could I have let it get this far without telling them?'

Good question.

'No, they're not,' I say, squeezing her hand, hoping she can't hear the doubt in my voice. 'They've come because they want to see their only grandchild marry. It's not important whether you're marrying a man or a woman, it's about your happiness.'

We had spent ten or fifteen minutes with them in the hotel room, chatting about their journey and the excitement of the day, somehow managing to dodge the issue of Remy's gender. Hannah barely said a word.

'God, what will they think when they see Remy walk down the aisle. Grandpa could have a heart attack.'

This is the closest to a panic I've ever seen Hannah – including the week of her law finals. She's normally so unflappable.

'You've two options,' I say, trying to sound composed, even though I can only see disaster whichever way I look at it. 'You can go up there now and tell them before the service begins or you can wait until Remy walks down the aisle. Which is best?'

'Whichever I choose they can still object.'

'On what grounds? It's not as if you're doing anything illegal.'

'They could demand all their money back.'

'So? Over time you could scrape it together. If that's the worst that can happen it's really not that bad a situation.'

'They could disown me.'

'I doubt that's going to happen. After all they have just flown from the other side of the planet to be with you. You clearly mean a lot to them. I mean, they might be a bit miffed with you for a while but, if I'm being honest, you probably deserve that.'

'You're right,' she says, shaking out her hands.

'What's going on down there?' calls Lizzie from the top of the oak staircase. 'The guests are waiting and Remy will be arriving soon.'

'What's it to be?' I ask Hannah. 'Tell them now or when Remy arrives?'

'I'd better do it now.'

'Then it's time,' I say, my hand on her back. 'For better or worse.'

She breathes deeply and gives the lapels of her jacket a firm tug. 'You're right. Time to face the music, whatever it may be.'

At the top of the stairs Kat is waiting outside the music room. 'Are you okay?'

'I need to speak to my grandparents,' says Hannah, whose body language has gone from rigid with fear to strong and determined, like a soldier going into battle. 'Is everything else in order?'

'Every detail duly attended to,' says Kat, with a playful salute.

'Good.' If anything can relax Hannah it's order and precision. 'Then I'm ready to tell them the truth.'

Kat opens the door to a perfectly proportioned wood-panelled room, with ten rows of elegant chairs, and a grand piano, which sits front and centre below a beautiful mullioned window. The pianist is playing Chopin, which I can hear underneath the babble of excited guests. It is the epitome of elegance and serenity, which could at any moment shatter into a thousand pieces.

'Good luck!' says Kat as Hannah walks towards where her grandparents are seated at the front.

I take Kat and Lizzie's hands and close my eyes for a moment, regaining my own composure. 'Please God, let them be kind to her.'

Even if I think she only has herself to blame for the situation, it doesn't make it any easier to watch. From where I'm standing I can't see the look on her grandparents' faces but the length of time it takes makes me think they're tough nuts to crack. But eventually she stands and takes her place at the front, her face a mask of determination.

'About time,' says Kat. 'The boys must be fed up with all the waiting.'

'You won't believe how hot Sebastian is!' says Lizzie, with a giggle.

Kat gives a look of 'she's not wrong', a playful twinkle in her eye. 'If you don't like this one, there's something wrong with you!'

In dealing with Hannah's predicament I'd completely forgotten about my own impending trial. 'Right, into the breach,' I say, girding my loins.

As I'm walking to the front I spot Simon among the guests, and next to him a woman about my age, taller and slighter than me with a pretty, old-fashioned face and a short dark bob. She looks as if she's just walked out of the 1920s. When I catch Simon's eye he smiles at me, a little nervously, and clutches the hand of his date a little tighter. *They look good together, better than we did.* I smile back, one of gladness coupled with regret.

'Bea, this is Sebastian,' says Kat, when I've reached our row. She's talking like a curator presenting a prize exhibit. And, to be fair to her, I can see why.

'Hi, Sebastian, how are you?' I shake his hand, which is warm and strong.

'It is nice to meet you, Bea.' His French accent is so thick that it takes me a moment to decipher what he's said, but his eyes are inky deep and his smile so sincere that it's impossible not to warm to him immediately. He bends to kiss me once on each cheek, his stubble tickling my skin, and his soapy scent filling my nostrils.

Kat raises an approving eyebrow at me and I flare my eyes wide in return.

'The bride, *elle arrive, oui*?' says Sebastian and I turn, not to see Remy but instead, to my surprise, Leo.

I have to catch my breath before replying. 'She must be.'

'It is exciting, *non*?'

More exciting than is good for me.

Leo is walking backwards down the aisle, his camera pointing towards the door, awaiting Remy and her bridesmaids. He is so close I can almost touch him.

'Please rise for the bride,' says the officiant. Hannah's grandparents share a perplexed glance at each other, as if the officiant has made a mistake.

As the rest of us stand, Leo crouches to the floor. My eyes should be on Remy's arrival but I can't peel them away from Leo's bum, a perfect peach in his stone-coloured trousers.

The pianist begins 'The Wedding March', so obviously Hannah's choice, and my attention is drawn away from Leo and on to the bridesmaids, who look effortlessly chic in ballet slipper pink, mid-length tulle dresses. As they near the front, Leo stumbles, and I reach out. Instinctively, he grabs my hand and, glancing up, breaks into that familiar lazy smile.

'Thanks,' he whispers. Our eyes are momentarily locked before the moment is broken by the pianist sounding out the arrival of Remy with three strong chords.

Remy is channelling the 'less is more' look in the lightest, full-length, pale-pink silk skirt, with a white slip of a top. She looks as light as a feather, as if the merest puff of wind would whisk her away. As she walks down the aisle on her father's arm, Hannah stands tall, brimming with pride, her eyes focused solely on her bride. Her grandparents' faces grow ever longer, clasping on to each other's hands as if their eyes deceive them.

The two of them come together in front of the officiant, and I see Remy give Hannah's hand a reassuring squeeze. The gaze of the whole room is fixed on them – but my eyes keep drifting to Leo. For the first time I notice that there's a girl beside him – all cheekbones and feline eyes – kneeling on the floor. She takes a lens from him and hands him another from a bag. There's something in the silent way the exchange takes place, a seamless transaction that screams of routine.

'Good afternoon,' says the officiant, drawing my attention back to Hannah and Remy, but before she can continue Hannah says, 'Wait!'

'Hannah?' asks the officiant.

Remy's face crinkles in concern.

'I have something I need to say,' she says, looking towards her grandparents and then turning to face her guests. 'I've done something of which I'm ashamed.'

A small murmur of intrigue scurries through the congregation.

'I hid the truth about Remy from my grandparents,

and in doing so I hid the truth of how much I love her.

'I don't know if my grandparents can fully forgive me for what I've done, but I know I couldn't fully forgive myself if I didn't stand here right now and say, in front of all of you, how proud I am to love Remy, how secure I feel with her by my side, and how I would sacrifice everything I have for her.'

She pauses, Remy squeezing her hand supportively, her eyes lit up in delight.

'I hope, Grandma and Grandpa, that you'll find it in your hearts to forgive me.'

A moment passes where every set of eyes in the room is focused on the grandparents. Her grandfather eventually steps forward and hugs her. Her grandmother only offers a benign look. It's impossible to tell what she's thinking.

'Thank you, Hannah,' says the officiant. 'Shall we proceed?'

Hannah clutches Remy's hand tightly and nods.

'We are gathered here today to witness the wedding of Hannah and Remy, but before we begin in earnest I *must* ask if anyone knows of any lawful impediment why Hannah and Remy may not be married today?'

Even though I know there's no legal reason for Hannah's grandmother to object, I still find myself holding my breath waiting for the wrap of knuckles on wood, like the sound that ricocheted through the church at Charles and Duckface's wedding.

The moment seems to last far longer than normal but Hannah doesn't once raise her eyes away from Remy's, as if the act of staring will compel her grandmother not to speak up.

'Well then,' says the officiant, after sufficient time has passed, a collective sigh pouring into the room. 'Shall we begin?'

IO

'Ah, there you are,' says Aunt Jane, in the courtyard garden, greeting me with a sharp peck on the cheek. Tom is standing behind her, watching with a benevolent smile.

'Hi, Aunt Jane. Tom, nice to see you again.'

'Hello, Bea. How are you?' he asks, kissing me gently on both cheeks.

'Glad to see Hannah married.'

'Without a hitch!' says Aunt Jane, raising her antique teacup.

'For one heart-stopping moment I thought all her worst fears were going to be realised.'

'I should have brought my gavel and given it a bang – that would have shaken things up even more!'

'Jane,' Tom says, reproachfully, unable to suppress a smile. There's a familiarity between them today that I can't help but notice, and it occurs to me that there might be something between them – but Tom said they were only friends, and Aunt Jane is so permanently single that I brush away the thought.

'Well, I ask you, seventy-three years I've been on this earth and not once have I heard anyone object at a wedding.'

'There's still time!' I say.

Aunt Jane indicates to Tom to fetch a plate of sandwiches. 'Who is your date?' she asks, when Sebastian waves at me from the other side of the courtyard where he's chatting with Kat.

'Sebastian. He's a friend of Remy's. French. Seems nice.'

'But?'

Hannah and Remy brush past us, holding hands and full of joyous relief, followed by Leo and the girl carrying his bag. The four of them disappear down the stone stairs to have their photos taken in the small garden below. My gaze follows Leo.

'Oh, I see,' says Aunt Jane, linking her arm through mine and directing us towards the stairs. 'Let's find a bench where we can watch the action.'

'They look good together, don't they?' I ask, once we've found a little bench in the corner of the garden.

'I must admit they do.'

Leo has set up a little table and chairs with the formal splendour of the Georgian house in the background and the informal afternoon tea in the foreground. Hannah and Remy are sitting at the table with their arms intertwined, sipping from each other's teacups.

'They look adorable,' I say, though in the most part I'm focused on Leo rather than Hannah and Remy.

'Who's the girl?' asks Aunt Jane, beckoning towards Leo's helper, who appears to be in charge of positioning props on his instruction.

'Photographer's assistant, I think.' I was aiming for nonchalant, but there's a definite note of jealousy.

Aunt Jane raises an eyebrow. 'Striking.'

'Very.'

'But not pretty, like you,' she says, patting the back of my hand.

'Thanks, Aunt Jane,' I say, my mouth smiling even if my eyes are not.

'Oh, and here comes trouble.'

I follow Aunt Jane's eyes to the couple walking towards us. Simon and his date. *That's all I need.*

'Aunt Jane, how are you?' says Simon, rather pompously. But then Simon always did do grandiose when nervous.

'Quite well, thank you.'

'May I present Edith Armitage.'

Aunt Jane chuckles. 'Have we fallen through the looking-glass into the Edwardian era?'

Simon seems blithely oblivious to her sarcasm. 'Edith, this is Bea and her great-aunt Jane.'

'I'm pleased to meet you both,' says Edith, her cut-glass accent pronounced, her voice small.

'Hi Edith,' I say, shaking her delicate hand. I wonder where they met, who introduced them and how she's never been on my radar before. 'It's really nice to meet you.'

'And you. I've heard a lot about you.'

'Really?' It surprises me that Simon would have told her anything at all. He's usually far more gallant than that. 'Nothing too bad, I hope.'

'Not at all.' She giggles demurely.

'We thought we'd join the queue to have our photo taken,' says Simon, reaching out his hand to her. 'We'll see you later.'

'Why not!' cries Aunt Jane, as they head off, and Kat joins us. 'Why not parade your new beau right under my niece's nose.'

'So, what's she like?' asks Kat, squeezing in beside me on the bench.

'Fuddy-duddy,' says Aunt Jane.

'Delightfully old-fashioned,' I say, reproachfully. 'They're probably the perfect match.'

'And how does that feel?'

I shake my head. 'Inevitable. Good for him. Bit weird for me.'

'But still for the best, yes?'

'Yes, I guess,' I say, uncertainly.

'Because remember: for every Simon there's a Sebastian,' Kat says, her face aglow.

'Absolutely.'

And for every Sebastian, there's a Leo.

'Kat!' calls Henry. 'We're up next.'

'Coming,' she calls back and runs towards him, greeting him with a kiss.

'It's nice to see them on good terms today,' says Aunt Jane. 'I sensed a lovers' tiff at Lizzie's wedding.'

'I know what you mean,' I say, watching the two of them embrace. Henry tickles her waist and pats her affectionately on the bum, which she playfully bats away.

'Though I still think it an unlikely match. I always

thought she'd plump for someone less high-maintenance.'
She nods towards Sebastian who is walking towards us.
'Perhaps this young man will turn out to be a good
match for you?'

'For that to happen I'd need to understand what he's
saying.'

'There are many ways of communicating, other
than speech!' She winks naughtily and I shake my head
despairingly.

'Bea, would you like to have your photo taken *avec
moi*?'

'Sure,' I say, stifling a giggle.

'Don't do anything I wouldn't do,' whispers Aunt
Jane.

'Who is the old lady?' Sebastian asks as we join the
queue.

'Don't let her hear you say that, whatever you do!'

'Why not? She is old, *non*?'

'Well, yes, but here we don't tend to say things so
frankly.'

'I see,' he says, his eyes dancing mischievously. 'For
example, in France we say *graisse* – fat – but here you
say, plump, cuddly, a little overweight. Never the real
truth.'

'It's called being polite,' I say, enjoying hearing him
say 'cud-lee'.

'Or dishonest.'

'A white lie.'

His brow furrows, giving him a puppy-dog appearance. 'I do not understand, white lie?'

'You know, something we say that is a *little* untrue but makes someone feel better.'

'But still a lie?' he says, tongue in cheek.

'Yes, still a lie,' I say, happy to give in.

'What did you think of the ceremony?' he asks, the queue inching forward.

'I liked the way it reflected both Hannah's and Remy's personalities.'

'One uptight, the other fun.'

'Oi!' I say, playfully hitting him on the arm.

'We French, we say it like it is.'

'So it would appear!'

We stand in line watching Hannah's grandparents having their photograph taken with Hannah and Remy. It's impossible to believe from their relaxed demeanour and joyous faces that they've only just found out their granddaughter is gay. The four of them look to be having a ball together.

'How do you like your little black suit?' Sebastian asks, looking it up and down.

'Well enough,' I say, a little self-conscious. 'How do you like it?'

He considers his response for a moment, studying it. 'It shows off your big chest and small waist. Of course, I like it!'

My blushes are spared by Leo's assistant calling us forward and we take the spot in front of him.

'Hi,' I say, trying to control the sudden tremble in my hands, but failing.

A slow smile forms on his lips. 'How are you?'

Why does it always feel as if he's undressing me with his eyes? 'Good, thanks. You?'

'Rolling with the punches. Trying to make this lot look presentable.' He nods towards the gaggle of increasingly tipsy guests waiting to be photographed.

'Well, we can't all be photogenic.' I give him a searching look.

His assistant comes up and turns me fractionally by the shoulders towards the camera, directing the position of my chin with a finger, which irritates me even though it shouldn't.

'Smile!' calls Leo, and just as soon as the encounter has begun it's over, and Remy's bridesmaids are in our place, striking yoga poses in their dresses.

'You look good together,' says Aunt Jane, once I'm back on the bench and Sebastian has gone off in search of an old friend.

'He's *very* French.'

'I wasn't talking about the Frenchman.'

My cheeks flush.

As luck would have it, Tom arrives back with a plate of sandwiches at that very moment, sparing me any interrogation from Aunt Jane about Leo.

'Where have you been?' asks Aunt Jane.

'I got caught by some old French broad. I think she said she's the bride's great-aunt but it was almost impossible to tell. She ate half the sandwiches; I had to go back for more.'

'So long as she wasn't hankering after anything more

than a sandwich,' says Aunt Jane, brushing a breadcrumb from Tom's tie.

'The days of anyone hankering for anything from me other than a sandwich are long gone!'

Aunt Jane pouts her lips. 'Perhaps.'

I swear something passes between them, which could be read as flirtation or, at the very least, a spark waiting to ignite. But really? Aunt Jane? England's most ardent spinster? Surely not.

'Last time a barn, today a canteen,' says Aunt Jane, on seeing the table arrangement for dinner. The music room has been cleared of chairs and set up with two long tables and a smaller top table.

'It's intimate,' I say.

'Or awkward!'

A quick scan of the seating plan shows that Hannah and Remy have broken up not just friendship groups but partners too.

'I've got you on one side and someone called Hermione on my other.'

'And I've got you and a Jean-Luc.'

'In we go then,' I say, knocking back the last of my champagne and handing the glass to a passing waiter.

I'm all in favour of wedding breakfasts when you're surrounded by friends and guaranteed a good laugh, but it's another thing entirely when you're seated beside a complete stranger for what could be the best part of two hours. Two hours is a long time to make small talk.

'Hi, I'm Bea,' I say to the whip-thin woman at the seat next to mine. Her arms are all veins and muscles.

'Hermione.'

'Are you a friend of Remy's?'

'She's my yoga instructor.'

Why doesn't that surprise me. 'I've known Hannah since school. She's an old friend.'

Hermione gives me one of those 'that's nice' smiles then casts her eyes away, further down the table, probably towards the person she came with, wishing she were with them instead of me.

I reach over the sweetpeas, offering my hand to the middle-aged man standing opposite me. 'I'm Bea.'

'George,' he says, in another impossible French accent. He immediately turns to the woman next to him and starts chatting in French.

'How are your lot?' I whisper to Aunt Jane, as Hannah and Remy enter the room to a chorus of cheers and applause.

'Dire. Let's hope there's plenty of wine.'

It turns out that neither Hermione nor Jean-Luc drink so Aunt Jane and I quickly snaffle their half bottles and knock it back like two teenagers on a night out in Newcastle. By the time the main course is served we're already pretty sozzled.

'Oh look, the photographer's coming to take a picture of us eating,' says Aunt Jane, absurdly.

I watch Leo make his way down the side of our table with his assistant behind him. He's keeping an unobtrusive distance and yet it feels to me as if he's about to press right up against me. The thought makes my legs feel like jelly.

'Hi, Hermione,' he says, momentarily moving the camera away from his eye to acknowledge her.

'Hi Leo, Brit,' she says, acknowledging the assistant. 'Good to see you back together.'

What does she mean, 'nice to see you back together'? Does she mean as his assistant or as his girlfriend?

He snaps her photo and looks at the image on the screen approvingly. 'It's a good one.'

'I should hope so,' she says, flirtatiously. I have to stop myself from stabbing her hand with my fork.

He's standing opposite me now, his assistant-slash-girlfriend by his side, his lens directly on me. I tuck my hair nervously behind my ears and try to look natural, which is a near impossibility.

'Take one of us together,' says Aunt Jane, leaning in and putting her arm round me.

'Got one!' he says, flashing a seductive grin at me. I swear the man is a walking hormone.

'The trick is,' whispers Aunt Jane, after he's moved on, 'to make insecurity look like disinterest.'

'I don't know what that means.'

'It means, don't allow him to see you like him, or feel self-conscious around him, or worry that he doesn't like you. Mask your insecurities, be imperious!'

'I'm not sure I have imperious in me.'

'Of course, you do! We're from the same stock, aren't we?'

'Yes.'

'Then channel your great-aunt Jane. When in doubt, think what I would do.'

'I'm feeling a bit lacking today, I'm afraid. Simon being here with his new girlfriend, Leo with his possible girlfriend/assistant, and girl in every port, and Sebastian, lovely as he is, but unlikely to turn out to be anyone special.'

'On days like these it can feel as if there isn't *any*one out there, let alone *the* one.'

I nod. 'Did you have days like these?'

'All the time. No one ever felt quite right, well . . .' Her eye wanders down the table towards Tom, a tiny smile forms at the corner of her mouth and her eyes twinkle. 'And there was more pressure then to settle down than there is now.'

I look at Tom and then to Aunt Jane. 'Is Tom your someone from "many moons ago"?'

Aunt Jane prickles and smooths out her napkin uncomfortably. 'For goodness' sake, Bea – absolutely not! We're friends, nothing more,' she says, briskly, spearing her salmon with just a little too much vigour.

11

'I might follow Aunt Jane and call it a night,' I say to Lizzie later in the small gallery space, where a DJ's been playing a mix of French hits and post-Brit-pop for most of the evening.

Lizzie's face crumples with disappointment. 'How come?'

'I'm not really feeling it and Hannah and Remy won't notice if I sneak away.'

'Wait . . .' Lizzie turns her ear towards the speaker in the corner. 'Christine and the Queens!' she shrieks, jumping up, hauling me with her. 'You're not going anywhere!'

One way or another Lizzie manages to get me on the make-shift dance floor with her bopping away to the first verse of 'Girlfriend', which is all pseudo 1980s synths and tinny beats, and me, shuffling around, doing my best not to look like a complete moron.

'Go for it, Bea,' she calls over the music, strutting her stuff as if no one were watching. Unlike Lizzie, who was always first on the floor at school discos, I have never had the ability to dance as if no one was watching and tonight is no exception, despite the amount I've had to drink.

'Wait! We need more people for the chorus,' calls Lizzie, leaving me alone on the dance floor while she gathers up extra participants.

Only a couple of metres away, Simon and Edith are dancing together, albeit modestly. I feel like such an idiot dancing on my own while they are standing face to face, all doe-eyed, even if their groins are a good distance apart.

'Jack, it's "Girlfriend". Come on!' calls Lizzie. Without further explanation he abandons the blokes he's talking to and heads over. 'Hannah, Remy – it's your song!' They too hurry over. 'And we need one more, for Bea.' Lizzie scans the room. 'Sebastian. Come, join us!'

Before I know it all four of them are on the dance floor and Lizzie is choreographing the routine with her at the front and the rest of us behind, copying her moves.

'You're not a very good dancer,' says Sebastian, a broad smile on his face.

I check out his attempt to mimic Lizzie's boxing moves. 'Nor are you!'

'Congratulations!' he grins.

'For what?'

'Not telling a "white lie".' He says 'white lie' in a cheesy British accent, causing me to laugh.

'What can I tell you?' I say, aware that I look as if I'm the uncoordinated muppet at the back of an aerobics class. 'You must do something for me.'

'*J'éspère*,' he says, which, if my schoolgirl French serves me right means, *I hope so*. He reaches out his hand and twirls me, and as I spin my eye falls on Kat and Henry, sitting to one side, locked in a heated conversation.

Once the track has finished and everyone, bar Lizzie, has left the dance floor, I tell Sebastian, 'I think I'll get some fresh air.'

'I'll join you?'

'Sure, why not?'

We venture out to the courtyard, criss-crossed with lanterns, and take a seat under the heated parasols.

'It's cooler than I thought,' I say, with a slight shiver.

Sebastian draws his chair a little closer and puts his arm around me. 'Is it okay?'

'Thank you, yes.'

'And "yes" means yes, not no?'

'Yes!' I laugh.

'Good, because . . .' Sebastian's eyes are oscillating between my eyes and lips when the front door of the mansion house flies open and Kat rushes out, followed by Henry.

'Kat, wait up!' he calls from the top step.

She's in such a fury that she doesn't even notice Sebastian and me as she storms past our table and out onto the small street beyond.

'Everything okay?' I call to Henry.

'Just a disagreement about wedding plans,' he says, lighting up a cigarette and joining us.

'Do you want me to go after her?' I ask, wondering why he hasn't.

He draws on his tab, lifts his chin and exhales the smoke into the cool night air. 'Would you mind? She might listen to you.'

On the side street there is no sign of Kat. I wander down to where a cluster of narrow roads diverge but I can't see her on any of them. When she doesn't answer her phone, I head back to the courtyard.

'Is she okay?' asks Sebastian. Henry lights up another fag.

'I can't find her. And she's not answering her phone. What do you think we should do?'

'Leave her, she'll be fine,' says Henry. 'She's a big girl.'

'But she looked really upset.'

Henry flicks his cigarette, ash falling to the floor, and shrugs. 'It's nothing worth worrying about. Let her cool off.'

It irks me that he isn't more concerned, but in my pleasantly prosecco-tinted haze I let it slide.

'Fancy a game of poker?' Henry asks Sebastian. 'There's a card table in the library.'

Sebastian looks to me for my approval. Given that the moment has passed between us and we're unlikely to get it back, I say, 'Go for it. I'll try and get hold of Kat.'

With the boys gone I put my feet up on the chair opposite me, wine glass in one hand, phone in the other, and start calling her. There is no reply. And the messages I send go unanswered.

'Here you are, I've been looking for you,' says Lizzie, a little while later, when I've given up and fallen into a drunken haze. 'Where's Kat?'

'Good question. She had a row with Henry and took off. I can't get hold of her.'

'What was the row about?'

'Their wedding.'

Lizzie ponders this fact. 'Really? Since when did Kat care enough about the details of her wedding to fight about it?'

It's a good point; one I hadn't thought of. 'So, if not the wedding, what?'

'I don't know,' says Lizzie, sounding oddly defensive.

It's then that I remember her snide comment about Henry this morning and her reluctance to meet my eye. 'Lizzie? Do you know something I don't?'

She shakes her head quickly, too quickly to pass as the truth. 'No.'

'Are you sure?'

Her shoulders immediately drop in surrender; she always has cracked under pressure stupidly fast. 'I might have heard a rumour at work, that's all.'

'About what?'

'About Henry.'

She pauses, probably trying to figure out whether it's a good idea to tell me or not. In the end, as always, she caves. 'Someone suggested that he might have been shagging one of the nurses – but it's probably just a malicious bit of gossip.'

'Or it could be true,' I say, because I have a horrible feeling that Henry might just be the sort of man who is capable of cheating on his fiancée.

I take in a lungful of crisp evening air, feeling my head begin to clear, listening to the muffled sound of the last few songs of the night and wishing my trousers were better insulated against the cold cast-iron. Lizzie tried to drag me back inside to dance, but one way or another it felt as if the evening was over. Hannah and Remy had left, Kat too, and Lizzie was only interested in boogie-ing the night away, not listening to my woes. Not that I blame her for that.

I've been sitting a while when Sebastian comes down the steps, his jacket slung over his shoulder. He has a certain James Bond swagger about him in the dim light.

'How was poker?' I ask.

'I didn't win.'

'Sorry to hear that.'

He shrugs. 'It was fun to play. Maybe I win next time.'

'Maybe.'

'So, I go now.' He makes a pattern in the gravel with his foot. 'Will you join me? Take a walk?'

It's a tempting offer but one I don't accept. 'Any other night.'

He takes the knock-back well, something that endears him to me even more. 'I see you again, *oui*?'

'*J'éspère*.' We both wince slightly at my pronunciation. Nevertheless, he comes towards me, places his hand gently behind my head and momentarily buries his nose in my hair. He then raises my chin towards him. For a moment our eyes meet and I think he's going to kiss me on the lips but, reading the situation correctly, he kisses me gently on the cheeks instead and says goodnight.

I sit a while longer, watching the last of the guests drift

out, full of happy, drunken chatter, all oblivious to me sitting back against the foliage.

In the end one person does notice me in the dwindling light. 'Why the glum face?'

In my stupor it takes a moment for me to figure out that the question is directed at me and that it's Leo, his camera bag in hand.

'Where's your assistant?' *Slash girlfriend*.

'I asked the first question,' he says, putting his bag on the table.

I shrug. 'Wedding blues.'

'How come?'

'Everyone seems to be growing up and moving on, finding what they want, except me.'

'I know that feeling,' he says, his eyes cast down.

'You do?'

'Sure! All my friends are getting married, settling, having kids. It sucks. Plus *I* have to go to client weddings too.'

I laugh. 'You may have the worse deal.'

'I *definitely* have the worst deal!'

A comfortable silence hangs between us. Maybe it's the wine I've consumed but tonight I don't feel nearly so awkward around him – I know this is just a perk of the job to Leo, a flirtatious wedding guest at every gig, but I can't help wanting to give in to the attraction, just for a moment.

'Where's your assistant?' I ask.

'Gone.'

'Left you?'

'Something like that.' He picks up his bag. 'I need to put my kit away but I'm not ready to head back yet. Fancy grabbing a bite?'

'I'm not that hungry, but a walk on the heath would be nice to blow away some cobwebs.'

'Sounds good.'

Once Leo is free of his gear we stroll past the red-brick mansion blocks towards Hampstead Heath.

'Do you usually take late-night walks with strange men?' he asks.

'I try not to make a habit of it!' I say, having to look up to talk to him. I hadn't realised how much taller he is than me, but then again, I am vertically challenged. 'How about you?'

He chuckles. 'The late-night walks, yes, the strange men? No!'

'Oh, just strange women?'

'Back home I used to walk barefoot along the beach at night with only the waves for company.'

'Sounds gorgeous,' I say, trying not to swoon too much at the idea of moonlit walks on the beach, hand in hand. 'Do you miss it?'

He hesitates. 'I miss the people, more than the place.'

I want to ask if he misses anyone in particular, but keeping in mind Aunt Jane's advice about being imperious, I keep quiet.

'Where's home for you?' he asks as we enter the park.

'Wiltshire.'

'Right, of course.' He clicks his fingers. 'Where Lizzie had her wedding.'

'We grew up together, Hannah and Kat too.'

'Kat?'

'The other "groomsman".'

'Gotcha. She asked today if I can do her wedding too.'

'Can you?' The pitch of my voice belies the composure I was aiming for. *Very smooth, Bea.*

'Usually at such short notice I couldn't – but I had a cancellation.'

'Lucky for Kat.'

'Although not so lucky for the other bride.'

'True.' I grimace.

We stroll quietly for a moment or two, me trying not to let my face show all the questions racing through my mind, he seemingly more comfortable in silence than I am.

'Your three best friends all married in one summer, huh?' he says, eventually breaking the lull in conversation.

'You see now why I have the wedding blues?'

'It's hard to see everyone settling down if you still feel restless. Sometimes it makes me wonder if there's something wrong with me.'

'Particularly when you're single.' I let the comment linger, hoping he'll agree and in doing so confirm that he and the assistant are not an item. But he doesn't. *Damn it.* 'It can make life a bit lonely.'

'You said Lizzie was your flatmate?'

I'm impressed that he's remembered. 'She was. Now it's just me.'

'And the guy who proposed . . .' Turns out he's remembered more than just Lizzie being my flatmate.

'Has moved on.'

'And now Hannah's married . . . and next it's Kat.'

'You get the picture?'

'What about the French dude? I thought . . .'

He doesn't finish, but I store away the fact he's had a thought about Sebastian and me. I allow myself a sliver of hope that the kiss wasn't quite as meaningless as I thought.

'He was just another wedding date. An improvement on the last, but ultimately just a date.'

'Looked to me as if he might have wanted to be more.'

Do I detect a hint of jealousy?

'I doubt it, and besides, as nice as he was, and pretty! I didn't get much sense of passion. He was a bit too *comme ci comme ça*.'

Leo offers me a quiet smile and we amble on to just beyond the mixed bathing pool, where we happen upon a late-night crêpe shack, the sweet smell of which makes my mouth water.

'Shall we grab one?' Leo asks.

'Absolutely. Just lemon and sugar for me, please,' I say to the vendor.

'And I'll have chocolate and banana.'

'Lizzie always made me pancakes when I was feeling down.'

'A stack of pancakes does it for me every time,' he says. *This man is too good to be true.* 'That is one thing I miss about home, the pancakes.'

With crêpes in hand we wander up to Parliament Hill

and take a seat on one of the benches, looking out over the city in the distance.

'It all looks so peaceful from up here,' I say.

'Hard to imagine ten million hearts beating among it.'

It's such a lovely way to think of a sprawling city that it brings me up short. For a moment all I can do is stare at the view and munch quietly on my crêpe.

'How's the jewellery designing going?'

'Mmm, good actually,' I say, wiping away a drizzle of sugary lemon juice that's escaped down the side of my mouth. 'I'm taking a refresher class and a little business course too.'

'That's great, Bea.' The sparkle in his eye makes me think he's genuinely pleased for me.

'Thanks.' It feels good to hear him being supportive. 'Sometimes I wonder if the girls think it's just a bit of a whim but I'd really like to give it a go. I know I have to start small but it's worth a shot, right?'

'I started out doing free shoots on weekends after working all week at a burger joint to make ends meet. But from that I got a portfolio and a website and then paid gigs started coming in. If you're passionate about it, it'll happen.'

'And now it's not just you, right? You have your assistant.'

'Exactly. And eventually I might get a studio manager and it will keep growing, so long as the desire is still there.'

I desperately want to ask if the assistant is anything

more to him, but I can't figure out how to steer the conversation without being completely blatant.

'Is it just weddings you do?'

'God no!' he says, wiping his hands on a paper napkin. 'Weddings are my bread and butter, the stuff that enables me to do the work I love. No, weddings will go just as soon as there's enough money coming in from the music photojournalism – that's what I really want to do.'

'Sounds cool. But weddings must have perks, right? Free food, free drink, lots of single girls looking for romance . . .'

He laughs, a coy smile forming. 'Well, I must admit there are certain bonuses.'

I offer a look that says, *go on.*

'Let's just say I've seen a lot of places *and* tasted a lot of different flavours.'

'Are we talking food, or girls?'

His eyes twinkle in amusement. 'Both.'

The scene in *Four Weddings* when Carrie discloses just how many men she's slept with springs to mind, and I feel a little as Charles felt, somewhere between baffled and unworldly.

'And was I just another of those flavours?' I ask, laying down the rest of my crêpe, suddenly not so keen to finish it.

He turns to face me, his amber eyes soft with concern, and brushes a thumb over my cheek.

'Once in a blue moon someone comes along who trips you up, someone who makes you turn around and look at where you've come from, someone who makes it crystal clear where you're meant to go next.'

'I don't know what you mean,' I say, my heart pounding.

From his expression I can tell a million thoughts are swirling inside his brain. I want to reach in and grab them and find out what they are. But before I can find the words he closes in and kisses me, and all million thoughts are forgotten.

12

'Good morning.' The voice drifts into my subconscious. 'Breakfast's up.'

'Huh?' I say, groggily, only just coming round from sleep.

'I made pancakes.'

I open my eyes to find Leo standing next to the bed holding a tray.

'You made me breakfast in bed?' I ask, sitting up and rubbing my eyes. *I must still be dreaming. He can't be this hot and thoughtful enough to make pancakes.*

'I figure after all the calories we burned last night we were entitled to some.'

'What time is it?' I squint at the clock, which reads just after eleven. 'How is that possible?'

'We didn't get in until after midnight and then . . .'

As he places the tray over my lap a smile spreads across his face.

'Oh God. Was I hideously drunk?' I paw at my cheeks. My skin feels dry and there's a faint pounding in my head. Lord knows what state my hair and make-up are in.

'Just drunk enough to be uninhibited,' he says, pouring me an orange juice.

Last night floods back to me. The kiss on the hill. The cab ride home. Stumbling in through the front door and frantically peeling off each other's clothes.

'Did we . . . on the stairs?' I ask.

'And in the shower, and on the bed, several times!'

I reach for the juice, the details slowly filtering back to me, and a smile twitches on my lips. 'Do you usually sleep with girls you consider unphotogenic?'

Leo climbs onto the bed beside me and starts kissing my upper arm. 'I was referring to the bloke you were with, what was his name?'

'Dave,' I groan, laughing at my paranoia.

'Right, Dave. *Dave* is definitely not photogenic. You, on the other hand . . .' He continues to kiss me, making his way up my neck until I push him away so I can tuck into my pancake. 'I was thinking,' he says, once he's got the message that food comes first, 'if you've nothing else to do, maybe we could spend the day together, here, in bed.'

I cast him an 'oh really?' look. 'I've someone coming round to look at the house, which won't take long. But I'm not promising anything until I've eaten *all* of these pancakes.'

'Fair enough!' he says, pinching one from the top of the pile.

'Oi! Watch it. That is no way to make friends with me.'

Leo showers while I eat and, on his return, with only a small towel wrapped round his middle, picks up the photo on my dresser of my mum.

'Is this your mom?'

'Uh–huh,' I say, focused on what's underneath the towel rather than the photo.

'You look just like her.'

'I hear that a lot, but my temperament is more my dad's.'

'How old did you say you were when he left?'

'Five.'

'Shit. How did your mum manage?'

I shrug. 'She didn't have time to wallow. She got a job at the supermarket and worked when I was at school. Then she came home and looked after me. I didn't think about it at the time but she had no life away from me. For ten years she did everything on her own. And I don't ever remember her complaining.'

'She sounds incredible.'

'Yeah,' I say, thinking about her resilience. 'I wish I had a tenth of her compassion and steeliness.'

'You strike me as having both those things.'

'Do I?' I laugh, surprised. 'I'm not so sure about that. But seeing my mum being stuck in one place and my dad being free to come and go definitely made me less inclined to want to be tied to one place or person, to be more self-sufficient.'

'I get that.'

'You do?'

'Mom was devastated when my dad took off. He sent money but I'm pretty certain she'd have chosen emotional support over cash any day of the week.'

'Do you have a photo?'

He scrolls through his phone. 'My father leaving made me determined not to be that guy – the guy who gives up on someone, who just ditches them on a selfish whim.'

He shows me a photo of him about ten years old in swimming shorts with two other kids, one older, the other younger, and his mom.

'She's very pretty,' I say, examining the photo a little more closely. 'Is this your garden?'

'Yeah, it's really just a deck that leads straight onto the sand. The beach was our garden.'

'Hence the late-night walks,' I say, glancing up to meet his eye.

'There's been quite a lot of those over the years.'

'And the people in the background?' I ask, referring to a family playing with a beach ball at the back of the photo.

'Our neighbours. When dad left they became a bit of a surrogate family.'

'Nice that your mum had someone.'

'Yeah,' he says, taking back his phone. There's an undercurrent to his voice that tells me he's left something important unsaid. 'Anyway, where were we . . .?'

He's clambering back under the cover when his phone pings. He ignores it, kissing my neck and snuggling in. The phone pings again and again.

'You should check it. It could be urgent.'

Grudgingly he turns from me to grab it.

'Shit,' he mutters, when he's read what it says. I pull the duvet a little closer around me, his energy suddenly different.

'What's up?'

He reaches for his trousers. 'I gotta go.'

The change in him is so abrupt that it makes me feel shut out, a bit vulnerable. And the memory of my father leaving, getting up and going without reason in the middle of us playing noughts and crosses one Sunday, comes racing back to me. In the end he stayed away for ever. 'Where to?'

'It's complicated,' he says, dismissively, his thoughts now occupied by something other than me. He comes over and kisses me sharply on the top of the head. 'I'll call you,' he says, leaving me alone with the disconcerting feeling that there's something about Leo that I don't know at all.

I can't pretend to be much in the mood for showing the house to a potential flatmate but it's all arranged – the guy coming is a friend of a friend of Bev's husband – so I bury my disappointment over Leo leaving and get the place ready, picking up the clothes I left draped over the bannister last night and shoving them into the washer.

It's almost three o'clock by the time the bell rings, which, given Connor was meant to arrive at two, doesn't exactly fill me with goodwill towards him. If you're trying to sell yourself as a flatmate you'd think the one thing you'd do is show up on time.

'Sorry I'm late, like,' says Connor, his Irish accent immediately soothing away any irritation I might have had. 'The Tube was feckin' heevin'!'

'No trouble,' I say, letting him into the hall. He shakes the rain from his black buzz-cut like a dog.

'It's lashing it down out there.'

It should bother me that he makes no effort to wipe his feet or remove his wet coat but there's something instantly likeable about his no-nonsense attitude that makes me put the thought to one side. I reckon if he was a dog he'd be a little Jack Russell, all wiry, yappy and spirited.

'Come through,' I say, taking him to the back of the house. 'The kitchen's small but it has everything you're likely to need.'

'Aye, that's grand,' he says, giving it a quick once over. 'I mostly have my scran at the pub anyway.'

Tick number one – unlikely to leave the kitchen in a mess.

'That's right, you said in your email you work at The Tup in Shepherd's Bush?'

'I'm the manager there.'

Tick number two – home late.

Tick number three – likely to get up late so won't need the bathroom when I'm getting ready for work.

I show him Lizzie's room, which has become something of a work area.

'Obviously all of this will be cleared,' I say, gesturing to the supplies and course notes scattered everywhere.

'Aye, no bother.'

He declares the rest of the house 'grand', and I find myself wondering if I'd inadvertently blown the whole 'finding a new flatmate thing' out of proportion.

135

'Have you any questions for me?' I ask, finally showing him the living room.

'Are either of these couches sofa beds?'

''Fraid not.'

'And no other mattress or fold-downs in the house?'

'No,' I say, a little alarm beginning to ring in my mind. 'Why?'

'Just that me brothers like to come over when they can, you know, go out on the tear from time to time.'

'How often?' I ask, trying not to let it show that he's just waved a major red flag at me.

'Ach, you know, maybe twice a month, three at most.'

I pause.

'And how many brothers do you have?'

'Eight.'

A look of horror must flash across my face because he quickly says, 'But don't fret, they wouldn't all come at once, like, maybe just half of them, maybe a few more at Christmas.'

Half?! You've got to be kidding me? You, plus four brothers, equals five drunken men in my front room. Not bloody likely, mate.

'Well, that's good to know,' I say, only just managing to hide the sarcasm.

'So, can I have the room? Me brothers'll be happy with a camping mat or that, they wouldn't need anything fancy.'

'I've just one other person to see,' I fib, showing him to the door. 'But I promise I'll let you know just as soon as I can.'

136

'Great,' he says, oblivious to my lie. 'Well, I'd better crack on.'

'Sure thing,' I say, closing the door behind him with a weary sigh, realising that Lizzie is even more irreplaceable than I thought.

13

'Thanks for coming with me, Aunt Jane,' I say, leaving the 1960s monstrosity of a building that is City University the following week.

'I see now why you needed the moral support,' she says, shaking off the tedium of the business class we've just sat through, and drinking in the warm evening air.

I managed to secure a place on a ten-week course soon after Aunt Jane and I discussed the idea of me focusing on jewellery design again, figuring it would be a good idea if I knew my proverbial arse from my elbow on all things business. Now, six weeks later, it's an understatement to say that my enthusiasm for spreadsheets, marketing and cash flow is waning.

'I can't wait to be able to focus all my energy on design and not on the tedium of websites and accounts.'

'All in good time,' she says, as we cross the square and stroll towards a gorgeous little coffee shop I discovered close to campus.

'Shall we treat ourselves to hot chocolate?' I ask once we're nestled under a heated parasol in the cafe's courtyard, its walls covered in ivy.

'Does this mean there's trouble afoot?'

I laugh at my own predictability. 'You never miss a trick!'

'So, what is it?' she asks, once the waitress has taken our order of two hot chocolates with all the trimmings.

'Do you remember the wedding photographer?'

'How could I forget!' she says, with a mischievous smile.

'Well . . .' I say, playing with a sugar sachet, trying to think of how to tell Aunt Jane I slept with Leo without shocking her too much.

'You went to bed with him,' she says, in her entirely matter-of-fact way.

'Aunt Jane!'

How is it that I'm the one blushing?

She shrugs with a little purse of her lips. 'I may be an old spinster but I'm not *completely* oblivious to the ways of the world.'

'Apparently not,' I say, bemused by how Aunt Jane is still able to shock and surprise me after all these years.

'So, do tell – what's the problem? Was he a selfish lover? Too big, too small, or maybe there was nothing at all!'

'Stop!' I say, my eyes wide, my cheeks reddening by the minute. 'It's nothing to do with his performance.' I cringe at the expression. Aunt Jane beckons with her eyes for more information. 'It's that he hasn't called since he left the next morning.'

'Ah,' she says, sitting back in her chair, absorbing the information. 'A hit and run!'

'Something like that.' I laugh, humourlessly.

'So you had a one-night stand – who cares!'

'I care.'

'Why?'

'Because I'd like something more with him.'

Our conversation is interrupted by the waitress bringing us our hot chocolates.

'Why would you want more with someone who sleeps with you then doesn't call?'

I scoop up a teaspoon of whipped cream. 'Because instinct tells me there's something more to his silence.'

'I'm not sure how much we should rely on instincts. In my experience they have a funny way of getting you into trouble. Maybe just chalk it up to being unlucky in love.'

'Maybe,' I say, thinking again about Aunt Jane and her someone 'many moons ago'. 'Is that something you've been, unlucky in love?'

At first Aunt Jane's expression is hard but it begins to relax as she wraps her hands around the warm mug, a memory coming back to her.

'Aunt Jane . . . was there someone special?'

'There was,' she says quietly, her eyes immediately softening. 'But I thought it was over a long time ago – until he came back into my life.'

'It was Tom, wasn't it?'

'Nonsense,' she says, blushing faintly.

'I felt the sizzle between you at Hannah's wedding, despite what you told me!'

'Don't be silly.'

'But it was him, wasn't it?'

She smiles coyly, taking a long sip of her drink. 'It was. We've known each other since we worked in an auction house on Lots Road, back in the late sixties. He was a porter, I was a secretary. At first we used to sneak out back for a cigarette together, that grew into lunch and then, before I knew it, we were eating dinner on the floor of my flat, which he helped me to decorate when I bought it.'

'Tom told me about the motorbike and miniskirt. I wondered then if you had been a couple . . . What happened? Why didn't it lead to more?'

'That's a good question.' It sounds as if she's not quite sure of the answer. 'I suppose it was to do with me having ambition. I dreamt of becoming an auctioneer; back then that wasn't compatible with being a wife, let alone a mother.'

'Did he ask you to marry him?'

'He did. And I was sorely tempted to say yes, but instead I asked him to wait, which *he* was happy to do but his family didn't like. In the end they forced him to find a better job, and he did. We saw less of each other and when someone else came along, someone more conventional, someone happy to be a wife, he started seeing her and eventually they married.'

'Did you know about her at the time?' I ask, wondering how I can have known Aunt Jane for thirty years and never heard this story.

'Oh yes, and she was nice. I understood. Tom asked me if there was any chance of me marrying him because he wouldn't marry her if he thought there was, but I told him no. By that time I was an auctioneer and I had my sights on my own business. I had no desire to be a wife, even if that did mean losing Tom.'

'So they married?'

'And had three beautiful children.'

'And did you keep in touch?'

She shakes her head, a slight sadness misting in her eyes. 'It was easier not to. We bumped into each other once on the King's Road, sometime in the eighties. We went for dinner, had a few drinks, and it was clear the chemistry was still there.'

'Did something happen?'

'No, but we were both tempted. We exchanged numbers but neither of us called the other. For months, maybe years after that meeting, I questioned if I'd made the right decision, putting my ambitions first.'

'And had you?'

'I think so. By that time I had the business, I was successful in my own right. Of course, it was easy to think I'd made the wrong decision, when it felt as if he'd slot right back into my life, but the truth is, if we'd married when we were young, I wouldn't have had my career and I'd have resented him for it. The relationship would have suffered.'

'So how did you get back in touch this time?' I ask, enthralled by Aunt Jane's story.

'Moira, his wife, passed away. It was his son who contacted me. He'd been given the job of calling his parents' friends. Tom had kept the slip of paper with my number on it, put it in their contacts book. His son must have thought I was a friend of his mother's.'

'Or maybe he knew his father needed you,' I say, caught up in the romance of it all.

'Well, whichever way, fate intervened. I didn't go to the funeral but we met up a few months later.'

'How did that feel?'

'It felt no different from when we were twenty-three or forty-three: the feeling was exactly the same.'

'And so you're back together?'

'Well, not exactly,' she says, and I feel as if a needle has just been ripped off a record. *How are they not together? I could have sworn something was going on between them!*

'I thought that's where you were going with this. He's been your wedding date twice . . . but you're not involved?'

She twists her lips uncertainly. 'Let's say we're exploring things slowly.'

'Why? Haven't you waited long enough?'

'Beatrice,' she says, in a tone that says 'be sensible'. 'I'm seventy-three.'

'So?'

'It's too late in my life for romance.'

'No, it's not!'

'I'm stuck in my ways,' she says, dismissing the idea. 'And I don't want to run the risk of losing him again.'

'Oh well, that's a great attitude. Why be with someone you've loved all your life when you could spend the rest of your life loveless and alone?'

'If it were meant to be, it would have happened long ago.'

'Aunt Jane, don't take this the wrong way but you're talking rubbish. Didn't I say falling in love is all about timing? Both you and Tom couldn't be more established, and for once in your lives you're both single. You have to grasp love whenever it comes, Aunt Jane. So, grasp it now!'

'I suppose you may have a point,' she says, stirring her hot chocolate in steady circles, a rogue sparkle forming in her eye.

14

'How was Bali?' I ask Hannah, a couple of days later, letting her into the hallway.

'Implausibly beautiful.' For once she isn't in her running kit and sporting a slick of sweat; her hair is swept back in a cloth headband, her skin clear and tanned.

'Did Remy subject you to endless yoga?'

'She knew better! I spent most of my time on the beach reading.'

'Sounds pretty great,' I say, taking her through to the dining room where Kat and Lizzie are busy unwrapping the Chinese takeaway for our girls' night.

'Hi, Mrs Remy,' says Lizzie, lacking her usual vim. I've asked her several times what's up but I can't get anything out of her.

'Hello, Mrs Jack.'

'You guys,' says Kat, with a shake of her head and a smile.

'You'll be Mrs Henry in a couple of months,' Lizzie reminds her. 'Then it will be three missuses and only one miss among us.'

'Speaking of which,' says Hannah, her eyes glinting

with mischief. 'How did you and Sebastian get on at the wedding?'

'Oh my God, he was so hot!' says Kat, pretending to fan herself. 'Tell me you've seen him again.'

The mention of Sebastian at the wedding brings Leo to mind and, inadvertently, a sheepish smile forms on my lips.

'Bea?' says Lizzie. 'Have you been keeping secrets?'

'No!' I blurt out, clearly not telling the truth.

'Bea Henshaw, we are not eating any of this food until you confess.'

'So you'd better start talking, because I'm starving,' says Hannah, already sitting at the table, loading up her plate.

'What happened, Bea?' Kat asks, with a slight look of disappointment in her eyes, as if, perhaps, she wishes I'd told her first.

I take a seat. 'Nothing happened with Sebastian . . .'

'But?' she asks.

'But something *might* have happened with Leo.'

'No way!' Hannah splutters, only just containing a mouthful of ginger chicken.

'Way,' I say, trying to sound breezy, helping myself to some special kung po.

'Exactly *what* happened?' asks Kat, always the first to know when I'm not sharing everything.

I circle my fork in the rice, avoiding eye contact.

'Bea?' says Lizzie.

'You slept with him, didn't you?' says Kat.

'I might have,' I say, raising my eyes sheepishly.

'How did that happen?' asks Hannah, putting down her fork. 'I thought he was just a crush.'

'I thought he was "out of your league",' says Kat.

'How is anyone out of Bea's league?' asks Lizzie.

'Thanks, Liz. I can always depend on *you* for support.'

'Bea . . .?' says Kat, in that way of hers that tells me she's not going to drop it until I tell her what's going on.

I finish a mouthful of rice, thinking where to begin. 'We kissed at Lizzie's wedding.'

'What?' cries Lizzie. 'How do I not know this?'

'How do any of us not know this?' asks Kat.

'Because I wasn't sure if it was just a "wedding thing". He made some comment that made me think he's slept with quite a few guests, *and* he told me during the day that I wasn't photogenic.'

'Well, that's bloody charming,' says Hannah, gnawing on a spare rib.

'Although kind of true!' says Kat.

'Kat!' says Lizzie. 'Don't be mean.'

'She's right, Liz,' I say, with a laugh, thinking of all the photos that make me look toothy with a double chin rather than broad-lipped and fresh-faced. There's one old school photo in particular that Kat loves to rib me about, where I look remarkably like Ken Dodd. 'Anyway, it turns out he was talking about Dave. After Hannah's wedding we went up to the heath and wound up, back here, in bed.'

'Oh God,' says Lizzie. 'Wouldn't it be amazing if Leo turned out to be the one, and we had our fourth wedding of the summer?'

I roll my eyes at Lizzie's wedding fever.

'I wouldn't jump the gun on wedding number four,' says Kat. 'I'm having serious doubts about whether number three is going to happen.'

Lizzy gasps, her hand covering her mouth; Hannah puts down the rib. It's something I've been wondering about ever since I saw Kat and Henry fight.

'What do you mean?' I ask, selfishly relieved not to have to tell them that Leo hasn't been in touch since he left, leaving me feeling that I'm just another of his many 'wedding girls'. But I'm also concerned about Kat. I called her a day or two after Hannah's wedding to make sure she was okay after her row with Henry but she brushed it off, saying it was nothing. I still haven't got to the bottom of what it was about.

She pushes her food round her plate. 'I don't know exactly. It's just a feeling. Something's not right.'

Hannah casts me an uncertain look. I glance down, remembering the rumour Lizzie told me.

'It's just wedding nerves,' says Lizzie. It surprises me that she sounds so casually dismissive, given what she's heard about Henry.

'But is it?' Kat asks, and I swear she's begging Lizzie to tell her what she knows.

I almost start to speak, but my mouth goes dry and I reach for my drink instead. I've always told Kat everything important – how can I keep this from her? But then again, I can't ruin her marriage on the basis of third-hand gossip.

'What's going on Kat?' says Hannah

'I just feel he's not telling me something.'

'Have you asked him?' I ask.

'Yes, but he says I'm being paranoid or making stuff up.'

'Being paranoid about what?' asks Hannah, and Lizzie shoots me a worried glance.

'Let's forget about it. I'm sure it's nothing,' she says, quietly returning to her food.

A slightly awkward silence falls over the table for a moment. I'm turning the rumour about Henry and the nurse over in my mind, and Lizzie is probably doing the same.

'Is married life still bliss?' Hannah asks, breaking the quiet at last.

'It's been better,' Lizzie says, which causes us all to do a double-take.

'Really?' I ask. 'How come?'

'We had a row.'

'Over what?' asks Hannah, completely incredulous. 'Who writes the best pillow notes?'

'Ha ha,' says Lizzie. 'Actually, it was about that tour I mentioned – it's to the States, probably for the best part of a year. I don't want him to go.'

'Wow!' I say, sitting back a little, taking in her news. 'A US tour is a big deal.'

'I don't think you can say no to that, Liz,' says Kat.

'We had an agreement,' she says, uncharacteristically staunch in her delivery. 'We couldn't live together before we married because of him touring and recording; he

promised we'd live together for at least a year before he
went away again.'

'Right, but he couldn't have foreseen a US tour,' I
say.

She shrugs. 'He needs to decide what's more important. Me or the band.'

'Good luck with that!' says Hannah, biting into a
prawn cracker with an enormous crunch.

'Anyway, in other news,' says Lizzie. 'Carburetor's
playing a festival in August near to home and I've got
tickets. I thought it might be nice for all of us to go, give
us a break from all this wedding malarkey.'

'Sounds great,' I say, thinking it's a great incentive
to get my collection together so that I might sell some
pieces while I'm there.

'I'm in. I reckon Remy will be too.'

'Me too,' says Kat. 'Regardless of what Henry thinks.'

'Then it's decided,' says Lizzie. 'Wellies and wigwams
ahoy!'

Kat and Hannah headed off together just a little after
ten-thirty, with Lizzie telling them she'd stay a little
longer to help clean up, though really it was because I'd
asked her to stay back so we could chat about Kat and
Henry.

'Should we say something to her?' I ask, scraping the
plates in the kitchen.

'What would we say?'

'That there's a rumour going around about Henry?'

'But it is only a rumour.'

'You haven't heard anything more?'

'I saw him with the girl in question the other day, in the canteen.'

'And?'

'Well, they weren't kissing or holding hands over their soup.'

'But did they look, I don't know, caught up in each other?'

'Not so much that I'd need to mention it to Kat,' she says, taking the plates from me and loading them into the dishwasher.

'But what if something is going on and we don't say anything?'

'It's not our place to say; it's Henry's.'

'We should just let him marry Kat even if he's cheating?'

Lizzie releases a long sigh. 'It's not as if we have any evidence.'

'Even though we had an inkling and she would more than likely eventually find out, and possibly get divorced?'

'Yes, because, otherwise we run the risk of introducing something that isn't real, that makes Kat look completely paranoid, and possibly blows up their relationship. At least this way their relationship stands a chance.'

'I'm not sure how much I want it to,' I mutter.

'Meaning?'

'Meaning I don't think he's that good for her. They're always at each other's throats. And that's not like Kat.'

'But Henry isn't our choice, Bea. He's Kat's choice.'

'You're right, I suppose.' *Though I don't like it.* 'So, we agree not to say anything?'

'Not unless there's something definite to tell.'

'Fine,' I say, twisting a dishcloth, not feeling fine at all.

15

'So? What do you think?' asks Kat, three days later, showing me her choice of wedding venue.

'Honestly?' I ask, looking at the beer-stained carpet and pine-clad bar of the hotel function room. 'I think it feels like the kind of place wakes are held for people without many friends or much money.'

Kat laughs. 'I admit, it is on the utilitarian side – but you know me, I'm not interested in all the trimmings and trappings of a fancy wedding.'

'I get that,' I say, imagining the place full of Kat's friends and family. Even then I can't quite imagine away the woodchip wallpaper.

She throws me a dubious look.

'I do!' I say. 'But Hannah's wedding wasn't big and yet it still represented what she and Remy are about.' I cast my eye round the bland walls and the net curtains obscuring the Westway beyond. 'This doesn't really say anything about either you or Henry.'

'But it will, once the tables are in and dressed and the flowers are in place. And besides, it's really practical for people getting here from home and there's lots of parking.'

I scoff tragically. 'Tell me you didn't choose a wedding venue on how much parking it has?'

'It's important!'

I incline my head at her, my eyebrows raised in a 'Really?' sort of way. 'What's important is that you can look back with no regrets.'

'Do you mean about the choice of wedding venue or the choice of husband?'

I know Kat's joking, but I can't find it in me to laugh. 'Bea?'

I pause, wondering how best to word my concerns about her husband-to-be. 'You don't think that maybe this place says something, subconsciously, about your feelings for Henry?'

'I don't think so,' she says, plumping down on the velour window-seat.

'You don't have any worries at all about marrying him?' I ask, sitting next to her.

She shakes her head. 'No more than most.'

'And the row at Hannah's wedding . . .?' I ask, hoping she doesn't brush me off again.

Kat releases a long sigh before telling me. 'I got it into my head that he was having an affair, or maybe not "an affair" exactly, but spending time with someone who could become *significant,* if you know what I mean.'

'And?'

She shrugs. 'He denied it and when I pushed him further he got mad and we ended up fighting about something petty instead, I don't even remember what it was.'

'And you're confident that he was telling the truth, that there isn't anyone else?'

It's obvious from her reticence that she's not convinced. 'I mean, what can I do? It's not as if I have any proof, it's just a feeling.'

I can't believe I agreed with Lizzie not to mention the rumour. Stupid, stupid me.

'Isn't it a feeling you should be free of come your wedding day?'

'That would make sense!' she laughs, dismally.

'Because you can't begin your life together on a doubt.'

She turns to me. 'You think I should challenge him again?'

'I don't see how it could hurt. If he really loves you he'll reassure you. And if he's having doubts, isn't it better you know now, rather than later?'

She laughs, soberly. 'Aren't I meant to be the pragmatic one in this friendship?'

'Yes, you are! So pull your shit together and let me be the ditzy one again.'

'Thanks, Bea,' she says, putting her head on my shoulder. 'What would I do without you?'

I place my hand on hers. 'You'd figure it out, hopefully before marrying someone who might be a complete pilchard!'

'I know he's not dementedly in love with me the way Jack is with Lizzie, or the way Simon was with you, but that works for me, you know? I'd feel completely hemmed in with someone like those guys.'

'I understand. I felt something similar with Simon. But maybe there's a halfway house? Maybe someone exists who gives you that space but also nurtures you. Because, from where I'm standing, I don't really see Henry doing that.'

'I think he leaves all his nurturing at work. But maybe I do too. Maybe we're both as bad as each other.'

'But does that make it right?'

She shakes her head. 'I don't know.'

'And you're sure you're not marrying him just because he's South African and it means great holidays for life?'

Kat throws back her head with a laugh. 'It's New Zealand I'm crazy about, remember? Not South Africa.'

We sit for a moment, both of us with our own thoughts: me thinking about Leo; she, I imagine, thinking how best to confront Henry.

'How did it feel seeing Simon with Edith at the wedding?' she asks.

'It wasn't the easiest.'

'I heard things are getting serious between them pretty fast.'

'That doesn't surprise me.' *Though it doesn't make it any easier to hear.* 'Simon wants a wife, and she looked like pretty good wife material to me.'

'You don't regret breaking up with him?'

An image of Leo flashes into my mind. 'No.'

'That sounds like a wistful kind of "no".'

I hesitate for a moment before saying slowly, 'But not for the reasons you might think.'

'So, enlighten me.'

156

I scrunch up my nose. 'It's been two weeks since I slept with Leo and he hasn't been in touch.'

She looks at me, surprised that I've kept this to myself for so long. 'Did he say he would be?'

I nod.

'Any idea why he wouldn't?'

'I've a hunch . . .'

'Which is?'

'That he might have a girlfriend?'

Kat contemplates this for a moment, looking at me watchfully. 'What makes you think that?'

'Just something about his assistant, the way they were together, and a comment a guest made about it being good to see them "back together".'

'But she could have meant them working together, right?'

'Maybe,' I say, tailing off. 'Someone messaged him the morning after we slept together, he rushed off saying it was "complicated" and that he'd explain later.'

'But he hasn't?'

'Nope,' I say, wishing desperately that I knew who he'd dashed off to be with. I could live with the answer, it's the not knowing that hurts.

'Sounds like you've got some questions of your own to ask.'

Don't I know it.

'Because you don't want to start a relationship with a two-timing twerp.'

She's right, so why do I still feel so crazy about the guy?

'Do you?'

'Of course not. It's just I can't quite get him out of my head.'

Kat falters before saying, 'If I'm honest, Bea, I don't really get it. He seems to pose more questions than he answers.'

'I know, it makes no sense, but . . .'

'What?'

'It's just something he said to me that made me think I might mean more to him than just a shag.'

'What did he say?'

'Something about me tripping him up, and making it crystal clear where he's meant to go next.'

Kat nods and then, as kindly as possible, says, 'You sure it wasn't just a line?'

I shrug, not knowing, but hoping that it wasn't.

We sit quietly, contemplating how best to get to the truth, until Sue, Kat's wedding coordinator arrives.

'Only eight weeks until "I do"!' she coos. I can almost feel Kat's restraint at not rolling her eyes. 'And as luck would have it your photographer has just arrived.'

A dim recollection of Leo telling me that Kat had booked him for her wedding is forming when Sue says, 'And here he is now!'

I turn to see Leo, walking across the dance floor, looking hotter than ever, my heart-rate off the chart.

'It's Leo, yes?' asks Sue, oblivious to my pounding heart and mind in overdrive.

'That's right,' he says, shaking her hand. He casts me a quick, apologetic glance before kissing Kat on both cheeks.

'And this is Kat's bridesmaid—'

'Bea,' he says, looking at me with a coy smile and a glint in his eye, which makes me glance nervously away.

Sue claps hers hands together. 'Very good. Shall we start by showing Leo the venue? Then you can decide where best to take your formal photos?'

'Let's do that,' says Kat. 'But Bea, there's no need for you to hang around, why don't you head to the coffee shop round the corner and *we'll* come find you after?' She exaggerates 'we'll' so heavily, with her head slightly pitched towards Leo, that there's no doubt in my mind that she's planning on sending him on his own.

'Good plan,' I say, trying to sound casual, gathering up my things. 'See you in a bit.'

The forty-five-minute wait in the dismal coffee shop near the Tube is torture. There are only so many emails you can reread, messages you can reply to, and Twitter feeds you can follow when your mind is half demented with thoughts of the man who slept with you and hasn't been in touch since. By the time Leo arrives, I've drunk three cups of coffee and I'm caffeinated to the hilt.

'Hi,' he says, pulling out the chair opposite mine. It scrapes loudly on the linoleum floor. 'Kat sends her apologies. She had to rush off to her final dress fitting.'

'Right,' I say, containing a laugh. It's such a plausible reason to anyone who doesn't know her, but to me it's the most blatant excuse to give us some space. 'Did you find somewhere suitable for the photos?'

He shakes his head with a little puff of resignation. 'It's not the most inspiring of venues.'

'Even by Kat's standards it's pretty basic.'

'But we'll make it work.'

We'll? Does he mean him and his assistant, or is he referring to himself and Kat?

There's a pregnant pause between us. I reposition the small vase of artificial flowers.

'I'll grab a drink. What would you like?' he says, when the moment becomes uncomfortable.

To know what's going on here. 'Nothing for me, thanks. I'm fine.'

He returns a few moments later with a large black coffee. My caffeine high has diminished, and the vibe between us feels less stilted.

'How have you been?' he asks. His eyes are full of warmth but he keeps his seat pushed back from the table, a safe distance apart.

'Okay.'

Bea, don't play it cool. Charles didn't. He told Carrie that he wished they'd rung each other. That she ruthlessly slept with him and never called. You can do the same.

'Though maybe a little confused,' I continue.

'About why I haven't been in touch?'

'Right.'

'I'm sorry about that, I've been meaning to, but I thought it might be better in person.'

Alarm bells start clanging in my head.

'What might be better in person?' I ask, not certain I really want to know the answer.

Maybe Henry was right, maybe it is kinder to be kept in the dark.

'You remember my assistant, Brit?'

As if I could forget. 'Uh-huh.'

'Our relationship is, like I said, complicated.'

'Relationship?'

'We work together but we also . . .'

There's a slight pause, while I feel my heart sink.

'We also have a kind of on–off relationship.'

'Okay,' I say, my voice tight. Aunt Jane would not be impressed. 'And were you *on* with her when we—'

'No,' he says, quickly. 'Definitely not. But she messaged me that morning, and I had to go. Not just because of her but because . . .' He falters. 'Like I said, it's complicated.'

'Are you with her now?'

He nods. 'I'm sorry, Bea. I didn't mean for you to be caught in the middle.'

'I don't feel caught,' I say, using my best imperious tone. 'It was a bit of fun, that's all. We're both grown-ups.'

Even if I do feel like running home and hiding under the duvet.

'I'm glad you feel that way.'

A moment passes between us where unsaid words seem to hang above us like cartoon speech bubbles, the only trouble being that the words are unintelligible. If Leo could understand mine he'd see that what I want more than anything is to climb back into bed with him and never let him go. I wonder what his might say.

If I were courageous, I'd put my heart on the line and deliver a speech, just like the one Charles delivered to Carrie on the South Bank, when he told her he thought he loved her but then realised how fruitless it all was, given that she was marrying Hamish. But I'm not courageous, and my life doesn't have a script to follow, so instead I sit, nervously twiddling my fingers, wondering how best to end the meeting without showing how hurt I am. Because it does hurt. The truth is that I want him and something, deep within me, tells me he might just want me too, even if he is with the strikingly beautiful Brit.

As luck would have it, fate intervenes in the shape of a phone call from Aunt Jane.

'Bea?' she says, when I answer.

'Hi, Aunt Jane,' I say, offering Leo an apologetic look.

'What are you doing on Wednesday afternoon?'

'I'll be at work.'

Not that that's much fun at the moment with Sir Hugh's ever-increasing forgetfulness and Simon trying to act as if everything's normal.

'Can you take the day off?'

'Probably. Why?'

'Because I'm getting married.'

She delivers this news completely matter-of-fact as if it were nothing out of the ordinary and warranted no reaction at all.

'What?' I blurt. 'To whom?'

'To Tom,' she says, as if it's me who's lost my marbles.

'But I thought—'

162

'Never mind what you thought, can you make it?'

'Of course, I can make it!'

'Good, and round up those girls of yours too. Every-one's welcome!'

JANE & TOM

Invite you to their wedding at
Chelsea Town Hall
& thereafter at The Palm Court
for a celebratory afternoon tea

Wednesday, 4 July

16

'This has got to be the most romantic wedding *ever*,' says Lizzie, admiring Aunt Jane's small bouquet of vibrantly coloured ranunculi on the coffee table. 'I still can't get my head around their story. Did they really meet fifty years ago?'

'Incredible, but true,' I say, adjusting my latest creation, a triangular fringe necklace of turquoise and purple beads and feathers, in the mirror above the record player.

'It couldn't have happened to a better person,' says Hannah, who's relaxing on the corner sofa, as much at home in Aunt Jane's flat as in her own.

'Aunt Jane, you're such a card,' Kat calls through to the kitchen. 'How could you keep this a secret?'

'Never mind me,' says Aunt Jane, bringing through a tray full of iced drinks and strawberries, her floral apron tied around her wedding outfit. She's chosen an elegant, high-necked, linen dress in navy blue and allowed me to choose her jewellery. I decided on a necklace and bracelet combo made of orange plastic that she's had since the 1960s. 'What I want to hear about is you girls.' She hands out drinks to each of us. 'Lizzie, how is married life? Should I be worried about what lies ahead?'

'It's more complicated than I imagined,' says Lizzie, flumping onto the sofa next to Hannah, briefly exposing the coloured layers of net beneath her bright summer skirt. She's unusually downcast again today and I don't know why.

'What's the matter?' I ask.

Lizzie explains to Aunt Jane about Jack's tour offer and the time it would mean spent apart, even though he promised her otherwise. I'm still not completely clear why she's so upset about it. 'And on top of that he's backtracked on starting a family, saying he'd prefer to be "financially stable" before we have a kid.'

'That's not such a crazy idea,' says Hannah, rubbing a tiny stain on the cuff of her floral chiffon dress. 'It's not as if the clock's *really* ticking.'

'It's a ludicrous idea!' says Lizzie, irritably.

If there are two people on earth more polarised in their opinions about money than Lizzie and Hannah I'd be very surprised. Hannah catalogues everything she spends; Lizzie's more your spend-and-think-later kind of girl.

'Starting a family in your late thirties is far more ex-hausting and stressful than doing it when you're younger. And besides, *I* am financially stable. *My* job is secure. I've no intention of giving it up; we'd be fine.'

'But what if he's touring and you're left bringing up the kid on your own while trying to work full-time?' asks Hannah. Sometimes Hannah really doesn't know when to keep quiet.

'I'd manage.' Lizzie sucks on her drink, sullenly.

'It sounds to me as if the two of you need to talk some more,' says Aunt Jane. It reminds me of the times she used to counsel us about boys, always reassuring us that no one could be good enough to deserve the time and worry we were giving them. 'Maybe it's not about the money *per se*, perhaps he's not feeling secure about his own future. That's very important for a man.'

'Thanks, Aunt Jane,' says Lizzie, finishing her drink with a slurp.

'And Kat, just two months until your big day. Are you excited?'

Kat fiddles with the bow of her high-waisted trousers. 'I'm not sure *excited* is quite the right adjective.'

'Why not?'

'Let's say we're trying to resolve a few differences of our own.'

'Well, what can I say – it all gets easier with age!'

'Let's hope so,' says Kat, and I give her an affectionate squeeze on the shoulder. Despite her best efforts she's no further forward with getting the truth out of Henry, making her more suspicious than ever.

'What's happening with you and Leo, Bea?' asks Lizzie. Last we spoke she only knew of us sleeping together. 'I thought after today we might be celebrating Five Weddings!'

'Well, if we are, it certainly won't be mine.'

'What's happened, Bea?' asks Hannah. In all the excitement of Aunt Jane's spur-of-the-moment wedding it hasn't felt appropriate to fill them in about Leo being back with Brit.

'He's with someone else.'

'Not the assistant?' says Aunt Jane.

'Yes, sadly. The assistant.'

'Bastard!' says Kat, loyal to the last.

'In truth, I don't think they were together at Hannah's wedding so . . .' I shrug. 'Anyway, they are now.'

'Has he rocks in his head?' asks Aunt Jane.

'Or his brains in his balls?' says Kat.

'I feel horrible for you,' says Lizzie, reaching for my hand. 'I really thought he could have been the one.'

'Right,' I say. *That old adage.* 'Maybe I did too.'

Maybe. But then again. Maybe not.

'Come on, Aunt Jane, look at us, the only one happy in her relationship is Hannah. You've got to cheer us up with the story of you and Tom. I've told the girls most of the story but we still don't know how you got back together? Who made the first move? What made you change your mind? And did Tom propose or did you?'

'Yes, please, Aunt Jane, tell us!' pleads Lizzie, her hands clasped together.

'Even I could do with hearing it,' says Kat. 'And romance and me are about as far removed as chalk and cheese.'

'Well, if you insist,' says Aunt Jane. She takes off her pinny and plumps a cushion to make herself comfortable on her chair.

'I phoned Tom a few weeks after his wife's funeral, when everyone else was returning to their own lives and not forgetting Moira but having no choice but to move on. The most I expected was a polite conversation, maybe a little fond reminiscing at most. What I didn't expect was for him to ask when he could see me.'

'Go Tom!' says Kat.

Aunt Jane casts her a playfully disapproving look. 'Well, naturally I put him off.'

'What?' I say. 'Why?'

'Christmas wasn't far away, it was a busy time, and I wanted him to think things through, be certain he wanted to visit his past when grieving for his wife. For all I knew he wasn't thinking straight.'

'So then what happened?' asks Lizzie, her hands on her cheeks, already absorbed in the story.

'He called me on New Year's Day. Said he couldn't wait any longer and when were we meeting.'

'Love it!' says Hannah. 'There's nothing like a persistent admirer.'

'And what did you arrange?' I ask.

'We met at the Tate Modern the following week. I thought it was a safe option – if our meeting was uncomfortable it would be easy enough to part without having to finish a meal or make some lavish excuse.'

'And was it uncomfortable?' asks Kat.

Aunt Jane throws back her head and laughs. 'Not at all! It was as if we'd never been apart. We chatted on ten to the dozen, barely stopping for breath. In the end they had to throw us out of the cafe at closing time.'

'How romantic,' says Lizzie, with a sigh. 'Was he desperately sad at the loss of his wife?'

'Of course, he was sad, but he was also relieved. Moira had been unwell for a long time, he'd become her carer;

171

the Moira he knew was gone well before she died.'

Kat allows Jane a moment of reflection to pass before she asks, 'What happened after you were thrown out of the Tate?'

'We strolled along the river for a time.'

'Hand in hand?' I ask.

I'm given a 'less cheek' look and I yield, despite the desire to tease her some more.

'We parted and agreed to see each other again soon for dinner.'

'Dinner?' says Kat, with a chuckle. 'Things must have gone well.'

'They had, and they continued to, until . . .'

'What happened?' asks Lizzie, quite breathless with anticipation.

'After a couple of months, Tom tried to kiss me.' Again, Aunt Jane pauses.

'And?' I ask, the suspense killing me, the others equally gripped.

'I froze,' she says, laughing foolishly at the memory.

'Why?' asks Kat.

Aunt Jane shakes her head a little. 'I was enjoying our get-togethers immensely, and it was clear that we both still had romantic feelings for one another, but I kept pushing those feelings aside, fearing I was too old for romance, too set in my ways.'

'But that's crazy,' says Hannah. *Exactly my point.* 'Why would you think that?'

'Being single is all I've ever known. It wasn't easy to consider living differently.'

'So, what changed?' asks Kat.

'It was something Beatrice said.'

'What did I say?' I ask, taken aback

'You asked me if I believed in "the one".'

The memory of us chatting at her flat after Simon and I broke up comes back to me.

'I knew in my heart that I did, but I couldn't allow myself to believe it. Even when you said, "your life has always been rich and varied" and my heart immediately reminded me that something, some*one* has always been missing, I still couldn't bring myself to be certain.' Aunt Janes pauses for a moment, appearing almost tired by the memory. 'But then you mentioned marriage being about timing—'

'That old chestnut,' says Lizzie, with a roll of her eyes, and Aunt Jane chuckles.

'But it got me to thinking that maybe this could be our time . . .'

'And?' I ask. 'What then?'

'I plucked up the courage to invite him as my "date" to Lizzie's wedding.' Aunt Jane looks pleased as punch at this decision. 'But I made him promise not to make it obvious, to say, if anyone asked, that we were simply companions.'

'I bought that line,' says Kat, selecting a strawberry.

'But then everyone knows you're completely oblivious to romance,' says Lizzie.

'Did *you* notice they were together, Miss *Brontë*?' replies Kat, poking fun at Lizzie's love of romantic fiction.

'I was too preoccupied with my new husband,' she says, her nose comically in the air.

'But wait, go back a step,' I say. 'Were you more than just friends at this stage? Had you . . .' I bottle asking about my aunt's sex life.

'We kissed after the wedding,' she says, putting me out of my misery.

'Oh, that's so sweet,' squeals Lizzie, at which point Kat throws a cushion at her.

'What can I say, all that mud and hay must have brought out some sort of natural instinct in us.'

'But then how come you weren't officially together at my wedding?' asks Hannah, never one to leave a thread dangling.

Aunt Jane shrugs a little. 'It all felt too new to tell. Tom had begun to stay over once or twice a week, and I loved sharing my life and home with him. It was as if in some way he had always been with me, always there at the back of my mind. And then he really was with me. It felt so personal, so momentous, I didn't want to share it. I dreaded losing what I'd dreamt of all those years.'

'How did you get from that place to your wedding day?' asks Hannah.

With her eyes full of admiration, Aunt Jane looks towards me. 'A little bird told me, "you have to grasp love when you can. Grasp it now", it said. So, I did. I rushed home to Tom and it all came pouring out. I told him I wanted to marry him. I proposed! Can you believe that? Me, a spinster all my days, proposed to the man I've loved since I was twenty-three.'

'Oh, Aunt Jane,' I say, reaching out my hand to her. 'I couldn't be happier for you.'

'It's incredible,' says Hannah. 'Completely remarkable.'

'And so nice to know that love is patient,' says Kat.

'That we should never give up hope,' says Lizzie.

'And that if it's meant to be, it *will* be,' says Aunt Jane, looking directly at me.

'Hmm,' I say, unconvinced.

'But for now, I have the perfect antidote to all your heartache—'

I raise an eyebrow expectantly.

'His name is Christopher, he's one of my up-and-coming auctioneers. Very charismatic!'

'Not another wedding date,' I say, despairingly.

'Trust me, Bea,' says Aunt Jane with a wink, 'this one's a goody!'

17

The five of us pile into a black cab, full of nervous excitement and chatter, and make the short drive to the Old Town Hall, where Tom is waiting in a high-ceilinged room with heavy drapes and Queen Anne chairs.

'Has she arrived?' he asks when I take my seat near the front with the girls.

'Yes!' I say. 'The wait is almost over.'

Tom is surrounded by his children, their spouses and his grandchildren, in varying degrees of patient expectation – one little girl in a frilly dress is swinging her legs, bashing them against the legs of the chair, there's a toddler staggering about at the front, and a slightly older boy slumped on his chair, desperate to be anywhere but here on such a beautiful summer's day. On Aunt Jane's side is a small hotchpotch of friends, young and old, from different stages of her life. I wave at a few familiar faces from years gone by, mouthing that I'll catch up with them later.

'You must be Bea,' says a voice from behind me.

I turn to discover a man, who's probably about my age but dressed in a three-piece linen suit and panama hat more suited to a man twice his age, and which certainly doesn't flatter his substantial bulk.

'I'm Christopher,' he lisps through a mouthful of protruding teeth.

'Hi,' I say, amazed at what Aunt Jane considers to be a 'goody'. Dave might have been a dork and Sebastian a bit bland, but Christopher surpasses both of them in the 'clearly not going to happen' stakes. 'Beautiful day for a wedding.'

'The very finest,' he says, over-annunciating every syllable, lisping on 'est' and spraying me with a shower of saliva.

'And here comes the bride,' I say, relieved not to have to extend our conversation further.

'Wonderful!' he exclaims, clasping his hands together in delight.

'A definite keeper,' Kat whispers into my ear with a giggle.

I give her a 'shut-up' nudge with my elbow and turn my attention to Aunt Jane, holding her brightly coloured posy, which looks brilliant against her navy dress and goes perfectly with the chunky orange jewellery.

'She looks amazing,' says Kat. 'I hope I look that good at her age.'

'Tom's a lucky guy.'

'Guess he's earned it, having waited for Jane for fifty years.'

'Yes,' I say, watching Tom's face as Aunt Jane arrives beside him. His devotion seems to radiate from every fibre of his being and I find myself wondering if I'll ever be lucky enough to find someone like Tom, someone who adores every inch of me and whom I adore equally in return. Because right now, with Christopher apparently my only option, the odds do seem impossibly small. The feeling I'd stored in my memory bank of Simon kissing me comes flooding back and I have to stop myself from wondering if I should have accepted his proposal after all.

'Good afternoon, and welcome to the marriage of Jane and Tom,' says the registrar. 'Before we begin I must ask if anyone knows of any legal cause why Jane and Tom should not be married today.'

'Oh goodie, my favourite bit!' says Aunt Jane, causing the guests to giggle. 'Nobody?' she asks, after no one is forthcoming.

'Then we can begin,' says the registrar with a smile. 'Jane, please repeat after me . . .'

After the briefest of vows Tom and Jane exchange rings.

'I give you this ring as a token of my love and friendship,' says Jane, threading the ring onto Tom's finger.

'And I give you this ring as a symbol of our love, friendship and support, promising to love and cherish you throughout our life together.'

The simplicity of their words and the conviction with which they're spoken causes my emotions to bubble over and before I know it tears are trickling down my cheeks.

'You big sap,' says Kat, handing me a tissue as Jane and Tom kiss.

'It's just the perfect love story,' I say through my tears.

Tom and Jane go to sign the register, a photographer documenting the moment.

'It feels odd to see a wedding photographer that isn't Leo,' say Kat.

'You're not wrong.'

I wonder where he is, if he's with Brit, and if so, what they're up to. My expression must give away what I'm thinking because Kat squeezes my hand and offers a supportive smile.

'Your turn will come,' she says.

'Maybe,' I reply, not quite able to muster the belief.

'Even if you do have to wait until your seventies,' she teases.

'With my luck I'll be dead and buried before anyone, let alone "the one" comes along.'

'Nobody knows *exactly* how afternoon tea came about but the Duchess of Bedford is rumoured to have started it,' says Christopher, who Aunt Jane has none too covertly positioned next to me at our table in the luxurious art deco setting of The Palm Court.

'Who was the Duchess of Bedford?' I ask, exchanging 'yawn' glances with Kat across the circular table.

'One of Queen Victoria's ladies in waiting.'

'Oh really.' I sip my champagne, trying to think of a reply. Queen Victoria's staff wouldn't be my first choice of specialist subject on *Mastermind*. 'Do you know why she invented it?'

'Dinner was served much later then, eight, eight-thirty

at night, sometimes even later. The duchess required sustenance mid-afternoon, hence afternoon tea.'

'Which is always a treat.'

'Mmm,' he says, salaciously biting into a smoked salmon finger sandwich, leaving me feeling a little queasy.

Kat raises her glass at me from across the table with a playful smirk. I could swing at both her and Aunt Jane!

Thankfully, midway through the afternoon, Aunt Jane and Tom decide to mix up the seating arrangement so, at last, Christopher is moved to the opposite side of the table and a lady, about my age, named Jessica sits next to me.

'How do you know Jane?' I ask, after we've established that Jane is my great-aunt.

'I manage her auction house,' she tells me, tucking her thick strawberry-blonde hair behind her ears.

'Oh, really!' I warm immediately to her gentle nature. Her unusual grey-blue eyes are full of kindness. 'How long have you been there?'

'I only moved down and started a few weeks ago. I think she took pity on me being the new girl in town, hence why she invited me here today.'

'Don't be silly. I'm sure she invited you so you could get to know everyone.'

Jessica casts a look towards Christopher on the other side of the table then whispers, 'There are some people I'd rather not get to know.'

I let out a laugh. 'You don't have to worry about Christopher. Aunt Jane is trying to set me up with him, he shouldn't give you any trouble.'

'Oh, no, I—' she says, taken aback. 'I didn't mean like *that*. I just meant, he's a bit full on and, given we have to work together, I'd quite like to keep a distance, personally, I mean. Besides, I think he's gay.'

'Really?' I say, kind of surprised, but then it dawns on me what Aunt Jane is up to. I shake my head, ruefully, and hatch a quick plan of retaliation before my thoughts return to Jessica. 'Where were you before you moved to the city?'

'In the north-east.'

'And have you settled into London life?'

'Not quite yet. I'm still in a hotel; it's hard to find an affordable place to live.'

'I have a room that's available,' I say, a slight feeling of trepidation in my stomach. Living on my own has been quite nice these last couple of months, but if I want to give up work and concentrate on my jewellery full-time I need someone to contribute to the bills, and Jessica seems pleasant enough.

'Oh really?' she says, her large eyes lighting up.

'Sure, why don't you come round and see it? I'm in Acton, not too far from the auction house.'

'That would be great, thank you.'

'What would be great?' asks Aunt Jane, drawing up a chair beside us.

'Jessica's going to look at my spare room.'

'Super,' she says. 'Now tell me, how are you getting on with Christopher? Quite charismatic, don't you think?'

At this point Jessica makes the wise decision of excusing herself.

'I think he's extremely charismatic,' I say, setting my plan in motion. 'In fact, meeting him makes me realise just how badly suited Simon and I were. It was obvious the moment Christopher introduced himself that I'd found my perfect match.'

A moment of panic flits through Aunt Jane's eyes.

'I'm definitely going to get his number,' I say, enjoying winding her up. 'In fact, I may ask him out for a drink this evening. It would be foolish to miss the opportunity.'

'Ah, Bea,' Aunt Jane stammers.

'Yes?' I reply, doing my very best innocent voice.

'Beatrice, Christopher is gay.'

'No!' I say, feigning shock, allowing my mouth to drop open.

'I was playing a little joke,' Aunt Jane continues. 'Only to cheer you up, you understand. I thought you'd realise the moment you met him that it was a wind up.'

'But Aunt Jane, why?' I say, amazed at my ability to act. 'Why would you do that to me after all I've been through?'

'If I'd thought for one minute that you'd like this man I'd never have done it. You must forgive me.'

I take out a tissue from my clutch bag and pull my best 'woe is me' face before very slowly allowing the tiniest glint to form in my eye, which Aunt Jane spots immediately.

'Beatrice Henshaw!' cries Aunt Jane. 'You scamp!'

'Me?' I cry back, slapping her on the hand, a broad smile on my face. 'You're the prankster!'

She laughs, and dabs her eye with a hanky. 'I just wanted to cheer you up. Despite his eccentricities, Christopher is a very good man.'

'I believe it,' I say, squeezing her hand affectionately, making it clear that there's no hard feelings.

'Now tell me, how are you? And how is Simon managing without you?'

'He's fine, I think. Happy with Edith.'

'And are you happy that he's happy with Edith?'

I sigh, putting down my champagne. 'I don't know, it does hurt a bit that he's moved on so quickly. And today, during the ceremony, I almost found myself wondering if I should have accepted his proposal after all. He used to look at me the way Tom was looking at you. He adored me.'

'But did you adore him?'

I shrug. 'Perhaps I was mad to throw that away.'

'There's no denying that for someone who doesn't believe in "the one" you do eliminate people very quickly. Nobody stands a chance.'

'Do I eliminate people?'

She casts me an enquiring look. 'Simon, Dave, Sebastian. The only one you seem really keen on is this Leo and, from what I can gather, nobody seems quite sure why.'

'No. I suppose on paper it doesn't read well. Why would anyone fall for someone who is clearly a player, and who slept with me when there was obviously someone else in the background?'

'It sounds far from ideal.'

'But . . . there's something about his spirit that seems to fit with mine in a way that Simon's never did, even with all his kindness, security and devotion. I think about Leo all the time. I can't help it.'

A smile twitches at the corner of her mouth. 'The heart wants what it wants, Beatrice. If you really think there's something there, you should fight for it.'

'I don't know, Aunt Jane. Didn't you say yourself that it's better to remain imperious?'

'Well, yes, but only when both of you are single. If he's with someone else then you need to let him know how you feel or else you run the risk of losing out completely.'

'But that doesn't seem fair to his girlfriend.'

Aunt Jane raises her brow. 'The operative word being *girlfriend*, not fiancée, not wife, *girlfriend*. And trust me,' she says, looking to Tom, 'Nothing is fair when it comes to love.'

18

Jane and Tom's reception was a special affair, one that will remain in my memory for many years to come. I could have sat into the evening watching the two of them casting tender looks at one another across the table, both of them with a look in their eye that told how utterly incredulous they both were that, at last, they were together again. What amazed me most was that neither of them seemed to resent the choices they'd made all those years ago, or feel as if time had been wasted. It was as if those fifty years spent apart only served to reinforce how precious their remaining time was together, rather than to underline how much they'd missed.

It was such a happy party, so full of hope and joy, that it felt impossible to head back to the flat and the humdrum of everyday life. But Tom's children had to take their kids home for supper and bed, and Jane and Tom were more than ready to return to the flat as husband and wife, to prepare for their honeymoon on the Amalfi Coast the following day.

'Let's go to a club,' I say to the girls, outside the hotel.

'Great idea!' says Lizzie. When Lizzie and I were at art college she used to go clubbing well into the small hours but always make 9 a.m. lectures, though generally with her hair in a mess, her PVC hot pants still on, and reeking of stale booze.

'I don't know,' says Hannah. 'I've work in the morning and Remy will be waiting for me at home.'

'So, call her and get her along too,' says Kat, already hailing a cab.

'I probably shouldn't . . .'

'Come on, Hannah!' I say, as a cab draws up. 'If I can, you can.'

'Yeah, come on,' says Lizzie, the three of us climbing in, waiting to see what Hannah decides.

'Oh, go on then!' she says, throwing caution to the wind. 'It's not every day a seventy-something woman marries the man she's loved for five decades.'

'Exactly,' I cry. 'Some things just have to be celebrated. Mahiki's please!'

It takes barely a minute for the cab to make its way into Mayfair and deliver us outside the club on Dover Street, just a stone's throw from the Ritz.

'God, how long's it been since we were last here?' asks Hannah, as we're waved inside by the doorman.

'Wasn't it here that you and Simon kissed for the first time?' asks Lizzie, as we head towards the lounge.

'Which was over four years ago,' I say, remembering the moment well. Simon told me sometime later that he'd been planning it for weeks but for me it had been completely out of the blue. At that stage he was just my boss's son; my *new* boss at that. I'd thought he was just being kind, making me feel part of the team by inviting me and my friends out to a club he liked. I had no idea he was *into* me.

'That kiss totally freaked you out!' says Kat, laughing at the memory.

'I was so paranoid that Sir Hugo would fire me if he found out! Or at least tell us to break it off.'

Entering the bar takes me straight back to that night. Simon and I had been sitting chatting, me thinking how nice it was of him to pay so much attention to the new girl; Simon, he told me later, trying to figure out how to kiss me. In the end he'd leaned over and placed the softest kiss on my lips, testing the water. I'd been completely taken aback but the kiss was so soft and tingly, and I'd had sufficient to drink that I'd leaned in and kissed him back. Before I knew it we were kissing in a way that probably wasn't appropriate for a public place.

'We spent days agonising about it at home,' says Lizzie. 'I'm certain there wasn't a potential scenario left undiscussed.'

'I was pretty freaked out, not just because of the work thing but because of how much I liked him and all his old-fashioned charm and respectability.'

'Do you remember how he used to jump up anytime a lady entered the room?' says Hannah.

'He was a regular jack-in-the-box!' says Kat.

'Up down, up down,' says Hannah, and we all laugh.

'That wasn't all that was going up down up down, if I remember rightly,' says Lizzie, a cheeky twinkle in her eye.

'He definitely had stamina!' I grin, but there's a pang

of regret too that I didn't expect. I haven't thought about the early days with Simon for so long, how new and exciting it felt. 'Anyway, I don't think we've been back since, so I guess it's been four years since we were here.'

'Four years,' says Hannah, with a whistle. 'So much has happened since then.'

'You and Lizzie married,' says Kat.

'Neither of us had even met Remy or Jack back then,' says Hannah. 'And you meeting Henry.'

'Simon and I splitting up,' I say, because I can tell no one else wants to. 'And him now so serious with Edith.'

'Let's order drinks,' says Kat, sensing my mood beginning to dip.

'Deadbeat daiquiri for me, please,' I say, as Kat takes the other's orders and heads to the bar.

'Things will get better, Bea,' says Hannah. 'If today teaches us anything it has to be that whoever is meant for you, will come to you.'

'Maybe it's neither Simon nor Leo,' says Lizzie. 'Maybe you're the one who's to have their "thunderbolt" moment.'

'Just like Tom in *Four Weddings*,' says Hannah encouragingly, though I can tell she's not that convinced by the theory.

'I think I might believe even less in "thunderbolts" than I do in "the one".'

'Then maybe you're just not ready,' says Lizzie. 'You always say it's about timing. Perhaps the person you're meant to be with isn't ready yet. And maybe you're not either.'

'I would like to get the jewellery business up and running,' I say. Over the last month I've had a few sales from the website I set up. It wouldn't take too many more to be able to go part-time at work.

'And have a bit more time to be sure you're fully over Simon,' says Hannah.

'Hmm,' I say, my tone suggesting they may be right but all I'm thinking is: *Maybe Leo just needs time to work things through with Brit, and to get rid of all the wedding work, before he's really ready himself.*

The thought bolsters my spirits a bit, as does the cocktail, and before I know it my dip in mood has gone. Remy made it after work and she and Hannah are now glued to the dance floor, unusually Lizzie isn't dancing but she's less concerned about Jack's tour, it's only Kat who can't quite get into the spirit of things.

'You need to confront Henry, Kat,' I say. 'Properly lay things on the table.'

'I've tried. It just makes him defensive. I've absolutely nothing to go on other than a hunch.'

I glance furtively at Lizzie who is sucking, surprisingly for her, on a mocktail, a look that doesn't go unnoticed by Kat.

'What's going on?' she asks.

'Lizzie . . .' I say, my tone suggesting that it's time she spoke up.

'Liz?' asks Kat, when Lizzie isn't immediately forthcoming.

'Okay, okay!' she says, cracking, and putting down her drink. 'Kat — I don't know how to say this, and I don't know that it's true . . . But there's a rumour going around at work that Henry is seeing one of the nurses.'

'Seeing?' says Kat, blood draining from her face.

Lizzie puts up her hands. 'I swear, that's all I know.'

'We haven't told you because there's been nothing to tell,' I say. 'It's only a rumour but—'

'Coupled with my hunch it could be everything,' she says, remarkably coolly.

'*Could* be,' I say, hoping to give her some reassurance.

Kat rifles around in her bag for her phone. 'I'll be back,' she says, heading outside.

'Do you think it was the right thing to do?' asks Lizzie, her eye caught by someone in the far corner of the lounge.

'I hope so,' I say, following her eyeline. My stomach lurches as I see who Lizzie is looking at.

'Is that . . .?'

'Leo,' I whisper.

Despite the noise of the bar Leo seems to hear me because at that moment he looks up, immediately catching my gaze, and acknowledging me with a nod.

'Who's he with?' asks Lizzie.

'Brit,' I say. She nudges Leo to gain back his attention and no doubt ask who it is he's staring at.

'Looks like they're coming over,' says Lizzie.

I grab my drink and hope to God my hair isn't a complete disaster.

In the words of Richard Curtis, *Fuck, Fuck, Fuck*.

'Hi,' he says, somehow conveying all his American charm and swagger into just one syllable. 'How are you?'

190

'Fine!' I say, overly brightly. 'You?'

'Okay,' he says. 'I don't know if you've met, Brit. Brit this is Bea.'

'Hi, how are you?' she says, shaking my hand.

'Fine,' I say, astonished that her voice in no way matches her appearance. She sounds sweet and likeable, not at all as I imagined her – distant and spiky. 'This is Lizzie. Leo did her wedding photos.'

'Oh yeah, I'd hoped to help out on that shoot but I wasn't able. I saw the images, you looked beautiful.'

'Thanks,' says Lizzie, finishing her drink.

'What brings you here?' Leo asks.

'Aunt Jane married Tom this afternoon. We've having a sort of post-wedding bash. You?'

'We're having one last London drink before heading home tomorrow,' says Brit.

'Home?' She doesn't know it but it would have been kinder to have blindsided me in the stomach.

'We leave for California tomorrow,' she says.

'For how long?'

'For good.' She smiles widely, like the cat who got the cream, while I search Leo's eyes for confirmation.

'Bea, Leo, why don't you get some more drinks in? I'd love another and I'm sure Bea would too,' says Lizzie, sensing my devastation, given that all hope of us being together has just disappeared down the proverbial plughole. She pats the chair beside her for Brit to sit down.

'Sure,' I say, glad of the intervention and the opportunity to collect my thoughts.

I follow Leo through the throng of bodies to the bar. Everything from the back of his tussled hair, to his strong broad shoulders and his pert backside is begging to be touched.

'Sorry, Bea,' he shouts, as we wait to be served. It's hard to hear him properly over the music. 'I wanted to tell you – to say goodbye.'

'It's fine.' I hope the fact that I have to shout helps hide the desolation in my voice. 'You don't owe me anything.'

'I do,' he says, the busyness of the bar causing his body to press close to mine. If it weren't for Brit I'd be making the most of the situation and moving even closer.

'You're definitely leaving for good?'

He leans in to speak into my ear, and I shiver. 'I never want to say never but, for now, yes.'

'So, you and Brit are serious this time?'

'Yes,' he says, but as he does his eyes fix on mine in a way that doesn't correspond with his answer; he looks as if he's thinking about kissing me, and my heart pounds in my chest. In that moment it's as if time slows, the rest of the world still spinning around us, and before I know it he's leaning in, his lips on mine, kissing me.

Sharply, I pull away, pushing him back, and time seems to speed up, the noise of the club at full force again.

'You can't do this. It's not fair to Brit or me.' A glance towards Brit and Lizzie tells me Brit couldn't have seen, there are too many people in the way, but still I feel awful, guilt and anger surging through me.

'You're right.'

'I know I'm right,' I say, my temper flaring. It's not often I feel cross but there's something about Leo's attitude tonight that reminds me of my father. That sense of entitlement, that he might have his cake and eat it. 'If you're choosing Brit, then choose her, don't eye me like something you fancy another piece of. Goodbye, Leo. I hope things work out for you.'

'Bea, wait, it's not that straightforward,' he calls, as I turn on my heels to leave.

I head outside for air, brushing past Lizzie and Brit, deep in conversation, and Hannah and Remy still tearing up the dance floor.

How could I be so stupid? I think, battling past a gaggle of women, ten years younger than me and dressed in impossibly small pieces of clothing. It feels as if someone's holding my head under the water, and I'm only released when I push the door to the club open and the warm evening air rushes into my lungs.

I cross the road and sit on the ground, next to a recycling bin outside Caffè Nero. I'm so past the stage of caring if my party dress gets mucky. My brain feels as if it's on spin cycle.

Did I really think there was still hope of us being together? How could I let him kiss me when he's with Brit? Does that make me as bad as him?

'Bea? What's going on?' asks Kat, crossing the road to join me.

'Leo's moving back to America, with Brit.'

'Ouch, that's got to hurt,' she says, squatting down to

join me. We must look a real sight, the two of us in our wedding gear, slumped beside the trash.

I pinch the bridge of my nose until it aches. 'I feel like such an idiot.'

'Why?'

'Because I knew before I slept with him that he was a player – he admitted as much to me.' I wish I'd confessed this to Kat before now. 'I allowed myself to believe that I was different, that we had some kind of "connection", that he didn't have with any of the other "wedding girls" he's slept with. Turns out I was just another notch on his belt.'

'I'm sorry, Bea. He is really nice, and super cool, I can totally see why you fell for him. You shouldn't feel bad.'

'Maybe I'm just a poor judge of character. I genuinely thought he was different. He told me he didn't want to be like his father, that he didn't want to ditch people selfishly. I respected that, you know? I thought he had integrity, that he was loyal. I thought, at last, I've met someone who understands what it was to have a shit as a father. I thought I'd found someone who might go out of his way to do good by me. But then, just now, he tried to come on to me when he's with Brit.' A thought pops into my mind, one I don't really want to entertain but find myself voicing regardless. 'I can't help wondering if I'm more like my mother than I thought.'

'How do you mean?'

'Not being able to see when someone isn't good for me.'

'People make bad choices, Bea.' Kat's tone is so full of regret that it makes me snap out of my upset.

'Kat?' Only now do I see that her face is puffy and her eyes bloodshot. 'What's going on? Is it Henry?'

She nods, casting her eyes sideways to meet mine. 'I just called him and pretty much forced him to tell me. Turns out the rumour was more than just gossip.'

'Henry was seeing someone else?'

'Yup. Her name's Lucille.' She says Lucille in a phony French accent.

'Yikes.' I pause, trying to think of something comforting to say. 'Bet she smells of garlic!'

Kat lets out a short laugh, shaking her head in dismay.

'Do you know when it started?' I ask.

'I'm not sure. It might be best not to know.'

'And is it over?'

'He says it is.'

'I'm so sorry.' I put my hand over hers. Even though I've always imagined it possible, the news still comes as a surprise.

'So, when you're doubting your ability to judge character just remember, at least you weren't about to marry a two-timing wanker. At least you only *slept* with one.'

I laugh, wryly. 'You had your suspicions.'

'True. But I allowed him to lie to me.'

'You didn't *allow* it. He's the one to blame here, Kat, not you.'

'Maybe,' she says, with a shrug.

I lean my head back against the warm concrete of the building. 'I'm sorry I didn't tell you when Lizzie first mentioned it. I wanted to, but she was worried it would do more damage if it wasn't true. That's why I kept suggesting you confront him.'

'I'm not mad about that. I'm not even that mad about him shagging someone else. I'm just mad about the lying. I should have realised at Lizzie's wedding, when he said Hannah shouldn't tell her grandparents about Remy, that he had a problem with the truth.'

'Hindsight is a wonderful thing,' I say, watching a pigeon peck at a McDonald's box. 'What are you going to do?'

'There's not much I can do. I guess I have to call off the wedding'

'Is that what you want?'

Kat leans her head back too, looking up to the sky. 'What I want is for all of this to be a dream, and for Henry to be the man I thought he was, not some screwed-up version I don't know.'

Pretty much exactly what I feel about Leo, I think, but I don't say it because Kat was prepared to marry Henry, whereas Leo was really little more than a figment of my imagination. Her problem puts mine nicely into perspective.

'Come on,' I say, getting myself up and holding out my hand to her. 'Let's go drink our entire blood volume in cocktails.'

'Bloody great idea!' she says, taking my hand to get up, the two of us going back into the club, our arms around each other in sisterly solidarity.

19

For a few days after *the kiss,* my emotions swayed between feeling gutted that Leo had left the country for good – clinging on to the idea that if we kissed there must still be some kind of connection – and feeling angry that he kissed me when he's with Brit, and the lack of loyalty that showed. But mostly I was cross at myself for spending too much time hoping for something that was never going to happen, and misreading his character so badly. In the end, despite the fact that I still fancied the pants off of him, I realised it was fruitless to hanker after him any more, and that it was far more important to channel my energy into something I could control.

'Just three more weeks to get this finished by the festival,' I tell myself, looking at the growing collection of jewellery laid out on the bed in Lizzie's old room. Over the last month the space has developed into a functioning studio with a work table, a shelving unit housing all my supplies, and the bed being used as a display area. Most nights after work, I've been putting in a few hours, managing to create a couple of pairs of fringed earrings or a bracelet each evening. My obsession with Native American beadwork, one I've had since Aunt Jane brought me back a beaded bracelet from Arizona when I was about nine, has led to a bold collection of brickwork pattern in turquoises, reds and gold. I'm trying desperately to create at least fifty pieces to sell at the festival, and since 'the kiss' I've been powering through pieces like there's no tomorrow. Trouble is, pieces keep selling through my website so it's a near impossible challenge to keep up. And to make matters worse, Sukie my business course tutor, tasked us with promoting our business models through social media, and now I've got several hundred followers all champing at the bit for new designs.

And all of this on top of work. Bev says most mornings I look as if I've spent the night in the desert, exhausted and disoriented from lack of sleep, sitting up half the night threading and looping and knotting. The other day Simon came by for a meeting with his dad and asked me if I'd been down with a stomach virus.

'No,' I said, too tired to be offended. 'Why do you ask?'

'You've lost your usual glow.'

I told him I'd been putting in lots of hours, trying to build a collection.

'Well,' he said, completely underwhelmed. 'Don't overdo it. Better to be healthy than . . .' he tailed off, uncertain what it is that I get from making jewellery.

'Happy and fulfilled?' I offered.

'Right,' he said, smiling, sounding supportive but his eyes sporting a slightly puzzled expression. 'Better get on, Dad's got something he wants to discuss.'

'Sure,' I said, getting back to my own work, realising

again that for all Simon and I were good together, it was never going to work long term.

I'm in the process of attaching a fishhook wire to my latest pair of earrings when the doorbell rings, and I remember that Jessica, the lady from Aunt Jane's wedding, is popping round for a viewing.

'Bugger,' I say, getting up from my desk and realising that the house is a pigsty. All the late nights spent working has meant little time to clean and tidy. It looks almost as bad as when Lizzie lived here.

I dash down the stairs, gathering stray bits of laundry and shoving them into the laundry cupboard, then I align my shoes at the door before answering.

'Hi Jessica, welcome!' I say, super cheerily, hoping that what the house lacks in neatness I might make up for in warmth.

'Hi Bea, it's so nice to see you,' she says, as I usher her in.

'And you. How have you been?'

'Good.' She looks up at the coving and ceiling rose, and I hope she doesn't notice the cobwebs. 'I've been enjoying the cricket. When I'm not at work, that is.'

'Great.' *Does that mean I'd lose the use of the telly for most of the summer?* 'Let me show you the living room.'

'It's just beautiful.' She casts her eye round the room, either not noticing or at least politely ignoring the design magazines and coffee cups abandoned about the place. 'I love your throws and choice of lamps. It feels really cosy.'

'Thank you,' I say, thinking how nice it is to have

someone who appreciates the place for what it is, rather than wanting it as a crèche or boarding house. 'Come through and I'll show you the rest.'

We head into the dining room, the table covered in boxes of wire and thread.

'Sorry about the mess, I've been super busy. If I'm honest I sort of forgot you were coming. I haven't had a chance to tidy.'

'Oh, don't worry about it,' she says, with a laugh. 'I'm more interested in the feel of the place, and this room feels full of happiness.'

'We have had a lot of laughs in here,' I say, impressed that she should pick up on that, and taking her into the kitchen. 'The kitchen is small but everything's here.'

'I know it's bad but I'm more of a ready-meal girl. You know how it is, once you're through with work, it's just easier to dash into M&S and grab a carbonara.'

Praise the Lord, the woman is sweet and kind and all she needs is a fork. 'Well, that just leaves upstairs.'

After I've shown her my room and the bathroom, I show her Lizzie's old room.

'Don't be put off by my work stuff, that will all be cleared, if, that is, you want the room.'

'My God, Bea,' she says, going over to the bed to look at my work. 'Have you made all this?'

'Uh-huh.'

'It's insanely good. How do you find the time?'

'It's a good question,' I say, with a little laugh. 'But you've seen the state of the place . . . it's not as if I've been doing much housework.'

'You're too hard on yourself. If I'd made all of this the dishes would be stacked to the roof and the laundry spilling out the front door.'

'Well, it's only me to look after, no one else.'

'What, things didn't work out with Christopher!' she laughs, and I do too, and I know she'd be the perfect flatmate: sweet, tidy, funny, a little bit like having Lizzie back, just without the mess, and probably a few less anecdotes about penguin-seeing patients.

'So, that's it,' I say, leading her back out to the landing and downstairs. 'You've seen all there is to see. Take your time making up your mind, there's no rush.'

'I don't have to think about it. I'd definitely like the room. Nothing I've seen compares to this, and it's half the price of most places.'

'Oh, right,' I say, feeling caught on the hop, because despite Jessica probably being the near-perfect flatmate, I'm hesitant.

When Lizzie moved out it was hard but, I don't know, over the last four to six weeks I've really grown used to it. It's nice not to feel guilty if the dishes aren't done, I like not having to think about when to use the bathroom, and, most of all, I've become accustomed to having Lizzie's old room as a place to work. Trouble is, if I want to transition from hobby jewellery maker to professional designer I'm going to have to give up my job, and I can't do that if I'm paying rent on both rooms.

'Or maybe you have someone else in mind?' she says, picking up on my hesitancy.

'No. No, that's not it.' Unlike with the others, with

Jessica I decide honesty is the best policy. 'I need to get my head around not having a work space. I hadn't realised how important it had become, until now.'

'I understand,' she says. 'If you want a flatmate *and* a work space then perhaps we could screen off part of the living room, it seems pretty big just for two people.'

'That's a really good idea,' I say, releasing the latch on the door. 'Can you give me a few days to think it over?'

'Of course. Call me, yes?' she says, stepping out front.

'I'll do that. Thanks for coming,' I say, waving her off, feeling a little guilty about making her wait for an answer.

'How long did it take for you to get shot of that hangover?' I ask Kat, who's come round for a 'Henry debrief'. It's been ten days since Aunt Jane's wedding and that eventful night at Mahiki's, and what with work, and jewellery making, and Kat dealing with Henry, it's the first real opportunity that we've had to chat it all through.

'It seemed to go on for days,' she says, taking a seat in the minuscule courtyard, which is only really big enough for the wheelie bins and an abandoned barbecue. 'Though I suspect some of that was the emotional hangover.'

I hand her a coconut Magnum and sit down beside her on a deck chair. 'What's Henry had to say for himself?'

'That it was a drunken one-night stand, that he's beyond sorry, that we shouldn't let one lapse in judgement stand in the way of our future together.'

The chocolate of my ice cream gives way with a satisfying snap. 'So he wants the wedding to go ahead.'

'Yup,' says Kat, catching a drip of coconut cream. 'He certainly does, he's been pretty persistent about that.'

'And what do you think?'

'I think lots about that.' She pauses for a moment, from both chat and ice cream, collecting her thoughts. 'I think he's a bloody cheek to think that I might still agree to marry him. But I also think he's right, why should one mistake cost us all we planned together?'

I sit quietly, allowing her to work through her thoughts.

'I want him to have some kind of a price to pay for what he's done, but I don't want me to be that price.'

'Sounds fair.'

'And I'd like to know for certain that his regret is sincere, that it won't happen again. But how can I ever know that?'

Her eyes will me to answer, to fix it all for her.

'It's not something you can ever know. No one can, not even in a marriage where two people have been faithful for decades. Ultimately, I guess, it comes down to faith in each other, and trust.'

'And what if the trust can't be restored. Won't I always be expecting the worst?'

'I think if you expect the worst, he's likely to deliver it.'

'But if I expect the best?'

'Then you might get it.'

'Might . . .' she says, drifting back into her thoughts.

'What does your heart tell you?' I ask, when we've both had some thinking time. 'Marry or not?'

'I have no idea.'

'And if Henry wasn't being persistent, if he had walked away?'

'Then I'd move on.'

I give her a look that suggests she might have found her answer.

'But doesn't his persistence, his willingness to fight for us, prove something?'

'Maybe,' I say, with a slight shrug, not wanting to lean either way, knowing Kat has to make this decision alone. All I can do is be a sounding board.

'Anyway,' she says, returning to her ice cream. 'What about you? How are you coping with the idea of Leo moving back to America?'

'Oh, I'm fine,' I say. *Am I?* 'You should see how many pieces I've managed to create this week now that I'm absolutely, one thousand per cent, sworn off men.'

'That's great, Bea. I'm so pleased that something good has come out of it. For a while there I was worried you were falling for a bit of a player. But don't be put off men completely, because I was thinking . . .'

'What?' I ask, detecting that tone in her voice that tells me she's got something afoot.

'Why don't we invite Sebastian along to the festival? He was really nice and not exactly hard on the eye!'

I hesitate, not that keen on the idea. 'I don't know . . .'

'Oh, go on! It would just be a bit of fun, nothing serious. We could all do with a bit of cheering up.'

I'm not really up for it, feeling too tired and fed-up with men to be bothered, but there's something about it that seems to light Kat up and she's right, we could all use a bit of fun.

'Go on then,' I say, devouring a big chunk of ice cream.

'Thanks, Bea,' she says, already digging out her phone, leaving me wondering what I've let myself in for and wishing, despite myself, that it was Leo not Sebastian who was going.

Apollo Music Festival

3rd to 5th August

New Grove Farm,
Gloucestershire

Saturday 4th August:

CARBURETOR

*and many more acts
to be announced*

20

I'd be lying if I said camping in a muddy field with several thousand other people had my name written all over it but, credit to Lizzie, she has gone out of her way to make it as comfortable as possible. She's hired a gigantic bell tent with four double beds and a wood-burning stove in the middle. We still have to share a toilet, and I'm not even going to think about with how many other people but, as camping goes, it's not that bad.

'Bagsy the bed furthest from the entrance,' says Kat, throwing her rucksack onto the bed.

'Guess that means I'm sleeping here too,' I say, putting my bag beside hers on the surprisingly soft mattress. Hannah and Remy take the bed nearest the 'door', Aunt Jane and Tom, just back from their honeymoon, decide on the one next to theirs, leaving Sebastian, next to mine, in a bed of his own, where he sits to slip off his shoes. I've learnt my lesson about sleeping with men I barely know, and it's not about to happen again anytime soon, regardless of how keen the girls might be for the two of us to hook up.

'Where's Lizzie going to sleep?' Hannah asks.

'She's in the band's trailer, with Jack,' I say.

'Ooh, that's cool,' says Remy, who's been tickled pink since I agreed that Sebastian should come along this weekend. Not that I'm certain why I agreed, other than the fact that I refuse to be stuck in the mud about Leo. That thing Aunt Jane said about me eliminating people too quickly has also been bothering me. I figure if I'm to give anyone a chance, I could do a lot worse than Sebastian.

'I slept in a band's trailer once,' says Aunt Jane, who, rather wonderfully, has embraced the whole shorts and wellies look, even if her shorts are a bit more 1940s Girl Guide than Kate Moss hot pants.

'Really?' I ask. 'When?'

'Mid-sixties, I imagine. I couldn't have been more than twenty-one.'

'Who were the band?' Kat is perched on the end of her bed, listening in.

'I don't remember its name, and they were quite tame by today's standards. Even so, I seem to remember we had a little fun!'

'What sort of fun, Aunt Jane?' Hannah looks genuinely shocked.

'Probably best we don't ask,' I say, preferring to leave Aunt Jane's wild days to my imagination. 'Who wants to help me set up my jewellery stall outside the tent?'

Kat wrinkles her nose apologetically. 'I need to call Henry. We've some stuff to sort out.' It's been over four weeks since she found out about Henry's one-night stand and she still hasn't made a decision about whether to go ahead with the wedding.

'And I've planned a little outdoor yoga session for Aunt Jane and Tom,' says Remy.

'Really?' I ask, incredulous at the thought of my great aunt stretching and bending in public.

'Tom and I made a resolution on our honeymoon to try as many new things as we could, while we're still able. Neither of us has been to a festival before and neither of us have tried yoga, so we're giving it a go, even if I do dislocate a hip in the process.'

'I'll be gentle,' says Remy. 'And if Hannah can do it then so can you.'

'Hey!' Hannah cries, in mock indignation.

'You know she's right,' I say, laughing. Hannah barely mastered a forward roll at school, she's about as supple as an eighty-year-old tortoise.

'I resent that. I'll have you know I've become quite nimble since meeting Remy.'

'Have you indeed?' I say, really not believing her.

'Yes, I have! Remy, do you mind if I crash the lesson?'

'Of course not. The more the merrier.'

Hannah sticks her tongue out at me playfully. 'Looks like Sebastian is your only helper.'

'I would like to help, if you don't mind,' he says.

'Why would I mind?'

After all there's nothing quite like a good-looking Frenchman to attract a few extra punters.

My stall is little more than a card table with a display board of bracelets, earrings, and necklaces. But despite its modest scale I feel a huge sense of satisfaction at what I've achieved in just a few months.

'You are very patient, *non*?' asks Sebastian, positioning his fold-out chair next to mine.

'What makes you say that?'

'Your work, it is, how you say, fiddle-y?'

His pronunciation of fiddly makes me laugh. 'Yes, I suppose it is, but I like the attention to detail, and creating something unique.'

'It would be very boring for me.'

I laugh, vaguely outraged. 'You don't mince your words, do you?'

'What does this mean?'

'It means you say what you think, even if it might offend.'

'Are you offended?' he asks, a concerned look in his eyes.

'Not at all! We can't all have the same passions. What do you like to do?' I ask, making minuscule adjustments to the stall.

'I like to travel to spectacular places like Iceland, Peru . . . I've a trip booked to New Zealand next year.'

'And when you're not travelling?'

'Then I like to play football at the weekend, basketball and Judo in the week. I run to work and go to the gym at lunch.'

'Gosh, that's a lot of exercise,' I say. *Stifling a yawn!*

'Which exercise do you like?'

The spectating from the couch kind. 'I swim from time to time.' *Can't actually remember the last time I went.* 'I've never really found a sport that fits me.'

'It's probably because of your body shape.'

'Really?' *Where the hell is he going with this?*

'Sure, you are short with big breasts. You're not fast or agile. Maybe weight-lifting would suit you.'

An enormous guffaw erupts from within me causing me to spit out my tea. 'Why weight-lifting?' I ask, still laughing, and wiping my mouth on my sleeve.

'Your centre of gravity is low.' He might be gorgeous, but I'm beginning to see why Seb is still single. 'Swimming is also good for you.'

'Because of my buoyancy aides?'

He shoots me a puzzled look.

I point to my breasts. 'These help me float!'

'Exactly,' he says, joining me in laughing. 'They are big "buoyancy aides".'

We have to rein in our giggles when a couple of potential customers stop by. They're younger than me – and far cooler than I ever was – but they're immediately drawn to the collection, cooing over the boldest designs.

The blonde girl tries on several of the beaded bracelets, holding out her arms to admire them. 'These would look so cool layered up with silver bangles.'

Her friend turns to me, holding up one of my favourites. 'You should make them really wide, more like wristbands than bracelets. I'd wear them all the time.'

'I could commission a piece for you, if you like?' I say, handing her my card, loving her idea.

'Could you?'

'Sure. Just select the colours and patterns you like from my website, then tell me how wide you'd like it.'

'Amazing,' she says, already on her phone, scrolling through my designs.

'And I'll take ten of these,' says the blonde, pointing to the bracelets. 'Just a random selection.'

'It feels good, non?' says Sebastian, once the girls have gone and I've squirrelled the cash into my money pouch.

'It feels bloody amazing!' I say, beaming from ear to ear, more thrilled than he could know.

As I'm rearranging the contents of the stall, a sound from within the tent causes me to turn, and I find Kat, her phone pressed against her ear, gesticulating to the empty tent.

'Hannah said she is having a tough time,' says Sebastian, noticing my look of elation turn to concern.

'And for once there is nothing I can do.'

In years gone by I've always been able to do something to cheer Kat up: ice cream and milkshakes when primary school got tough; Haribo and Coke during school exams; chips and alcohol when revising for uni finals. For once in our lives this isn't something that food or drink or even the world's largest stack of pancakes is going to sort out. For once she's going to have to tough it out on her own.

'Just being her friend is enough,' says Sebastian, sincere and sensitive in his response, his eyes full of tenderness.

'Yes,' I say, the softness of his gaze pulling me in. Despite the weightlifting comment I can still see his appeal.

Just then I catch sight of Lizzie, hurrying down the avenue of tents, waving at me.

'Isn't this great!' she says, breathless from her walk and

holding onto her straw pork-pie hat. 'I knew this was exactly what we needed.'

'I can't deny it, it *is* nice to get out of the city.'

'Hi Seb.' She greets him with three kisses. 'Where's everyone else?'

I gesture towards the small enclave where Remy is conducting a yoga session for Hannah, Tom and Jane, and, as it happens, a few others who've tagged on. Remy is positioned in a perfect triangle, feet wide apart, arms perpendicular to the ground. The others are in various imitations of the pose, some more successfully than others.

'Is Hannah's spine fused?' asks Lizzie, and I laugh. Despite her protestations about being 'quite nimble' these days it's really very hard to see any difference from the Hannah of old, who never could touch her toes despite being able to run a marathon in under three and a half hours.

'Check out Tom and Aunt Jane, they're totally on it,' I say.

'I expect bedroom gymnastics has increased their flexibility.'

'Lizzie!' I cry, trying to erase the image that jumps into my mind.

'Don't be such a prude, Bea, older people can have a healthy sex life too—'

'Moving on,' I say quickly, changing the subject. 'When's Jack's set?'

'This evening, nine thirty. They're totally psyched about it.'

'I'll bet, a band's first time on the main stage is a big deal. Their trajectory is incredible.'

'Right, it is,' says Lizzie, the excitement slightly edging from her voice, causing me to wonder, not for the first time, what's up with the girl.

Lizzie was quick to whisk Remy and Hannah away after the yoga class, leaving me with Seb at the stall, Kat still on the phone, and Aunt Jane and Tom having a late morning cat-nap – Aunt Jane might have taken the downward dog in her stride, but I'm worried that Tom might never recover. Word seemed to be spreading about the stall and over the course of the next hour or so Seb and I were inundated with crop-topped teenagers, glitter-painted twenty-somethings and some of the older bohemian crowd.

'I heard about you down at the main stalls,' says a middle-aged woman, pushing her Armani shades up onto her head. She's dressed casually in denim shorts and a cheesecloth top but the designer wellies, knuckle-duster diamond, and expensive haircut tell me that she's either successful in her own right or married to someone wealthy. 'Thought I'd better come check out what all the fuss is about.'

'It's nothing really, just a little hobby,' I say, anxious that she might be festival police, if there is such a thing, about to fine me for not having a licence.

'It doesn't look like just a hobby – some of this is very detailed. What's your background?'

'Oh, you know, graduated art college, couldn't afford my rent, got a job, stopped making stuff . . .'

'What changed?'

'It's a long story.' I figure she doesn't need to hear about the girls' mad notion of all of us marrying in one year, and me then realising how trapped it made me feel in all areas of my life, not just my relationship with Simon. 'But it got me creating again, pushing for my dream of becoming a designer.'

'Whatever happened, it's clearly ignited something strong. Your work really captures the current zeitgeist.'

I nod sagely. *I don't know what that means but I'll go with it.*

She reaches her hand out to me. 'Hillary Bentham.'

'Hi, I'm Bea. Bea Henshaw.'

'Bea Henshaw,' she says. 'That's a strong name. I could work with that.'

I have no idea what you're talking about.

'Forgive me, I haven't said what I do. I'm the buying director at Whimsy & White.'

I must stand gaping for an inappropriate amount of time – Whimsy & White is one of my favourite boutique chains, and they're big on pushing independent designers – because eventually Seb has to nudge me back to life.

'That's impressive,' I gabble.

'And I'm certain my team would be interested in considering your collection. Do you have a card?'

'I do.' My fingers seem to turn to butter as I fumble around for it in my bag. In the end it's Sebastian who hands one to her.

'Very nice to meet you, Bea. I'll be in touch,' she says, returning her sunglasses to her face and walking away.

'Did the buying director of Whimsy & White just imply she might be interested in buying my work?' I ask Seb, once Hillary is out of earshot.

He puts up his hand for me to high five. '*Oui, c'est vrai*,' he says, clasping my hand and giving me a very unromantic hug. 'Maybe your dream will come true!'

'Maybe it will,' I reply, imagining handing in my notice at work, and dreaming of designing full-time for a living.

21

'Who fancies a game of Truth or Dare?' asks Kat, once we've finished our dinner of baked potatoes and bananas cooked in the ashes of the stove, and we're waiting to head down to the main stage to see Carburetor's set.

'I haven't played that game in decades,' proclaims Aunt Jane, who's putting on her cardy, the evening air beginning to cool. 'Count me in!'

'And me,' says Tom, warming his yoga-tired muscles by the fire, his toes wiggling.

'Do we have two more takers?' Kat asks.

Sebastian takes a seat next to Tom. 'I will play.'

'And me,' sings Remy, her hand in the air.

'Hannah, Bea, Lizzie – majority rules,' says Kat, tearing up a piece of paper into bits and handing them out. 'Everyone, write down one question and one dare and then place them in Tom's hat if it's a truth, and Lizzie's if it's a dare.'

'I feel drinks are required for this,' says Hannah. She passes round cans of G&T and lager.

I draw up a chair by the stove, taking a G&T. 'Couldn't agree more!'

'Not for me, thanks,' says Lizzie, positioning herself next to me.

'You okay?' I ask.

'I just don't want to be drunk when Jack's onstage. I don't want to forget his big moment.'

'Jack doesn't know how lucky he is,' I tell her, reaching over to rub her arm.

'No, you're right,' she says, staring in the flames. 'He doesn't.'

Before I can challenge Lizzie on what she means, Kat is up in the middle of the huddle, shaking the hats from side to side. 'Who wants to go first?'

'Oh, go on then, I will,' says Hannah.

'Truth or dare?'

'Truth.'

Kat pulls a question from Tom's hat theatrically. 'If you had to choose between going naked or having your thoughts appear in bubbles above your head for everyone to read, which would you choose?'

'Boo-ooo,' cries Aunt Jane. 'Too easy!'

'Is it?' I say, with a chuckle. 'Both seem terrifying to me.'

'I'd go naked,' says Hannah, which is met with general cheers and whistles.

'Why?' I ask.

'Because I wouldn't be much use to my clients if the opposition could read my thoughts.'

'I'm not sure you'd be much use to your clients in the all-together,' I say, laughing at the thought of Hannah in court in the buff.

'Who's next?' asks Kat, and Aunt Jane raises her hand. 'Truth or dare?'

'Dare!' says Aunt Jane, her eyes wide in anticipation, a decision that is met with a collective, 'oooohhh.'

'Eat a mouthful of crackers and then try to whistle.'

'Now *that's* too easy,' says Hannah, as Kat hands Aunt Jane the crackers.

We sit compelled by the sight of Aunt Jane methodically pushing crackers into her mouth. If it were me, I'd get the giggles and not be able to do it, but Aunt Jane, composed as she is, troughs them in, then slowly, carefully, purses her lips to blow.

'Jane!' cries Tom, when he's showered in cracker crumbs. She leans in closer, a cheeky, wicked look in her eye and blows again, so that Tom is left with crumbs inside his ears and all over his hair. 'Get away with you, woman!' he says, his arms flailing about trying to get rid of her.

'How can you do that without laughing?' I ask.

She masticates quietly, quite soberly, until the mouthful is gone when she breaks into a giant smile, arms aloft with a satisfied, 'Tah-dah!'

'Very impressive, Aunt Jane,' says Kat.

'A little too impressive,' Tom grumbles, though the twinkle in his eye belies his irritation.

'Your turn next,' Aunt Jane says to Tom. 'Truth or dare?'

'Truth!'

Kat removes a small piece of paper from the hat and reads aloud, 'What is your guilty pleasure?'

'Intriguing,' I say, an eyebrow raised at Aunt Jane in curiosity.

'He'll probably say the newspaper in bed on a Sunday morning.'

'Well, yes. But . . .' says Tom, and a hum of interest grows around the tent. 'I do also like . . .' he hesitates, uncertain whether to tell or not.

'Go on, Tom,' says Hannah. 'You're among friends.'

'I wouldn't be so sure,' says Aunt Jane, a naughty glint in her eye.

'What is it, Tom?' I urge.

'I do quite like having a bath and then . . .'

'No!' says Aunt Jane, reaching over to place a hand over his mouth. 'Stop right there. I won't allow it.'

'Hurry, Tom, tell us!'

From behind Aunt Jane's hand he mumbles, 'Slipping on your aunt's silk dressing robe and climbing into bed beside her.'

'Oh, Tom,' says Aunt Jane, removing her hand, perfectly mortified. 'How could you!'

'What?' he exclaims, a wide smile on his face. 'I do!'

'Love it,' says Kat, after our laughter had died down. 'There's nothing like a male septuagenarian in a lady's dressing gown. Who's next?'

'Can I go next with a dare?' I ask, spurred on by Tom's confession.

'Okay,' she says, reading one from the hat. 'Eeek! This is horrid . . . smell the feet of everyone in the room and rank them from best to worst.'

'Oh, that's cruel,' says Remy.

'Very,' I say, getting down on my hands and knees and doing a cursory inspection. 'But easy in the end. Hannah, definitely has the worst, and Remy has almost no odour at all.'

'Thanks very much, Bea,' says Hannah, her voice loaded with sarcasm. 'I think it's fair to say I won't hear the last of that for some time to come!'

'It is true, you do have "stinky" feet,' says Remy, with a laugh. 'But you know I love you all the same.'

'Moving swiftly on,' says Kat, when Remy goes in for a full PDA. 'Who's left?'

'Sebastian,' I say. 'Truth or dare?'

'Truth,' he says, and Kat offers him the hat.

'Do I fancy anyone in the tent,' he reads, and a light blush colours his cheeks. Aunt Jane's eyes dart towards mine, believing his crush to be me, but I have an idea of my own.

'Well, do you?' presses Kat.

Seb raises his eyes slowly towards her and with a quiet intensity he slowly says, 'Yes.'

'Who?' asks Kat, astonished, she too looking at me.

'The question only asks if I do, it doesn't say, who.'

'Smart-arse,' says Kat, a cheeky smile on her lips and a flirtatious glint in her eye. I can't remember the last time I saw her look that way at Henry. 'Lizzie, truth or dare?'

'Truth.' It's only now that I realise Lizzie hasn't contributed to the game so far, which is very unlike her, she's usually crazy for it.

'Ooh . . .' says Kat, intrigued by the question. 'Are

you currently keeping a secret from someone in the group?'

Lizzie's delay in answering causes the mood in the tent to shift from light-hearted to something more serious. Everyone's eyes are on Lizzie, who's sitting quietly, staring into the fire.

'Lizzie?' I ask. 'Are you?'

'I need to get out of here,' she says, pushing back her chair.

'Oooh,' says Hannah, her voice crescendoing, the effects of the G&T kicking in. I shoot her a look to be quiet; Lizzie is clearly not in the mood for being teased.

'All right, all right,' says Kat, regaining our attention once Lizzie has gone. I wonder if I should go after her but my hunch is that she'd prefer some time on her own. 'Only two more left in the hat. Whose go is it?'

'It's mine,' says Remy. 'I'll have a truth.'

'All righty. If you had to choose between Bea and me, which of us would you go out with?'

'Bea,' Remy says, quick as a flash.

'Take your time to think about it why don't you!' says Hannah, with a scandalised laugh.

'The choice wasn't between *you* and Bea,' says Remy, stroking Hannah's arm.

'But even if it had been she probably would have chosen me!' I say, enjoying poking at Hannah's wounds.

'Children,' says Aunt Jane, clearing her throat, and we all fall into line.

'And last, but not least,' says Kat, producing the final slip of paper from Lizzie's hat. 'A dare for me!' She holds the piece up and reads it to herself, her expression turning from one of glee to trepidation.

'What is it, Kat?' I ask. 'What's the dare?'

'Kiss Sebastian,' she says, quiet as a mouse.

'Drum roll!' says Hannah, starting a 'drrr', the rest of us joining in and drumming our fingers and feet too until there's a swell of noise in the tent.

Kat kneels down in front of Sebastian, placing her hands on his cheeks, giggling nervously. Seb's eyes dance over hers, Kat's are focused on his lips, and then slowly she leans in, and he does too, and they kiss, a kiss that is more tender than hurried. The kiss doesn't end there, and just as it's developing into something more, and all of us are screeching with surprise and delight, a voice from the entrance of the tent shouts, 'What the fuck is going on here?'

Kat turns sharply. 'Henry!' she gasps, pulling away from Seb and getting up. 'What are you doing here?'

'I thought it would be a good opportunity to get things back on track . . .' He stares at Sebastian. 'Guess I was wrong.'

If there was such a thing as a communal wince, we'd all be partaking in it right now. I've never seen so many people dissipate to take care of unnecessary chores in my life.

'We should go elsewhere,' says Kat, ushering Henry away from the tent. 'Bea, apologise to Lizzie for me, will you?'

'Of course, take your time,' I say, watching them leave.

*

'I'm so excited for you, Beatrice,' says Aunt Jane, on the walk to the main stage, the rest of the group walking ahead of us in the fading light, everyone still a little shell-shocked from Henry's arrival. 'Maybe Hillary will propel you towards being a famous jewellery designer after all.'

'Let's not jump the gun, Aunt Jane. She may not call. For now, I'm still Sir Hugo's assistant,' I say, though secretly, all afternoon, I've been imagining handing in my notice and working from home developing designs for Hillary.

'How is Sir Hugo?'

'Driving me mad with his increasing forgetfulness.'

'And Simon?'

'Full of chat about what he and Edith are up to. I don't think it will be long until they get engaged.'

'Good heavens! That's fast,' she says, wearing a fantastic look of amazement. 'I never doubted your decision to break up with Simon – but imagining *you* engaged to him, and marrying in pomp and ceremony really does solidify the fact that you made the right choice. Can you imagine, you walking down the aisle of a large church in a giant meringue of a dress?'

'I know!' I say, hoping to sound as if the idea is preposterous but, one way or another, I end up sounding unconvinced. For all my designs to put men out of my life I find myself questioning if splitting up with Simon was the right decision.

'Bea, what's the matter?'

'Nothing.'

Because how can there be? How can I find myself doubting my break-up with Simon when I've just taken a huge step towards fulfilling a life goal?

'Nothing my eye! Come on, tell your Aunt Jane. What's going on?'

As we trudge through the mud towards the main stage, I try to recall my motivation behind the break-up. 'I can't quite remember why I threw away someone so good and kind and reliable.'

Aunt Jane takes my hand and gives it a squeeze. 'Because the spark had gone.'

'But lots of people have successful marriages that are built on other things, like friendship and respect and loyalty. We had all those things.'

'And yet the idea of marrying him filled you with dread.'

'But I don't know why.'

'Because you want a creative life, one with freedom and space, and maybe a little passion too. Simon's bound by tradition and convention. Even with all the money in the world you wouldn't feel truly free with him.'

'But everyone needs some kind of anchor in their life, or else they drift.'

'Or, alternatively, the anchor prevents us from moving forwards.' She eyes me cautiously. 'What became of the wedding photographer?'

I release a sigh. 'He wasn't who I thought he was.'

I can tell from the pregnant pause that Aunt Jane wants to ask more, but she knows better than to probe too deep.

'And Sebastian?' She beckons towards him up ahead, walking with Tom.

'I have a funny feeling he's into someone else, don't you?'

Aunt Jane flashes her big playful eyes, 'Talk about setting the Kat among the pigeons!'

I grimace. 'She's got some talking to do, that's for sure.'

'My advice to her would be the same as it is for you – when you follow your heart, all the rest has a strange way of following on behind.'

Even though I don't fully believe it, I take some comfort from Aunt Jane's words of wisdom, and I can feel my head begin to clear, enabling me to focus on the buzz of discovering how much people love my work – and, more pressingly, on enjoying Jack's big night.

'What are you guys talking about?' asks Lizzie, who's somehow managed to find us among the throngs heading towards the stage. She seems in much brighter spirits and immediately wraps herself around me, stumbling in the process.

'The excitement of Beatrice making it as an up-and-coming designer,' says Aunt Jane.

'Whimsy & White is perfect for you,' says Lizzie, slurring slightly. I figure she must have taken off earlier for a drink or two. 'You've always been the one who was a little bit different.'

She means it as a compliment, I'm sure, that I had the potential to do something unusual, but given my current anchorless state it feels more like an insult. Hannah was always going to be a professional; Kat's always been happy so long as she's healthy, undefined by what she does; Lizzie was determined to be an art therapist. It was only ever me who didn't quite know where I belonged, either at work or in relationships; being a jewellery designer felt more of a dream than something achievable, and I've always doubted myself. I guess it didn't help that all my mother really wanted was a husband and family — and look how that turned out.

'How much have you had to drink?' I ask Lizzie, after she trips and I catch her just before she falls.

'Nothing. I just went to see Jack. We needed to talk.'

'And you're sure you didn't have anything to drink while you were with him?'

'As if I would!' she says, defensively.

What does that mean? Lizzie's always been so proud of how much she can drink, given she's so small; it's unlike her to be so hostile about it.

'Okay,' I reply, not wanting to goad her any further in fear of spoiling the evening she's been looking forward to for so long.

The three of us press through the gathering crowd, as close to the front as possible.

'Isn't this brilliant?' Lizzie shouts as Jack and his mates run on to the stage, the crowd going wild.

'It is!' I yell back, remembering their first few gigs to an audience of ten or twenty people to this, thousands of people all knowing their name and singing their songs.

As the set progresses I step to the side, away from the horde, watching my friends from a distance: Hannah has her arms draped over Remy, the two of them swaying in time to the music, lighters held aloft; Seb is singing along, lost in the lyrics, and then there's Aunt Jane and Tom, their eyes brighter than any of those around them, even those who are a third of their age.

Towards the end of the set I catch sight of Lizzie, right at the front, screaming for Jack's attention, seemingly even drunker than before. When he eventually glances down, she lifts up her shirt, braless, and starts gyrating in front of him.

'Jesus,' I mutter, when her image is blasted over the wide screens at the side of the stage. 'Excuse me,' I start yelling, pushing my way towards her. It takes a while to reach her but when I do I pull her top back on and take her off to the side.

'What the hell?!' she says, angry at me for spoiling her fun.

'You're making an idiot of yourself,' I say, holding on to her arm when she tries to break away.

'No, I'm not!'

'Fine, you're not, but you *are* making a fool of Jack. Now come on, I'm taking you back to the tent!'

'Lighten up, Bea! Try having a little fun for once,' she yells, this time getting away from me and running towards the trailer park.

'Shit,' I say, watching her run, as the heavens open and the rain soaks us all.

'Why would Lizzie behave like that?' asks Remy, back at the tent, our wet clothes hanging round the stove.

'Because she's clearly drunk her way through almost an entire brewery.' I sit cross-legged on my bed, my hands wrapped round a mug of hot chocolate, which Aunt Jane has made to repair my emotional wound.

'But why? It's so unlike her.'

'She has been kind of weird recently,' says Hannah, reclining next to Remy on their bed. 'I'm guessing things aren't resolved between her and Jack over the tour.'

'Where is she now?' asks Aunt Jane.

'She went off in the direction of the trailers. She must be with Jack.'

'Do you think he'll go to America?' asks Hannah.

'I don't see how he can't. You saw how the crowd reacted to them tonight, they're big news. Why would he opt out of that?'

'Because he promised his wife he'd stay home.'

'I can't figure out why Lizzie's so adamant about him being here,' I say. 'They know they can make long-distance work, they've done it before.'

'Maybe it's more about the kid thing,' says Hannah. 'You know she's always been crazy about having a family.'

'Lizzie's maternal instinct is pretty strong. I think she's genuinely keen to make it happen sooner rather than later.'

'Well the drinking won't help,' says Hannah, ever the pragmatist.

'Now, now, children,' says Aunt Jane, resplendent in a pair of silk pyjamas, her hair in a plait, rubbing face cream into her cheeks. 'Perhaps we should hear it from the woman herself.'

'Here, here,' mumbles Tom, sleepily, already tucked under his duvet for the night.

I'm just about to snuggle down myself when Kat returns, an almost empty bottle of wine in hand.

'Hey,' I say. 'What happened?'

'It's over. I called off the wedding.'

Her news is met with a chorus of groggy affection and hugs, which she soaks up limply, before sitting on the corner of Sebastian's bed. I know she's hurting and it's not the right time to say it, but I do feel she's made the right decision.

'And where's Henry?' asks Aunt Jane, climbing into bed.

'Gone.'

'What can we do to help?' asks Hannah.

'Nothing much. I'll be fine.'

'Let's call it a night, shall we?' suggests Tom, kindly.

'I agree,' says Aunt Jane, turning out the retro-style bedside camping-lamp. 'Everything will be clearer in the morning.'

'I might sit up a little longer, just in case Lizzie comes back,' I say.

'I'll join you,' says Kat. Sebastian pats the duvet beside him to indicate that Kat is welcome to make herself more comfortable.

We chat for a while about what transpired between her and Henry – she'd been leaning towards forgiving his one-night-stand, but his apoplectic reaction to her kissing Sebastian honed her sight and she knew she had to call the wedding off. But it's quite tricky to talk while the others are trying to sleep so in the end I resort to reading, while Kat and Sebastian whisper quietly in the dim light of the tent.

I'm beginning to drift into sleep when the sound of someone staggering into the tent jolts me awake.

'Lizzie?' I ask.

'What's going on?' asks Kat, who's still sitting up with Sebastian.

'Hey guys,' slurs Lizzie. 'Took me for ever to find you. I've been into every fecking tent on the avenue.'

'Bloody hell, Liz,' says Kat, getting off the bed. 'Why didn't you call?'

'Lost my phone,' she says, with an exaggerated shrug, swaying ominously.

'Is everything okay?' I ask, fetching her some water.

'Never better.' Water dribbles down her chin. 'Jack's going on tour and I'm staying at home. Simple.' She stumbles towards my bed then falls face first onto it before passing out.

'Well, at least we know why she's been so weird,' says Kat, both of us staring at Lizzie.

'Although there is still one problem.'

'What's that?'

I point to where Lizzie is on the bed. 'That's where you were meant to be sleeping.'

'Don't worry,' says Sebastian. 'Kat can sleep next to me.'

Kat shrugs an okay.

'Are you sure?' I ask, concerned she might not be thinking straight after calling off the wedding.

'I'm sure.' She reaches over to give my arm a reassuring rub, her eyes glinting in the dark.

22

I wake to the sound of Aunt Jane stirring porridge on the stove, the morning light filling the tent with a mellow glow. Tom is up and dressed, reading a paper, while Kat, Sebastian and Lizzie are all still dead to the world.

'Where are Hannah and Remy?' I ask, sitting up and rubbing my eyes, noticing their empty bed.

'Hannah's gone for a run and Remy's holding an impromptu yoga class outside,' says Tom, accepting a bowl of porridge from his wife.

'Bit too eager if you ask me,' says Aunt Jane. 'I'm certainly not doing one of those rhinoceros positions, or whatever you call them, until I've had my breakfast.'

'Agreed,' I say, stretching myself awake.

'What happened here?' she asks, beckoning towards Kat and Sebastian.

'Lizzie passed out next to me,' we both look at Lizzie, breathing fumes, her face squashed against the pillow, 'so Kat had to bunk in with Seb.'

'*Had* to?' she enquires, bringing me some porridge.

'I think it's fair to say it softened the blow of ending things with Henry!' I fell asleep listening to sounds of them fooling around underneath the blankets.

'You don't mind?'

'Not at all, I'm not interested in Sebastian in that way and besides, I reckon it's just a rebound thing for Kat.'

Just then Kat's phone pings, causing her to stir, her hand fumbling on the floor for it.

'Oh shit,' she mumbles, reading the text, still half asleep.

'Everything okay?' I ask.

Sitting up, her hair a fantastic mess, she tries to focus on the screen. 'Henry wants to talk.'

Kat looks to Sebastian, still fast asleep.

'Did you . . .?' I whisper, my eyes lowered towards Sebastian's nether regions.

She nods sheepishly, flushed with embarrassment.

'Wow! This should really give Henry something to think about.'

'Maybe,' she says, biting her bottom lip. I hope she's not thinking of changing her mind.

'What's going on?' asks Lizzie, prising her cheek from the pillow where she's lain motionless since she fell face-first into it.

'Kat called off the wedding, but Henry wants to talk things through,' I tell her, quietly so as not to hurt her head any more than it already appears to be hurting; her eyes are narrowed and bloodshot.

'Tell him to fuck off,' she mutters, putting her head back onto the pillow. 'You're better off without him. We're all better off without men. Hannah's the only sane one among us.'

'Speak for yourself,' says Aunt Jane, swinging Tom's hand.

'Things aren't that bad, are they?' I ask, offering her a bottle of water.

'Jack has to tour or else he loses his place in the band, I'd say it's pretty bad. We had a big fight.'

I stroke her hair. 'Sounds like he's stuck between a rock and a hard place.'

She lets out a little grunt of grudging acceptance.

'Remember your vows, "to move forward . . . ready to risk, dream, and dare". Maybe this is one of those moments where you have to risk letting him go for a bit, dare to be brave, to let him dream. You know he'd do the same for you.'

Lizzie puts the pillow over her head to block my voice out but then she reaches out a hand. 'Sorry I was mean to you last night.'

'Forgiven,' I say, squeezing her hand, thankful that I'm single and not having to run the gauntlet of emotions a relationship can bring.

I'm trying to coax water into Lizzie when Hannah returns from her run.

'I don't think you'll believe who I've just seen,' she says, reminiscent of Martin, the hapless bookshop assistant in *Notting Hill*.

'Who?' asks Lizzie, managing to sit up enough for a bit of potential showbiz gossip. 'Was it someone famous?' Lizzie loves a celeb.

Hannah stretches out her calf muscles. 'Nope.'

'That would have been a bit of excitement,' says Tom. I can't tell if he's being sarcastic or not.

'I once saw Paul McCartney,' says Lizzie.

'Where?' I ask, surprised I haven't heard this story before.

'In Regent's Park.'

Kat and I exchange sceptical looks.

'Least I think it was him, though it might have been that Den Watts from *EastEnders*.'

'You mean, Lesley Grantham?' I have no idea if Lizzie is deliberately rewriting the scene or if she's just seen it so often that it feels like something she'd say anyway.

'Right, that guy.'

'Liz, Lesley Grantham and Paul McCartney look nothing alike,' says Kat, playing along with a laugh.

'He was quite far away.'

'So what you're saying is, it may not have been either.'

'Guess not.'

'Not a classic anecdote, Liz!' says Hannah, throwing a sweaty balled-up running sock at her.

'So, who did you see, smartarse?' says Lizzie, lobbing the sock back at Hannah.

'Leo.'

For a moment no one says anything, everyone discreetly looking in my direction to see what my reaction might be.

'What's he doing here?' I ask, trying for cavalier, but not pulling it off.

'Working, I guess,' she says, rubbing her face with a towel.

'Did you stop to talk to him?'

'Sure.'

'What did he say?'

'Not much. Something about a photo-shoot opportunity that delayed his trip back home.'

Suddenly my chest feels tight and my mind is turning over a thousand thoughts.

'He said he'd try and find the tent later, stop in and say hello.'

My heart skips a beat. *So he could arrive now, with me in my knackered pyjamas and bird's nest hair? Though why I should care so much I've really no idea.*

'Fuck,' I mutter, grabbing a towel, change of clothes and loo bag, and running for the shower block.

A half hour later, washed, dressed and with a skim of make-up on, but not so much that looks as if I give a damn, I mosey out of the shower block feeling ready to face Leo head on, and confront him about his behaviour at the club. That is, until I see him lazing on the grass opposite, seemingly without a care in the world, and at that point my stomach flips like a pancake.

Shit, he's hot, I think, my amygdala getting the better of me. *Get it together, Bea. Hot or not, the guy has issues.*

'Hi,' I say, curtly, making it clear from the start that he's not in my good books.

'Hey,' he says, getting up and nervously wiping his hands on his jeans. He leans in to kiss me on the cheek but I swerve and he ends up kissing my ear. 'I stopped by the tent,' he says, tentatively, sensing my mood. 'Your aunt said I might find you here.'

'Well, here I am,' I say, flatly. I have no intention of making this easy for him, even if everything about him does make me quiver.

He shifts awkwardly for a moment, shoving his hands into the pockets of his jeans, his shoulders raised. 'Would you like to grab some brunch? There's a churro stand just over there.' He indicates to a converted old van.

'Sure,' I say, shrugging my shoulders as if I'm not that fussed, though quietly I'm pleased by the offer, never being one to turn down sweet carbs.

On the way to the stall I relent to some polite chit-chat about the festival, the atmosphere, the bands, but still making it perfectly clear from my tone that I'm anything but pleased about him kissing me when he was with Brit.

Once we've grabbed our churros, Leo's with coffee and mine with hot chocolate, we take a seat at the colourful, if rickety, wooden tables and chairs beside the van.

'So, how come you delayed going back home?' I ask, wondering if something has changed between him and Brit.

'I got a shoot for a big magazine – a backstage piece of the summer festivals.'

'Congratulations,' I say, unable to conceal my happiness for him. 'Will you head home after it's done?'

He nods. 'The wedding season is almost over. Kat's was the last in the diary and I got a message late last night to say that's been cancelled . . .'

'Right, I can't pretend to be overly disappointed,' I say, hoping not to come over too harsh.

'No?'

'Henry was cheating on her,' I explain, feeling a little of my hostility towards him waning. 'And, if I'm honest, they never seemed like a good fit. I don't know how it went on as long as it did.'

'It's not always easy to know the ins and outs of other people's relationships.' There's something in his tone that makes me think he's had some experience of this, causing me to wonder what he's not saying.

We sit quietly for a moment, both of us drinking, watching passers-by milling around, perusing the stalls.

'How's the jewellery going?' he asks, after a time.

I tell him about Hillary Bentham and Whimsy & White.

'Congratulations, Bea!' His eyes brim with admiration and before I know it he's reached over to hug me, and a tingle of desire rushes through my body. I hold the embrace longer than I should and he does too. We pull apart to explore each other's eyes, trying to read the other's mind, and wondering if we're both feeling the same thing.

'We should consider Brit,' I say, breaking away when it becomes obvious we're about to kiss again. I want to shake myself – this is exactly the kind of behaviour I've always hated. The kind of thing my father would have done. *So why am I still interested in this man?*

'You're right, we should,' he says, pulling away, and there's a slightly awkward pause. 'I'm sorry if my behaviour's been a bit erratic.'

I shirk the comment away. 'It hasn't really shown you in your best light.'

'I can imagine.'

'What's going on? You don't really seem sold on your decision to settle back home with Brit.'

He indicates to the vendor that he'd like a refill, then takes a second to gather his thoughts. 'It's a long story, but I'd like you to hear it,' he says, an earnestness in his eye. 'It's important to me that you should understand why I've behaved so badly.'

'Then go ahead.'

'Do you remember the family photo I showed you?'

'Sure,' I say, recalling the picture of him with the beach in the background.

'And you remember you asked about the other family?'

'Uh-huh.'

'Brit is part of that family. We've known each other since we were kids. When Dad left us, Brit's dad stepped up and filled the gap he left.'

'He sounds like a good guy.' *But I'm still none the wiser.*

'When we were about eighteen we began dating and not long after I started doing my first photography gigs. Brit would help me out, it was a bit of a slog at times, long hours, long drives, but it made us pretty tight. Then after a few years I decided I wanted to go travelling, Brit wanted to stay home with her family, we just began to drift apart, and eventually we broke up.'

I nod along, following the story, wondering where it's going.

'Fast forward three years and I get a call to say that her parents have been involved in a road accident, so I rushed home to be with them. When I saw her dad in the hospital, he asked me to promise that I'd always take care of her, to help in any way I could.

'In the end both her parents passed away. Brit's brother was sixteen at the time. She had to look after him, and to do that she needed money, so I offered for her to work as my assistant again. Since that time, we've been on and off.'

'You were right when you said it was complicated!' I say, sympathetically.

'Right,' he says, with a dismal laugh. 'And what makes it more complicated is that Brit now wants to start a family.'

'Wow!' I let out a whistle. 'How does that fit in with being a photojournalist?'

'It doesn't really. But until this summer I was prepared to give up on the dream so that she might have hers. Given she helped me get mine kick-started I figured I should do the same for her.'

'What happened this summer?' I ask, my upset over him kissing me beginning to dissipate.

'Lizzie's wedding – and the thunderbolt that was you.' He pauses, drinking me in as if I were something completely unobtainable. 'I knew exactly what I wanted but wasn't able to have it.'

'Once in a blue moon . . .' I begin, remembering what he said to me on Parliament Hill.

'Someone comes along who trips you up, someone

who makes it crystal clear where you're meant to go next.'

'I thought that was just a line to get me into bed,' I say, relieved to learn that my instincts were right, that he isn't the self-centred, womanising arse I made him out to be in my head.

'No, never,' he says, his eyes full of sincerity. 'But Brit and her family have been there for me since my father left. She helped me get started in photography, I owe her, and them, *so* much. The last few years have been the worst years of their lives, and she in particular has needed me.'

'But her brother is an adult now, she's no longer his carer?'

'He is, and gradually they're all moving on, but I don't see how I can just drop her like a stone just because I've found someone I'm more passionate about.'

'You *refuse to be the person who gives up on someone*,' I say, remembering what he told me the morning after we slept together. And suddenly it all makes sense: those things that I thought he lacked – loyalty, a sense of integrity – are actually the things at his core, but they're also the root of our struggles.

'I promised her father, you know? And I refuse to be like my own father. I refuse to go back on a promise.'

'But you promised him you'd *care* for her, not *marry* her,' I say, hoping my support doesn't come over as self-interest, hoping he knows how much it means to me that he is nothing like his dad or mine. 'Just because you fall for someone else doesn't mean you can't be a good friend to her.'

He looks at me as if he's in a dream. 'You're so sweet, Bea – so understanding and considerate, not to mention sexy!'

I laugh off his adulation. 'And what about Brit? She sounds like she's all of those things too.'

'She is,' he says, his brow furrowed in thought. 'But lots of people have those qualities, don't they? Ultimately, if there isn't the spark, the passion, then what is there?'

'I can't answer that, I'm afraid. Only you can.'

There's a moment of quiet between us that's broken by the call of my name. I turn to find Remy running towards us.

'Bea,' she says, breathless, clutching her side. 'You have to come quick! Lizzie is sick.'

'What do you mean?' I ask, assuming it's alcohol-induced.

'She's unconscious,' she says, reaching out her hand. 'Come on!'

23

Remy grabs my hand and runs, leading me through the dawdling festival-goers, the stalls, the tents, and past the stages. By the time we get to Lizzie an ambulance is already there with paramedics working on her. Jack is stroking her hair, Hannah and Kat are by her side, and the rest of the gang are standing around, hands on faces and each other, staring blindly at her body.

'What happened?' I ask, barely able to breathe at the sight of her lying motionless on the ground. Aunt Jane wraps an arm around me.

'We think someone spiked her drink last night,' says Kat, looking up from where she is beside her. 'It's only caught up with her now.'

God, that explains why she was so adamant about not drinking. 'Who would do that?'

'We don't know. All we know is that she's unconscious and showing no sign of coming round.'

My heart freezes as I look at Lizzie's limp body – beautiful, irreverent, joyous Lizzie. I can't bear to think about what might happen, or about the fact that I've been with Leo while she's been lying here.

'They need to get her to hospital,' says Kat, as Lizzie

is wrapped in a red blanket, which Jack tenderly tucks around her.

I watch as the paramedics ask everyone to stand back and they transfer Lizzie from the cold, muddy ground to a trolley. Jack wears the look of a man who's just had his entire world blown apart. Then, as Lizzie's about to be taken to the ambulance, I can hear a choppy sound in the distance.

'That's the air crew now,' says one of the paramedics.

'Air crew?' I utter.

'They'll take her on the helicopter to Bristol. It's quicker that way.'

I know nothing about medicine but even I know that when someone needs an air ambulance, it's not good.

It doesn't take long for the ambulance to land and the doctor, in bright orange overalls, to reach Lizzie. After gathering information from the paramedics, he crouches down beside her.

'Lizzie?' he calls, opening her eyes and flashing a torch into them. 'Lizzie can you hear me?'

Come on, Lizzie, say something!

'Let's get her on the aircraft,' he says. 'We need to get her scanned ASAP.'

Scanned? Scanned for what?

Before I have the chance to question what's going on the doctor asks, 'Does anyone have a medical history for this woman. Medication, allergies, implants?'

My mind goes blank. *Come on, Bea, think! You lived with her for years, you must know if she takes any medicine.*

'She's asthmatic,' says Hannah.

'And allergic to codeine,' says Kat.

'Any metal implants?'

'No,' says Hannah.

'And could she be pregnant?'

They both shake their heads.

'Actually,' says Jack, stepping forward, all of us listening to what he's about to say. 'She's eleven weeks.'

'Thanks,' says the doctor, ushering Jack forwards. 'Come on. Let's get going.'

I watch Lizzie being taken to the helicopter, Jack by her side, and ask myself, how could I not have known? How is it possible that I didn't notice that one of my best friends was eleven weeks pregnant? As she's loaded into the back of the chopper I run through the last few months in my mind, and suddenly it becomes clear, not only her hesitancy about Jack leaving for his tour, but the little things too – not drinking or dancing at Mahiki's, a sense that Jack didn't know what side his bread was buttered, no G&T during Truth or Dare. All the clues were there, I've just been too self-absorbed to notice.

We all head back to the tent, me flanked by Hannah and Kat, the others following on behind.

'I'll make hot chocolate, it'll help with the shock,' says Aunt Jane, when we arrive back. The memories of the four of us drinking hot chocolate after school at Aunt Jane's house makes me burst into tears. How petty all our teenage angst seems now.

'She's in safe hands,' says Kat, sitting next to me on the bed, gently rubbing my back.

'But she looked so lifeless.' I can barely believe the words I'm saying.

'Her body was in shock. Sometimes bodies look like they've shut down but really they're busy repairing themselves. Give her time.'

'I can't get my head round who would do such a thing,' says Hannah. She and Remy are huddled on their bed, a blanket over their shoulders, like survivors of a shipwreck.

'Maybe it was a prank gone wrong.'

'Poor girl,' says Tom, his eyes hazy with moisture. It's the first thing he's said since she left.

'But she's strong,' says Remy. 'If anyone can get through this it's Lizzie.'

'You're absolutely right,' says Aunt Jane. 'It's important to remain positive for her.'

'And the baby,' I say, causing everyone to fall silent, the magnitude of the news too great to make sense of.

'Did anyone know?' asks Sebastian, hugging a pillow.

'I had no idea,' I say, accepting a hot chocolate from Aunt Jane. 'But if she's eleven weeks then it must be a honeymoon baby.'

'It certainly clears up why she's been so keen for Jack not to go on tour,' says Kat.

I blow on my hot chocolate, lost in my thoughts.

'We should decide who's doing what, make a plan, somebody needs to be with her,' says Aunt Jane.

'It doesn't make sense for all of us to go to the hospital. Jack is with her, and her parents will be there within an hour or so,' I say.

'I have a deposition in the morning,' says Hannah, her voice heavy with regret. 'I really have to get back to the city.'

'I'll drive,' says Remy.

'And I can take Jane and Tom home,' says Sebastian.

'Thank you,' says Aunt Jane, already packing her bag.

'That's kind,' says Kat, getting up to go over and kiss him on the cheek.

'It is not a problem,' he says, giving her a warm hug. They look so good together, snuggled up close but, despite their dalliance, my hunch is that Kat's heart is with Henry.

In spite of our best intentions to remain positive, the mood is still pretty solemn by the time we've packed our backpacks, ready to leave. The excitement of yesterday seems like a lifetime ago, and the fun of the festival, still going on around us, feels remote, as if there's a force-field between it and the seven of us.

'Knock, knock,' says a voice from the entrance to the tent, breaking the heavy silence in which we've all been packing.

'Hi Leo,' says Kat, putting on her backpack and securing its waistband with a click.

'Hey,' he says, his voice quiet, sensitive to the mood.

'Come in.'

It's obvious to everyone that Leo's here to see me so, with their bags packed, they begin to filter out.

'You let me know if you need anything at all,' says

Aunt Jane, with a kind wink and a stoic rub on the arm. Tom hugs me gently. I bite hard on my lip; it's all I can do to stop myself from brimming up again.

'I'll take care of them,' says Sebastian, kissing my forehead and following them out.

'And I'll wait a few tents down,' says Kat, out of earshot of Leo. 'Take your time.'

'You have great friends,' says Leo, once everyone's away and the two of us are alone in the tent, which without the others just feels large and cold.

'I really do.' My voice breaks, and tears flow freely down my cheeks. 'Sorry,' I say, laughing at my own fragility, clumsily wiping my eyes.

'Don't apologise.' He puts his hands on my arms and squats a little to bring his eyes level with mine, brushing away a hair that's stuck to my damp cheek. 'You've had a terrible shock.'

I nod, inhaling sharply, trying to gather myself as Aunt Jane would have me do. Leo's eyes are still level with mine and as I attempt to pull myself together I see a look of desire grow in them; an affectionate, sincere look that says he wants to kiss me. And in that moment, feeling lost and afraid, I almost let him.

'What about Brit?' I ask, gently, not wanting to create conflict.

He sighs, sounding weary.

'Brit and I need to talk.'

'Yes, you do,' I say, stepping back. 'And if you choose to help her fulfil her dream, then I'll accept that decision, with no regrets.'

He laughs wryly. 'At least one of us would be free of regret.'

I take his hand in mine and, looking deep into his eyes, I offer him the words Aunt Jane gave to me, 'Follow your heart, and the rest will follow.'

'I just need to figure out exactly what my heart is telling me,' he says.

'Only you can do that.'

'Yes,' he says, looking at me longingly.

'And if it makes you feel any better, I'm not interested in anyone else. Once Lizzie is better I plan to focus on me for a while, call Hillary Bentham, eventually hand in my notice, make a name for myself.'

'You're following *your* heart.'

'For once I am.'

'I'll try and do the same,' he says, his watch buzzing a reminder. 'Shit, is that the time? I have to go.'

'Of course,' I say, for once feeling that I'm the one in control of this relationship. I can see from Leo's rapid eye movement that his mind is working overtime, that he's agitated at having to rush our goodbye.

'Goodbye, Bea,' His voice is strained. We both know that after today that's it, he flies back to California. More than likely we'll never see each other again.

'Take care of yourself,' I say, my thoughts turning to Lizzie, wanting desperately to be with her.

24

Kat's ancient Land Rover Defender, just like Tom's in *Four Weddings*, is noisy and uncomfortable but she's had it for such a long time and we've shared so many memories in it that it's almost like a piece of home. We're bombing down the motorway towards the hospital.

'Do you remember when we almost careered into the sea at Cromer when the handbrake failed?' I ask, my knees tight against the green metal dashboard.

'Don't remind me!'

'And the time the four of us all had to sleep in it when we ran out of petrol?'

'We were like sardines in a tin.'

'And Lizzie spent the night convinced that someone was going to slaughter us in our sleep because the doors wouldn't lock.'

'Lizzie's imagination always has got the better of her,' says Kat. 'Remember when we hid Hannah in that cupboard at Aunt Jane's and told Liz it was haunted? And every time Lizzie asked it a question Hannah would push one of the top drawers open as if the ghost was communicating with her.'

'God that was funny. We were cruel to her sometimes.'

'Only ever with affection.'

'Life wouldn't be the same without her,' I say, swallowing back a huge lump in my throat.

Kat glances over to me, reaching out a hand. 'She'll be okay, Bea.'

'Yes,' I say, determined to remain positive. 'I'm sure you're right. It's just . . .'

'What?'

'I can't help thinking, all this Four Weddings business, I hate to be the one to say it but there was also a—'

'Don't even go there,' says Kat, staring, unblinking, ahead.

'No, you're right, of course she'll be fine.' I shake away the thought. 'And the baby too.'

'They'll both be fine.' It's clear from Kat's slightly aggressive, positive stance that she's as frightened as I am.

'Can you imagine Lizzie as a mother?' I say, trying to lighten the mood.

'She'd probably keep misplacing the baby!' Kat laughs. She doesn't know it, but I see her hurriedly wipe away a tear.

'She'd leave it in the supermarket trolley, or at the side of the road . . .'

'Or by a park bench!'

'Oh jeez, it has disaster written all over it.' I laugh at the endless baby-related catastrophes Lizzie could be capable of.

'But the truth is she'd be the most doting, loving mother a child could ever wish for.'

'You're right,' I say, my mind drifting to the thought

of her in a hospital bed, fighting for both their lives.

'Fill me in on what happened with Leo,' says Kat, sensing my darkening thoughts and trying to take my mind off them.

I explain about how things stand with Brit. 'He needs to figure out what he wants. I can't do that for him.'

'And what about you? Are you getting any closer to what you want?'

'Do you know, I think I am,' I say, breaking open a packet of Liquorice Allsorts, which we picked up at the petrol station to keep ourselves going. 'Once we know how things stand with Lizzie, I'm going to work my arse off to get my collection complete. If Whimsy & White are interested, then that's brilliant and if not, I'll do it alone.'

'Good for you, Bea!' She pops a Bertie Basset into her mouth. 'So, Leo's forgotten?'

'A flight of fancy,' I say, sounding completely over him, even though a little pang in my heart hopes he'll choose me over Brit.

'And Simon?'

'What about him?'

She grips the steering wheel a little tighter. 'If I'm completely honest, Bea, I never really understood why you broke up with him.'

'The spark had gone.'

Though he was completely stable. If my father taught me anything, it's that stable matters.

Kat considers this for a moment. 'You've mentioned that before.'

'It's kind of important, don't you think? It looked to me as if you and Seb might have it . . .'

She drums her fingers on the wheel. 'Henry really wishes I hadn't called off the wedding.'

'Do you want it back on?'

'I'm not sure. I don't want to be with him; I don't want to be without him.'

'Do you want to know what I think?'

She laughs. 'I'm not sure about that either!'

'I think you should tell him to wait and explore things with Sebastian a bit more. If that doesn't work out, and it's meant to be with Henry then it will happen.'

'Sleeping with Sebastian was just a tit-for-tat. I really should tell Henry.'

'I think that's a bad idea.'

'I have to; I feel so bad about what I did.'

'Really?' I ask, surprised. 'It's not as if you and Henry were together. And you've fancied Seb since Hannah's wedding. You have loads in common, and, dare I say it, he's far kinder than Henry. Remember that halfway house we talked about?'

She nods, her mouth tight in thought.

'Maybe Sebastian is that,' I say.

'I don't think so . . . I think he's more into me than I'm into him, and besides, there's too much unresolved with Henry. We've both made a mistake. I owe him more time.'

'Kat, you know I don't believe in "the one" but surely if what's happened to Lizzie shows us anything it's that there is something *close* to the perfect match. We rib

Lizzie and Jack relentlessly for being so loved-up but maybe if we can't be like them we should just let it go.'

'You sound a lot like Charles after Gareth's funeral.'

I laugh; she's right, I do.

'But like Tom, I never really expected a thunderbolt,' says Kat. 'I've always leant more towards meeting a guy I liked the look of and making a go of things. My parents don't have a really romantic relationship, and it works for them.'

'What do I know?' I say, giving up. It's not that I want Henry to be romantic, I just want him to be less of a shit. 'Given I'm the only one of us not even close to marriage you're probably better without my advice. Maybe Charles was right in the first instance, maybe this waiting around for one true love stuff gets you nowhere.'

'Does that mean you'd marry Simon?'

I look at her as if she'd gone mad. 'Simon is with Edith.'

'And if he wasn't?'

'I have absolutely no idea.' Though right at this moment, with Lizzie being as she is, I'd give anything for the warmth and security of his arms.

The drive took less than an hour but it felt like an eternity. Knowing I can wait no longer, Kat drops me at the entrance of the A & E before going to look for a parking place.

'I'll be in as soon as I can,' she calls, and I slam the car door, running inside as fast as my legs will carry me.

'Where can I find Lizzie Strachan?' I ask, at the reception desk.

The woman, in an uncomfortably tight blue uniform, punches her name into the computer.

'She's still with us,' she says. I know she means she's still here in A & E but for one heart-stopping moment it sounded as if she was saying, 'She hasn't died, yet.'

'Can I see her?'

'You are?'

'Her sister,' I lie, vindicated by the fact that though we may not be biologically related, we're as good as the real thing.

She eyes me warily but then sees the desperate look in my eye. 'Let me get someone to take you through.'

I pace the waiting area until a nurse appears and escorts me into the part of A & E you never want to see. The part where people are having their hearts restarted and major blood loss stemmed. Whatever I was expecting to see when I arrived, I wasn't prepared for this.

Lizzie is lying on a bed in the middle of a curtained area, surrounded by medics, machines and tubes. She looks unrecognisable. The only thing that's familiar is the little butterfly tattoo on her ankle that she forced me to have done with her when we were sixteen.

Jack comes over to be with me. 'How is she?' I ask, putting my arm around him.

'It's a bit early to say,' he says, his voice frail. 'She's just had a scan. We'll know more soon but for now the doctor's say it's touch and go.'

I stare at the butterfly on Lizzie's ankle and for the first time in a long time, I pray.

25

I wake in the morning to a message beeping on my phone.

'Is it Jack?' asks Kat, sitting up.

'It's Simon,' I say, barely awake. 'He's heard about Lizzie. He's asking if there's anything he can do.'

'That's sweet of him.' Kat rolls her neck and shoulders with a satisfying crack.

'Isn't it,' I say, wishing, a little, that he was here. He always was the adult of our group, and we could have used a grown-up yesterday.

The results of the scan came back clear and the doctors told us that all they, and we, could do was to wait. It was likely, they said, that Lizzie would make a full recovery but there was a chance she would remain in an unconscious state, a coma. The baby, they went on, appeared unharmed but at such an early stage it was impossible to be sure. If Lizzie did remain in a coma it was possible for the baby to grow normally and be delivered by Caesarean section. It was all too much to take in.

After a few hours in A & E, Lizzie was transferred to intensive care, where only Jack and her parents were able to be with her. Kat and I ate a miserable meal in the hospital canteen before bunking down in the back of the Land Rover for the night. The word 'coma' kept me awake into the small hours, with Kat tossing and turning beside me.

Once we've unravelled our stiff bodies from the back of the Defender, and I've asked Simon to let Sir Hugo know I won't be in, we freshen up in the hospital toilets then head up to ICU. With Lizzie's parents catching up on some sleep we are allowed in to be with Jack, who is sitting attentively by Lizzie's bedside, holding her hand.

'How is she?' I ask

'A little better, she came round earlier, they think she's almost out of the woods.'

'Thank God,' I say, slumping into one of the chairs on the opposite side of the bed, Kat taking the one next to me. 'And the baby?'

'They think it's fine.'

I close my eyes for a moment, relief washing over me, saying a silent prayer. 'Are you any closer to knowing what happened?'

He shakes his head. 'We probably won't ever know. Most likely some idiot mucking around backstage. The doctors think her size, and being pregnant, made the effects much worse. She's just been unlucky.'

'Had you guys made up?'

'Yes,' he says, slowly. 'She came over in the morning, she seemed fine, and we were fine too; I was over the initial shock of the pregnancy. We hadn't figured things out, but we knew we would, and then . . .' Jack tails off, the memory of finding her too raw to talk about.

'What matters is that she's doing so much better,' says Kat.

Jack's eyes fill with tears, his hand shaking over Lizzie's.

'You look exhausted,' I say. 'Why don't you take the keys to the Land Rover and grab a few hours' kip. It'll do you the world of good.'

Hesitantly, Jack accepts the offer leaving just Kat and me with Lizzie. Within only a few minutes of him leaving, Lizzie mutters something in her sleep.

'Lizzie? What is it?' I ask.

'Whimsy & White,' she whispers.

'What about it?' I ask, laughing at her saying such a peculiar thing when she's still recovering.

She opens her eyes a peep and offers a crazy smile. 'Call them.'

I take her hand in mine. 'Liz, it's really not important right now. Save your energy for getting fully better.'

'Live life now,' she says, squeezing my hand. A smile forms on her lips and as she tries to sit up, one of the nurses rushes over.

'Hi, Lizzie, how are you?' she asks, supporting her decision to sit.

'In need of pancakes,' Lizzie says, weakly, and Kat and I laugh, and then we cry, because both of us know that pancakes means Lizzie is well and truly out of the woods!

'I'm not sure we have those,' says the nurse. 'But maybe when you're back on the ward, which won't be long now.'

'Thank God,' I say, once the nurse has gone. It feels as if I've been walking around since yesterday with an elephant on my chest. 'Lizzie, you can't know how much you scared us.'

'Did I?' she says, completely oblivious to what she, and we, have just been through.

'Yes!' says Kat, who's messaged Jack with an update, and got Hannah on Facetime. 'Look who's back in the land of the living,' she says, showing Hannah Lizzie sitting up in bed.

'Oh my God,' squeals Hannah. Hannah never squeals. 'You can't know what a weight off my mind that is.'

'Do you feel like a rhino's been sitting on your head these last twenty-four hours?' I ask.

'Like you wouldn't believe,' she says, her elbows resting on her desk, her hands pushing back her hair. 'My God, Liz, you properly scared me!'

'Enough for you to make me pancakes?'

'Wow,' I say, amazed at the intensity of her craving. 'That baby in there must be really hungry.'

Lizzie's brow crinkles in confusion.

'Jack had to tell the doctor you were pregnant, and we heard,' I explain, worried she might be upset that we found out before she was able to tell us.

'Oh yeah,' she says, slowly, clearly still enjoying the effects of the medication. 'I'd completely forgotten about that.'

'You're going to be a mummy,' cries Hannah down the phone. 'And we couldn't be happier for you!'

'Not at all,' I say, pressing my cheek against Lizzie's, and Kat does the same on the other side, so that the three of us are all facing Hannah on the screen. 'Hashtag

Three Weddings and A Baby!' I cheer, and Hannah and Kat do the same.

'I'm still gunning for four weddings,' says Liz, ever the optimist, even after what she's just been through.

I'm just about to question who's to be wedding number four when another visitor arrives, someone it takes me a moment to place.

'Dave,' says Lizzie drowsily, drifting back to sleep. I'm surprised at how different he looks out of wedding clothes.

'How is she?'

'She's going to be okay,' I say, getting up to greet him.

His shoulders drop by about a foot. 'Thank God. I saw Jack on his way out. Poor bloke looked knackered.'

'That's an understatement. It's good of you to come.'

'I don't live far away. When I heard, I wanted to be here, for Jack's sake. How is she?'

'Doing much better, but in need of pancakes.'

He laughs lightly, understanding. 'I'll go get some, it's the least I can do to help.'

There's something in Dave's compassion for his cousin and in his desire to help, that makes me wonder if I got him wrong at Lizzie's wedding. And a flicker of a thought occurs to me of something I might do for him.

I leave Kat sleeping with Lizzie and head downstairs for a coffee. Lizzie's words, 'Live life now,' seemingly on loop in my head. They remind me that every part of my life needs some adjustment: a flatmate at home; a plan about work, and an emotional check-up about the men in my life.

And then, accepting my drink, I'm hit with a desire to heed Lizzie's advice. Sitting at a wobbly table I scroll through my phone to Jessica and without a second thought I call her.

'Hi Jessica,' I say, when she answers.

'Hi Bea, how are you?'

'I'm sorry it's taken me a while to get in touch. Are you still looking for a place to live?'

'I am.'

'Would you like to take the room?'

'I'd love to! I was hoping you'd call. Yours was the only place I've seen that felt like home.'

'That's so nice to hear,' I say, thankful that I called her, feeling the decision that I've been procrastinating over since she viewed the flat is the right one. 'You can move in any time. I'll partition off the living room as you suggested. Just let me know when suits.'

'I will, thanks Bea. You've made my day!'

The next call feels harder, and it takes me a moment to locate a number that might work. In the end I find the switchboard for Whimsy & White's head office.

'How may I direct your call?' asks the receptionist.

'Hillary Bentham, please,' I say, hoping she doesn't detect the tremor of fear in my voice.

'Please hold.'

My heart leaps as I'm transferred away from reception and onto another line, which is answered remarkably quickly.

'Hillary Bentham's office, Abigail speaking.'

'Good morning,' I stammer, doing my very best to sound composed. 'My name is Bea Henshaw—'

'Oh, hi, Bea.' Abigail immediately switches from formal to friendly. 'Hillary asked me to call you today. Actually, you were next on my list.'

'That's wonderful,' I say, relaxing a little.

'She'd like to set up a meeting, as soon as possible. How are you placed for Wednesday?'

'I can do that.'

'Shall we say two o'clock?'

It feels as if I've run a marathon by the time we've finished the conversation so, instead of dashing straight back upstairs, I sit for a time, relieved to have things in order but unable to shake a niggling sensation that I'm tying myself down, or over-committing myself. As I'm trying to pin down the feeling, a voice says from above me, 'Hi Bea, I thought I'd find you here.'

I look up to find Simon, standing protectively beside me.

'Simon, hi!' I say, bewildered at his sudden appearance. I kiss him on both cheeks.

'How's Lizzie?'

'Getting stronger.'

'And you?' he asks, his eyes tender.

'I'm getting stronger too. How are you?'

He inclines his head to one side. 'If I'm honest, I've been better.'

'How so?' I ask, indicating that he pull up a seat.

'Edith ended our relationship.' He runs his hands anxiously through his hair.

'She what?' I ask, completely taken aback. 'Why?'

'That's an excellent question.' He laughs awkwardly, the way he used to, when he wasn't telling me something, usually to protect me.

I reach out a hand to him. 'Are you okay?'

'Not really.' His eyes are full of remorse and searching mine for an answer. 'I'm in a bit of a knot as it happens.'

'I'm so sorry, Si. First me, then Edith. You don't deserve that.'

'No. I don't believe so,' he says, managing a humourless laugh. 'Still, life goes on.'

'Yes,' I reply, Lizzie's advice of 'live life now' still ringing in my ears.

26

No offence to Kat but it's much more comfortable driving back to London in Simon's plush new Volvo than it would be in her Defender.

'Thanks for sticking around these last couple of days,' I say, as we cruise along the M4. 'And for the hotel room for Kat and me. There's nothing quite like spending a night in the back of a Land Rover to make you appreciate a comfy bed.'

'It's the least I could do. I'm just glad Lizzie is on the mend.'

'Me too. She should be home tomorrow, and everything will be back to normal.' I pause, realising for the first time how much things have changed. 'Well, other than the fact she's pregnant!'

'I'm pleased for the two of them,' he says, casting me a sideways glance. 'I can't wait to start my own family.'

The scene from *Four Weddings* with Charles and Tom flashes back into my mind, and it occurs to me that Simon is a bit like Tom in his total confidence that he'll find the right girl and get married.

'You don't ever worry that you won't find the right person?'

He's watching the road, but still I catch a quizzical look flash across his face.

'What is it?' I ask.

'It's just it's curious to me that you don't know.'

'Know what?'

'That I've found the right person already.'

'You mean Edith?' I ask, my heart aching a little for him.

He laughs, a little sadly. 'No, not Edith. You, Bea.'

I struggle to catch my breath, bowled over by this declaration.

'But I thought . . .' I begin, but don't know how to finish. 'I—'

Simon chuckles. 'It's not often you're tongue-tied.'

'No,' I say, laughing too.

'Edith ended the relationship because she knew, in her heart, that I love you.'

'Oh God, Si, that's awful,' I say, trying to imagine how that must feel. 'I'm so sorry, for both of you.'

And then, glancing over, looking at Simon so strong and dependable, taking me home, I'm filled with a desire to reach out and wrap my arms around him, to bury my face in his brushed-cotton shirt. 'Can we pull over?'

'Of course,' he says, indicating for the next exit, looking over at me a little anxiously.

We stop at a service station. 'What's wrong, Bea? Are you hungry?'

I take off my seatbelt and reach over. 'I just wanted to hug you.'

'Well, that's allowed,' he says, a little bashfully,

wrapping his arms around me. 'What's brought this on?'

A thought of Leo pops into my head, passionate and good-looking but torn between Brit and me. But Simon isn't torn: in all the time we were together, he's never been anything other than 100 per cent true. 'It just feels good to know you're on my side.'

'I'm always on your side, Bea,' he says, looking deep into my eyes.

And before I know it we're kissing, and though it's completely unexpected it's also familiar and comfortable, and far more secure than the perilous passion I felt with Leo.

'I'll call you,' says Simon, leaning in for a kiss after he's pulled over on Chiswick High Street. 'Good luck!'

'I'll need it,' I say, wishing I'd had time to nip home and change out of my festival clothes. I'm not sure a denim pinafore dress and gypsy blouse shouts professional.

'You'll be terrific!'

As I watch him roar off I can't help wishing Simon would come back and hold my hand, to take care of the corporate speak that I've never got to grips with in all the time I've worked for Sir Hugo.

I take a deep breath before entering the head office, which is shiny and new, and makes me feel ultra-shabby.

'I have an appointment with Hillary Bentham,' I tell the perfectly turned-out receptionist. Her nails have an immaculate French manicure; mine have bits of mud ingrained in them. 'My name's Bea Henshaw.'

'Take a seat,' she says, picking up the telephone.

I've pulled out a pocket mirror and am tweaking my hair when it occurs to me that this is my one opportunity to realise my dream, that's there's no point in wasting energy on worrying about the wrong clothes or nails or hair. The only thing that matters is selling my product, and me, to Hillary.

'Live life now,' I whisper to myself, snapping my mirror shut, just as Abigail arrives in reception.

'Hi Bea,' she says, smiling warmly, paying no attention to my dishevelled state. 'Come on up.'

Take strength from Lizzie, I tell myself as we ascend in the lift, trying not to focus on the contrast being Abigail's professional attire and mine. *She fought for her and her child's lives, the least you can do is fight for your dream.*

'Hillary's really excited to hear more about your designs. Everyone who's seen the images has loved them.'

Abigail shows me in to Hillary's office, which is ridiculously large and bright.

'Bea, how are you?' She extends her hand to mine, shaking it firmly.

'I'm okay. Straight back from the festival, as you can see.'

'Perfect! Your style really captures the zest that we're always looking for. Come in and tell me all about your work.'

I spend a few minutes explaining about my passion for jewellery that I've had since I was a child, my time at art school, my detour into becoming a PA, and the events that led me back to design again.

'And the Native American influence?' asks Hillary.

'My great-aunt brought back a bracelet from Arizona when I was small, which I treasure to this day. It's something I've always had an interest in but hadn't found the right moment to explore.'

'And that exploration is really important,' she says, sucking on the end of a leg of her glasses. 'I'm wondering if it might be worth exploring that a little further, taking a trip to the States maybe, seeing if you can push the designs past great and into something more extraordinary.'

'Okay,' I say, trying to rein in my disappointment that she's not biting here and now, and wondering how I'll ever afford the travel.

'It's not a no, it's a very definite maybe,' she says, picking up on my disappointment. 'I just want to see the designs developed a little more before committing. Let's arrange to meet again before Christmas. Bring your sketches, some new products if you have them, and we'll make a decision then.'

'Okay, I'll do that,' I say, trying not to doubt myself, resigned to the fact that the dream, to hand in my notice and design full-time, will have to continue to wait.

27

'Come in, come in,' says Tom, waving me into the flat, four days later. 'Your aunt is desperate to see you.'

'I'm desperate to see her,' I say, going into the living room, which has had some subtle changes made since Tom's arrival. Gone are some of the more 'subjective' pieces of artwork and in are pictures of Tom's grandchildren and, pride of place on the record-player cabinet, is Tom and Jane's wedding photo.

'Jane!' Tom calls. 'Bea's here.'

'Oh, thank heavens,' says Aunt Jane, coming out of the kitchen, a gin and tonic in hand. 'You can't know how much I've been worrying about all of you these last few days.' She hands me the drink and indicates for me to sit down on the sofa, where she parks herself beside me. 'How is Lizzie?'

'She's home,' I say, clutching her hand, trying to reassure her.

Aunt Jane looks to Tom, her eyes overflowing with relief. 'Thank God.' He strokes her hair and sits in beside her, his arm round her back.

'And the baby?'

'Unaffected.'

Tom gives her a squeeze. 'That's the very best news,' he says.

'She's taking a week off work just to rest but, after that, everything should be back to normal.'

'She's always been strong,' says Aunt Jane. 'It's the farmer's blood that does it.'

I laugh. 'I'm not sure she'd thank you for that but, yes, for someone so small, she is particularly steely.'

'Any news about Kat and the good-looking Frenchman?' Aunt Jane's eyes twinkle mischievously, and Tom chuckles.

'If there is, she's keeping tight-lipped about it. I think her heart's still with Henry, though I've no idea why.'

'And Leo?'

'Gone back to California, to figure out what he wants out of life.'

Aunt Jane gives my back a supportive rub. 'And how was your meeting with Whimsy & White?'

I knock back a swig of G&T before telling her about Hillary's plan.

'What's wrong with that?' she asks, sensing my frustration.

'It just feels as if the dream is always out of reach. I don't really have the time or the money to take a trip before Christmas. It's hard to see how I'm going to conjure up something "extraordinary" by then.'

'That's not the fighting spirit, Bea.'

'Probably not. And Simon did say he'd be happy to help but I don't know . . . it doesn't feel right.'

'Simon?' she asks, sitting erect.

Sensing an impending battle, Tom excuses himself, and Aunt Jane and I distance ourselves from each other on the sofa.

I pause, hesitant to tell her about Simon and me, knowing exactly what she'll have to say about it.

'Should I gather from your reticence that you're back together?'

I nod, sheepishly. The day after the meeting, and over one of our Thursday night suppers, Simon and I agreed to give things another ago.

'Why?' she asks, sharply.

'I feel safe with him. And I don't know if you've noticed, but it's been a pretty rocky summer. A bit of security isn't such a bad thing.'

Aunt Jane scoffs derisorily. I should be mad at her but I can't, because the truth is I know what her reservations are. Those same feelings have been niggling away at me over the past few days.

'He's really trying to support me,' I say, a bit too eagerly, no doubt signalling even more clearly to Aunt Jane that I'm concealing my real feelings. 'He doesn't really get my creative side, but he's trying to. Offering to pay for me to take the trip is incredibly generous of him.'

Aunt Jane gets up, whisking away my glass. 'Are you back with him out of love or because there's a free ticket on the table?'

'That's a bit harsh!'

'Only because you know there's an underlying truth to it.'

'I haven't agreed to marry him,' I say, aware that my vitriol isn't helpful. 'We're just seeing how things go.'

'Well thank God for small mercies,' she says, turning on her heels and disappearing into the kitchen.

28

'These cuff bracelets are insane,' says Lizzie, picking up one of the pieces from my new work station in the living room. When Jessica moved in at the weekend we rearranged the room together, using the end with the window for my studio space and the opposite end as our snug. It works surprisingly well.

'Insane good or insane bad?' I ask, placing a huge bowl of popcorn on the coffee table.

'Insane amazing!' she says, trying one on, and I must admit, it looks good on her. For someone who was in Intensive Care two weeks ago she looks the picture of health. It's too early for her bump to be showing but she's got a glow about her that can't go unnoticed, even after being so poorly.

'The inspiration came from something a customer said at the festival. I wasn't sure if I'd gone too wide.'

'Not at all. They're proper statement pieces. Like beaded wrist warmers.'

'That's what I was going for,' I say, relieved that someone gets it.

'It's cool, Bea. Properly different. I bet Hillary will love them!'

It's nice to hear Lizzie's enthusiasm because, since my meeting with Hillary, I've been a bit up and down. After what happened to Lizzie I know I've no real reason to complain, my life is pretty damn good: I'm working towards my dream; I have a job that pays the rent; I have a nice home and a great new flatmate, and I'm back with Simon, *but*, some days I'm not that good at appreciating it. My dream of a nomadic, creative existence still feels just out of reach and I can't figure out how to bring it closer, other than by plugging away at my design work and squirrelling away towards a research trip to the States, because I don't feel fully comfortable accepting Simon's offer, and, if I'm honest, I feel anxious about travelling on my own. Aunt Jane tells me to be patient, that 'all good things will come' and all that, but some days it's harder than others.

'I hope so,' I say, trying not to doubt, trying to take each day step by step. 'Anyway, how are you feeling? How was the twelve-week scan?'

'The scan was incredible. Wait, I have a picture, somewhere . . .'

Lizzie disappears out to the hall, where I hear her muttering to herself about where she's put the photo, and I call the others through. Once Lizzie has eventually found it, the five of us huddle onto the sofa, Lizzie in the middle, the photograph in hand.

'Here's Bean!' she says, holding out the image of the scan.

'Oh my God,' I squeal, looking at the tiny critter lying on its back with its feet pointing upwards. I lean my head on Lizzie's shoulder, 'I actually think I'm going to cry.'

'Babies have a way of doing that,' says Jessica, marvelling over the photo. 'I love them so much I almost trained as a nanny.'

'Am I missing something?' asks Kat, taking the picture and squinting at it. 'All I can make out is a grey mass.'

Jessica leans in beside her, already part of the gang. 'This is the head, body and toes.'

'Huh,' says Kat, continuing to stare. 'Oh yeah . . . I see it now.' And I swear I see her eyes mist over.

'It's a miracle you kept the baby safe, Liz,' says Hannah. 'You can't know how scared we were.'

'I do know.' Lizzie leans her head against mine. 'But I think, in some small way, we're all a bit stronger for it.'

'Have you and Jack figured out what to do yet?' asks Hannah, as we begin to find more comfortable spots on the sofa.

'Not yet, but we will. Plenty of women have babies on their own, so I'll be fine. If nothing else, I'll have moral support on the end of the phone.'

'And we'll always be here to help out,' I say.

'Bagsy not doing the night shift!' says Kat. 'Or nappies.'

'Just you wait until the baby comes,' says Hannah, laughing. 'You'll be the first to want to get stuck in.'

'Seriously doubt it.'

'Don't believe you,' I say.

'Don't really care, Mrs Simon!' she sings, and I throw a handful of popcorn at her.

'It's nice that you and Si are back together,' says Lizzie.

'I didn't like to say at the time, but I kind of missed him being around. You guys are strong together.'

'Does it feel right, Bea?' Hannah asks, knowing my previous doubts better than anyone else.

'It's fine,' I say, my voice a little tight. 'Life pretty much continues as normal.'

'Thank Christ for that,' says Kat. 'We've had enough bumps in the road this summer. It's good to have some sense of normality again.'

'So long as that's what Bea wants,' says Hannah. She's watching me carefully, probably sensing that the normality I craved when everything was up in the air with Lizzie, isn't necessarily what I'm looking for now.

'Of course it's what she wants!' says Kat.

'And Leo's back in California?' asks Lizzie.

'Yup,' I reply, nibbling my bottom lip.

'And he hasn't been in touch?'

'Nope. I figure he's settled down with Brit, planning a family.'

'Nice that you had a little summer romance though.' Lizzie gives my wrist a shake and a squeeze. 'No harm done.'

'Right,' I say, nodding, hoping they don't hear the faint change of pitch in my voice. 'No harm done.'

'Speaking of summer romances,' says Hannah. 'Kat, have you heard from Sebastian? Remy tells me he's pretty keen.'

'I don't know what you mean,' says Kat, shaking her head, the muscles in her neck tensing a little, the way they do when she's under strain.

'Remy told me he wants to see you again, by all accounts he's smitten.'

'Well, too bad,' she says on an outward breath. She stretches her arms out in front of her, her fingers locked, as if she's about to do some intense exercise. But I can tell it's not exercise she's thinking about, it's something else, something she knows we're going to find hard to swallow. 'The wedding's back on. Henry and I are getting married.'

Her news is greeted with a wall of stunned silence, until Jessica chimes in.

'That's wonderful news,' she says. Our eyes flit between each other in shock. 'When's the big day?'

'September the eighth, same as it was before.'

'Gosh, so soon. You must have a lot to organise.'

'Actually, no. I called the wedding coordinator, it's all taken care of. The only thing outstanding is the photographer.'

'Well, good for you.' Jessica casts me a terse smile that says, 'say something, please'.

'What made you make your mind up?' I ask. I remember when she announced her engagement and I struggled to be pleased, and now, with the wedding being back on, me finding it even harder to be excited by the news. She must think me such a rubbish friend, but all I want is for her to be happy.

'It wasn't any one thing, exactly,' she says, a little on the defensive. 'But when Lizzie was sick, it got me to thinking about how fragile life can be, how we can lose everything in a blink of an eye, and it's over. I don't want to lose Henry. He makes life difficult sometimes, it's true, and he does have a way of blowing things out of proportion but I don't want to give up on us, not after all we've been through.'

'Sounds like a good enough reason to me,' says Lizzie.

'Does he know you slept with Sebastian?' I ask.

She nods. 'Funnily enough, I think it made the decision simpler for both of us. We're even, you know? It's easier to be forgiving when you've been in the same situation.'

'Sure,' I say, not wanting to put a damper on things, even though being even doesn't sound like a good enough reason to me. Also, I can't help thinking that confessing to sleeping with Sebastian wasn't such a great idea. But Kat's always been a believer in making a go of things and not making a fuss, so if that's what she wants, who am I to criticise?

'To Kat and Henry,' says Hannah, raising her glass. 'And to wedding number four!'

'To wedding number four!' we chorus, chinking each other's glasses, the feeling of excitement less than it should be.

'You know what's rubbish?' asks Lizzie, and I can tell she's about to say something inane.

'What's that?' I ask.

'The fact that you're back with Simon.'

'Why's that rubbish?' asks Hannah. 'I thought we just agreed that was a good thing.'

'Right, it is, of course it is, but it does mean we can't set Bea up with wedding date number four!'

'Damn that Simon!' says Kat, with sufficient good humour for me to know she's not completely mad at me for lacking enthusiasm about her wedding.

'But I have an idea . . .' My eyes wander towards Jessica.

'Such a good idea!' says Lizzie, immediately picking up on my thinking.

'What?' asks Hannah.

'Jessica is single,' I explain. 'And I reckon I know just the person to set her up with at Kat's wedding.'

'But I'm not invited,' she says.

'You are now!' says Kat, holding out her hand for Jessica to shake. 'And I'm telling you, with these girls' track-record, you may just live to regret it.'

KATHERINE & HENRY

Katherine & Henry invite you
to their wedding at

St Mary's Church

And for their wedding breakfast at

The Westway Hotel, Acton

❦

Saturday, 8 September

29

There's something about the urban church setting and
the eight of us all huddled on and around the bench in
the graveyard that makes me feel as if I've been propelled
into the scene before Charles's wedding. Except I guess
if my life was following the same course as Charles's it
would be me getting married, not Kat. But there is the
similarity of her marrying someone I'm not that sure
about, in the same way Charles decided to marry Duckface, much to Fiona's despair. Though I can't pretend
despair is what I'm feeling, just a mild disappointment
that my best friend has chosen someone who doesn't
seem to ignite much passion in her.

'A church wedding, at last!' says Aunt Jane, pouring
hot tea from a flask. She looks spectacularly bright today
in a jade-green kaftan dress and wide-brimmed straw
hat.

'Yes, it does seem odd that we've come through so
many weddings this summer without one,' I say, brushing a crumb of pain au chocolat off the grey silk of my
bridesmaid's dress.

'I'm just can't believe we've made it to wedding
number four!' says Lizzie, who's looking lovely in an

empire-line bridesmaid's dress with a black ribbon under her growing bust. She's really begun to throw herself into preparing for the baby. Not a day goes by where she isn't online looking for some piece of paraphernalia or other, reading about the birth or considering colour schemes for the nursery. She's like a woman possessed. 'It's a dream come true, almost . . .' she says, glancing to where Simon and I are sitting propped up against a gravestone.

'You've not to expect wedding number five anytime soon,' says Simon. 'Bea's made me promise: no more proposals until next year, at least!'

'Quite right, no need to rush,' says Aunt Jane, and I know exactly what she's thinking – don't do it at all! But, I've been thinking, maybe a traditional marriage and life with Simon wouldn't be so bad. I wouldn't have to work so I'd have plenty of time to concentrate on my jewellery and to travel, and I'm sure Simon would help me set up a little business. Still, it's not what Aunt Jane wants for me, despite having apologised for being so harsh.

'Four weddings are definitely enough for one summer,' says Hannah.

'I don't know,' says Remy, balanced on the arm of the bench, next to Hannah in her grey silk maxi-dress. 'I have loved this summer and all the love we've shared. It would be good to have another.'

'How about Jessica and Dave?' I say, indicating to the church gates, where the two of them are arriving, looking very sweet together for a couple who only met ten days ago. 'I'm feeling quite proud of my match-making skills.'

'Don't try to dodge the topic of you and Simon,' says Lizzie. 'We all want it to happen.'

'Simon's going to be far too busy to even think about a wedding,' I say.

'Why so?' asks Tom, his arm around Aunt Jane, supping his tea.

'He's taking over from Sir Hugo as CEO!' I say, in a sort of proud-spouse sort of way, which makes me feel at odds with myself, and the ideas I've been churning over.

'Congratulations!' says Hannah.

'Very impressive,' says Aunt Jane, somewhat dry in her delivery.

'Congrats, man.' Jack bumps fists with Simon, which makes Simon look ridiculously awkward and more old-fashioned than ever.

'It's not that impressive,' says Simon. 'My father's had enough. The stress of it all is making him tired and forgetful. I was always going to take over, it's just come a little earlier than planned.'

'But it's still a big deal,' I say, trying to show my support, even though I have serious reservations about Simon being CEO and how he'll be even more married to his work, not to mention my concerns about whether I'll have a job after Sir Hugo retires.

'When does your tour start, Jack?' asks Simon, deflecting the attention away from himself, and us, which is a relief.

'Next month,' he says, pulling Lizzie a little closer.

'You're leaving when your wife will be five months pregnant?' asks Aunt Jane, clearly horrified.

'He's not leaving me; I'm going with him.'

Lizzie's news leaves us all in suspended animation for a moment.

'You're going on tour?' asks Hannah, once she's computed what Lizzie has said. 'When was this decided?'

'Last week,' shrugs Lizzie, as if the idea of touring America on a cramped, smelly tour bus with a baby due in four months was the most normal thing in the world.

'Have you completely lost your mind?'

'Lizzie's up for the adventure,' says Jack, supportively. 'We're really excited.'

'But what if you go into labour when you're out there?' asks Hannah, still incredulous.

'They do have hospitals in America,' says Lizzie, with a laugh. 'And management is fine about paying the extra cost for insurance.'

'I think it's a brilliant idea,' I say, happy to see Lizzie and Jack so tight again after their little hiccup. 'Now is definitely the time for taking a risk, and daring to dream. When the kid is older you won't be so free to move around as you are now.'

'Hear, hear,' says Tom. 'Life is meant to be lived.'

'Absolutely,' says Remy, raising her cup of tea and we all join her, lifting our plastic cups to Lizzie and Jack.

'Live life now,' I say to Lizzie with a fond smile.

'Live life now,' says everyone else, Jack leaning in to Lizzie, the two of them sharing a kiss.

As we're focused on Jack and Lizzie, a car pulls up

outside the church and Henry and his brother climb out, joking and slapping each other on the back. Henry looks as if he's still pissed from his stag-do last night.

'Gosh, is it that time already,' I say, getting up, and wiping down my skirt of crumbs. 'Time we got this show on the road.'

Kat decided to go fairly minimal on the flowers, which felt like a mistake in such a large church, but by the time the guests have arrived, and the colour of their outfits and the murmur of their excitement is filling the space, it no longer looks so bare and uninviting.

'Everything's in order,' says Hannah, having helped to seat the final elderly guest. 'Now we just need the bride.'

'She'll be here,' I say, waiting by the entrance, able to see both the church gate and where Henry is sitting at the front. He keeps glancing furtively in my direction.

'Let's hope so.'

'Everyone knows Kat's not a great timekeeper.'

Hannah checks her watch. 'She's already ten minutes late.'

'Which is nothing for Kat,' I say, trying to pull off jokey but unable to hide a note of concern.

'Should we call her?'

'Give her five more minutes,' I say. 'Go tell Henry the car was delayed, or something that helps him relax. He looks petrified.'

I pace the vestibule, out of sight of Henry, wondering where she might be. *Traffic could be bad*, I tell myself. *She could have a nervous tummy. Or maybe she's just doing plain old-fashioned late*. But whatever I come up with, nothing abates the anxiety in my stomach that something is up.

When her car eventually arrives outside the church, the congregation is beginning to get restless, the quiet excited murmur having changed to louder, nervous chatter. Rather than signal to Lizzie and Hannah that she's arrived I nip down to meet her, to check that she's okay.

'What's going on?' I ask, after her parents have got out of the car and headed inside, looking frostier than anyone might expect parents-of-the-bride to look.

'Everything's fine.' She climbs out of the car, carrying off her wide-legged, bridal jumpsuit in white silk as only Kat can.

'Where's your bouquet?'

'Didn't bring it.'

'Why not?'

She shoves a hand into a pocket of her jumpsuit and walks towards the entrance. 'It felt too fussy.'

'Okay,' I say, not wanting to make a thing of it, hurrying to keep up with her. In fairness, she does look stunning. The halter neck shows her sinewy arms to full effect and the low V displays just enough of her toned stomach without being risqué. If I had a body like Kat's, I wouldn't want to hide it behind a bunch of flowers either.

She's just about to go inside when we hear another car draw up and we both turn to see Sebastian getting out of a taxi. I'm surprised to see he's been invited and wonder if Henry knows. He jogs towards us, holding on to his top hat.

'God,' he says, panting slightly. 'I thought *I* was late!'

Kat laughs, her face lighting up.

'*Bonne chance*!' he says, briefly ducking in to kiss her on the cheek. Then he slows, admiring her. 'You look incredible.'

Kat blushes lightly. 'Thank you.'

'You are welcome.'

Sebastian lingers for just a moment, the two of them holding eye contact.

'It is time, *non*?' he says.

'Yes,' she agrees, almost tentatively. He kisses her once more and heads in.

'Are you ready?' I ask, once Sebastian is out of sight.

'Guess so,' she says, which isn't quite the emphatic response I was looking for.

She's about to step inside the church when I reach out and grab her by the wrist. 'Wait.'

'What?' she asks, her voice catching just a little.

'Kat, I've known you since we were four years old. I know when something's not right. What's going on? Tell me.'

She shakes her wrist free of my hand, her eyes narrowed. 'It's nothing. Come on. I'm late enough.'

Before I have the chance to say anything more the organist has begun to play, and Lizzie and Hannah are processing down the aisle in front of Kat, me following on behind. I admire my friend walking down the aisle alone, a modern woman in her statement 'dress', not wanting the fuss of flowers or her father's arm. I wonder when the moment will come in my life where I have that much inner confidence.

'Why the delay?' whispers Aunt Jane, when Kat has reached the front and I've taken my seat.

'I don't know,' I say, glancing towards where Sebastian is seated. 'But intuition tells me something isn't right.'

'Welcome to St Mary's on this glorious day,' says the vicar, my mind wandering as she offers her thoughts on God's will for marriage. At this point during Lizzie's wedding I remember her and Jack being utterly trans-fixed on each other, the same was true of Aunt Jane and Tom, and Hannah was busy proclaiming her undivided love for Remy. It worries me that Kat has barely glanced at Henry since arriving at his side, seemingly more inter-ested in the tiles on the floor than in her husband-to-be.

'Let us turn to the order of service and sing "All Things Bright and Beautiful".'

As the organist opens with the first four bars, Aunt Jane stage-whispers, 'Not the most original of hymns.'

'Kat hasn't been invested in the detail. It's all a bit of a formality.'

Aunt Jane locks on to Kat's outfit. 'That's clear to see.'

I nudge her disapprovingly. 'I love the jumpsuit; she looks beautiful.'

'Proof that beauty is definitely in the eye of the beholder.'

I shake my head and sing along to the rest of the hymn,

watching Kat and Henry, standing shoulder by shoulder but still managing to look a mile apart.

'We come now to the part of the ceremony where I must ask if anyone knows of any lawful impediment as to why these two people may not be joined in matrimony,' says the vicar.

I'm so busy watching Kat and Henry that it escapes my attention that Aunt Jane has reached into her handbag and pulled out a gavel, which she is now banging on the pew.

Gasps of shock fill the church, the vicar scans the congregation to see where the sound is coming from, and Kat and Henry both turn to face their families and friends. Before I can stop her, Aunt Jane has her hand in the air waving at the vicar.

'Do you have something you'd like to say?' the vicar asks Aunt Jane.

Kat glares at me furiously. I shake my head wildly, trying to tell her that this is all Jane; I haven't put her up to this.

'I don't believe the bride wishes to marry this man,' says Aunt Jane, bold as brass.

'Aunt Jane,' I hiss, the eyes of every member of the congregation on us.

'And what makes you believe that?' asks the vicar, who is shaking like a leaf. It's hard to imagine that she's dealt with something like this before.

And that's when it happens, our very own *Four Weddings* moment, when Aunt Jane says, 'Because I suspect the bride doesn't love the groom.'

'Is this true, Kat?' asks the vicar.

For a moment, I think she's going to say, 'Of course I do, don't be so ridiculous' but she doesn't. Instead she looks, not at Henry, but straight at Sebastian, whom Henry clocks for the first time, and says, 'I think she might be right.'

After that the script alters, and the moment where everything feels frozen in time rapidly accelerates and suddenly Henry is running down the aisle, grabbing hold of Sebastian's lapels with his fist held back.

Then he hits him, hard.

So hard that the next thing I know Sebastian is lying, flat on his back, passed out on the floor.

30

'Jesus, Henry!' yells Kat, the vicar flinching. Kat races towards them, immediately crouching next to Sebastian's head. 'What's the matter with you?' she shouts at Henry.

'What's the matter with me?!' Henry shouts back, his voice ricocheting off the rafters. 'You're the one who slept with him!'

Oh Kat, didn't I say telling Henry about Seb was a bad idea?

'While we were on a break!' she spits, getting up. Kat's poor mother sinks into her pew in despair. 'At least I haven't hidden anything from you.'

'Meaning?'

'Meaning, how many times did you sleep with Lucille?'

Henry flounders, unable to come up with an answer.

Kat releases a sigh of contempt. 'So, it *was* more than once?' she says, more quietly now, resigned to her fate. 'I figured as much when you sent me a message last night that was clearly intended for her.'

'No, I, uh—' Henry burbles, trying helplessly to fudge a way out. But he can't, the truth is out at last and there's no taking it back, particularly in a house of God.

'I can't believe I didn't realise sooner. I can't believe I

was prepared to forgive you for a one-night stand, when you'd been cheating for . . .' she stops, unable to finish. 'For how long?'

He looks at his shoes, aware no doubt that the entire congregation is now looking at him, each one of them waiting for his answer.

'It's not important,' he mutters.

'It bloody well is important,' I blurt. Aunt Jane takes hold of my wrist, tightly, urging me to control myself, which seems rich given what she's just done. Simon places a placating hand on my shoulder which I shake off.

Kat stares at Henry, her brow raised, waiting for an answer.

'Almost a year,' he says, and a quiet groan of 'there's no coming back from that' reverberates round the church.

'Fine,' says Kat, standing up, unyielding in her stance. 'Let's chalk this up as a near miss, shall we? You get on with your life, I'll get on with mine.'

'Come on, Kat, we can—'

'No. I don't want to hear it. I'm done. Let's call it quits while we still have an ounce of respect left for each other.'

'She's quite right,' says Aunt Jane, her voice cutting over the melee. 'Better to walk away while you still like each other.'

'I'm not sure we need *your* opinion,' says Henry, scathing in his delivery.

Aunt Jane shrugs. 'Well, whether you like it or not, young man, I'm offering it. Best you run along, before all this shock turns to anger and you find yourself lynched.'

'She's right,' says Kat, when Henry turns to her for backup. 'It's best you go.'

Henry's about to put up a fight when his brother steps in to guide him away.

'Let's go,' he says, leading Henry down the aisle, past friends and family members, who no longer know quite where to look.

With Henry gone, I go to Kat, trying to put an arm around her, but she's so full of fiery indignation that I quickly let go. She squats down beside Seb, who is beginning to groan on the floor.

'I'm sorry,' he whispers, raising a hand to his face to assess the damage.

'Don't be. You and Aunt Jane did me the biggest favour of my life.'

Slowly, Seb sits up, clutching his jaw. 'Let me take you away from here.'

'No, I have to stay, pick up the pieces.' She glances towards her parents and Henry's, who are huddled together, no doubt trying to figure out what to do next.

'That's what we're here for,' I say, Hannah and Lizzie joining me on either side, our arms wrapped around each other. 'You go with Sebastian. We'll take care of the rest.'

'Are you sure?' Kat asks, helping Seb up.

'Of course,' I say. 'Leave it to us.'

'I expect the "reception" will feel more like a wake,' says Hannah, when we're finishing up at the church and the congregation has left.

Kat's choice of a 'one-stop shop' wedding venue proved pretty useful in the end. A single call to Sue and everything was taken care of. Kat and Henry's parents decided it wasn't good form to send their guests back home without feeding them, so a few stragglers have wound their way over to the hotel for a non-wedding breakfast.

'It's a good place for a more sombre occasion,' I say, ambling outside, uncertain what to do next. As bridesmaid, I should probably be at the reception, but something tells me nobody's going to be too concerned about customs and protocols considering what's just happened.

'I can safely say that I didn't see any of that coming,' says Simon, as we park ourselves on and around the same bench as earlier.

'I can't figure out who to feel most sorry for,' says Jack.

'What do you mean?' asks Lizzie, outraged by his comment. 'Henry doesn't deserve any sympathy. He's a bare-faced lying shit!'

'Steady, Liz,' I say, all of us astonished by her language.

'Well it's true!'

Baby hormones have certainly made her less shy about speaking her mind, that's for certain.

'Kat knew about the girl at work. And Henry knew about Sebastian,' I say.

'Henry cheated on Kat and only confessed when she confronted him about the rumour. *And* he lied through his teeth about how long it went on. Kat didn't cheat on Henry, they were separated.'

'She has a point, Bea,' says Hannah.

'Still,' says Jack. 'He really did want to marry Kat.'

'How can you be so sure?' asks Lizzie, still incredulous at her husband. 'He's proven himself a liar.'

'I know the guy,' says Jack. 'And yes, he's kind of proud and a bit of a misogynist but underneath it all, I really believe he loves Kat.'

'Well, he's got a fucking funny way of showing it,' says Lizzie.

'I agree with Jack,' says Simon.

'What do you mean?' I ask, bewildered by this outpouring of misplaced male sympathy.

'I think he does love Kat, and I also think it's incredibly bad form to jilt someone at the altar.'

'You can't take someone's side based on what Debrett's might have to say about it,' I say, irritated by his stuffiness.

How much more insufferable will he be when he's the CEO of his father's family business?

'You can all blame me,' says Aunt Jane. 'I acted on instinct, and I always say, instincts get you into trouble.'

'No one should be blaming anyone,' I say. 'If Kat hadn't found out today she would have found out after they were married. Better to call it off now than to go through an expensive divorce.'

'Better the parents pick up today's bill than Kat and Henry pay for the dissolution,' quips Hannah, causing a nervous ripple of laughter.

'I feel bad that my Four Weddings scheme has brought all of this about,' says Lizzie. 'It caused you and Simon to break up too. I should have kept my mouth shut.'

'Rubbish! Kat was engaged before you mentioned the idea; Henry's behaviour was always going to come out in the wash. And as for Simon and me, I needed some time to figure out what I wanted. It's all worked out for the best.'

I think.

'And besides,' says Aunt Jane. 'I wouldn't rule out another wedding one day. I'm convinced Kat and Sebastian are right for each other.'

'Or maybe . . .' says Hannah, looking towards the church gates.

'Is that who I think it is?' asks Lizzie, squinting against the sunlight.

'Who is that?' asks Simon.

'It's Leo,' I say, reining in my excitement, because what I really want to do is to scream, really yell out my delight! But instead, I stop myself, not only from screaming but also from rushing towards him and wrapping myself around him, just as Scarlett did when Chester rocked up unannounced to Charles's wedding. It takes every inch of my self-restraint to control myself.

'Hi,' I say, getting up off the grass to greet him, my heart feeling as if it's trying to break through my ribs.

'Bea,' he says, his arms outreached, ready to meet me with a generous hug. My slightly stiff body language, feeling Simon watching me from behind, tells him it's not the right time, and he kisses me awkwardly on the cheek instead.

'Did I make it in time?' he asks, glancing over my shoulder at the small gathering on the bench, the church door closed behind them with no sign of the bride or groom.

'Things didn't go exactly to plan,' says Hannah.

'How come?'

'Aunt Jane's gavel got Henry in trouble,' says Lizzie, who's got up to give him a hug.

Leo squints, none the wiser. 'Kat found out at the altar that Henry's been cheating on her for a long time. And Henry found out that Kat has feelings for Sebastian,' I explain.

'The French guy?'

'Exactly.'

'I thought he was your date—'

Simon clears his throat. 'I think you'll find that's me,' he says, eyeing Leo suspiciously from his place on the ground.

'Simon, this is Leo. Leo, Simon.'

Simon gets up and stands, territorially beside me. 'How do you do?' he says, slightly overblown in his delivery.

'Nice to meet you,' Leo replies, not making the connection about who Simon is. 'Mind if I grab a quiet word with Bea?'

'Not at all,' Simon replies, even though it's patently obvious that he does.

Leo takes me to a corner of the graveyard, a safe distance from the others.

'How are you?' he asks, taking hold of my hands. He

looks at me as if he's just found water after days in the desert, a sense of relief, or release, pouring out of him.

'I'm a bit shell-shocked, if I'm honest. Kat jilting Henry, and now you turning up out of the blue . . . it's all a bit much. I didn't realise Kat had invited you.'

'She didn't.'

'Then why are you here?'

He squeezes my hands a little tighter. 'I ended things with Brit.'

'Wow,' I say, staggered by the news. 'That's big.'

'She realised, in the end, that she was clinging to the past; she knows it's for the best, even if it is hard.' He brushes his hand lightly round my face, drinking in every detail of it. 'You told me to figure out what my heart wanted, and I did: it wants you.'

I nod slowly, mesmerised by every inch of him, my heart wanting to burst with delight but my head tempering it.

'And I was kind of hoping you might want the same,' he says, when I've failed to say anything.

'Wow.' I sit down on the grass before my legs give out beneath me.

'You said that,' he says, with a laugh, joining me on the ground.

'Right, yes, I guess I did. Um . . .' I bite my lip, and glance towards my friends, and Simon in particular.

Leo follows my line of sight. 'Is there something I don't know?'

I exhale long and slow then tell him, 'Do you remember I told you about turning down a proposal?'

'Sure.'

I indicate towards Simon.

'That's the proposal guy?' he asks, a hint of disbelief in his voice. I try to see Simon, all stiff and British and upper class, through Leo's eyes, and how odd it must seem to him, the two of us together.

I hesitate before answering, and when I do I'm surprised just how loaded my voice is with regret. 'Yes.'

Then slowly he says, 'You're back together, aren't you?'

I wince. 'Our timing isn't great, is it?' I say, hoping to sound light, when really I feel totally weighed down.

'You can say that again.'

We sit quietly for a moment, both uncertain what to say, every possible scenario and outcome I can imagine bombarding my mind.

'There is one other thing I wanted to tell you,' he says.

'What's that?' I ask, not sure if I can handle another bombshell.

'I got my first tour.' His eyes can't conceal his delight.

'You did?'

'With Carburetor. Their management asked me to do the US tour with them.'

'Oh, that's amazing, Leo. Congratulations! You know Lizzie is going along?'

'Right, I did hear that, and I was thinking,' he pauses, his eyes flitting over mine. 'Would you like to come too?'

It takes a moment for the question to sink in and then,

once it has, my mind fills up with thoughts of Hillary Bentham and her wanting me to travel to develop my collection, and suddenly there seems to be creative potential everywhere and freedom and, most important of all, someone who's passionate about me and who I'm passionate about in return. But then Simon's laugh filters over from where they're sitting, and I'm reminded that I've responsibilities here – Simon, my job, Aunt Jane, Kat, even Jessica – and I know I can't do it, even if I might be beginning to believe in 'the one'.

Leo must see the decision in my eyes because before I can respond he chuckles wryly and gets up. 'Guess it's been a wasted trip then.'

'I guess,' I say, standing. 'I've always been a believer in things happening at the right time. Maybe now just isn't our time.'

'Maybe not,' he says, his head low, his eyes raised hopefully towards me.

I place a hand lightly on his shoulder and kiss his cheek. 'Goodbye, Leo.'

'Goodbye, Bea,' he replies, his voice breaking.

As he turns to go, Aunt Jane gets up, meeting me in the middle of the graveyard.

'What's happening?' she asks, watching Leo heading off.

'He broke up with his girlfriend.'

'So why is he leaving?'

'I told him I'm with Simon.'

'Why?'

'Because I am. And besides, Leo's going off on tour. I

can't just drop all my responsibilities to be with him on a whim.'

'Responsibilities?' she questions.

'Sure, I've Simon, work, and you. Kat's going to need my support and I've Jessica to think about too.'

Aunt Jane eyes me as if I've lost my marbles. 'Firstly, I have Tom, I am *not* your responsibility. Secondly, you don't care about your job, it's not what you want, and with Sir Hugo retiring it's on the line anyway. I'm not even going to waste my time on Kat because, as is patently evident after today, she's perfectly capable of looking after herself. And as for Jessica . . .' She dispels the thought with a wave of the hand but as she does I remember Jessica saying how much she loved babies, and then Eva with baby Whitney pop into my mind . . . could they be the perfect flatmates, if Eva hasn't found a place already? 'And Simon? Really?' She looks at me in a lovingly aggressive way. 'Beatrice, don't settle. You didn't want Kat to do so, so why would you do it yourself? You've just watched your best friend make the right decision at the very hardest time; don't let that go to waste.'

'What do you mean?'

'I mean, if Kat can let go of Henry at the altar you can certainly let go of Simon now, before you really break his heart. Harness Kat's inner strength.'

I'm loath to admit it but I know she has a point, and something, a feeling I can't identify, begins to swell inside of me.

'Is your loyalty to Simon, and his secure, sensible

ways, really worth letting go of the one person you have a real connection with, the one person you're whole-heartedly in love with?'

'I'm not certain,' I say, my head beginning to pound. 'The only thing I know for sure is that I want to focus on my career. Just like you did.'

'But you have the choice to have both, Bea. I didn't. You can have your career and your man – and he'll only help develop your work, all that travelling, new inspiration . . .Will Simon do that for you?'

'Simon would be able to help in other ways, even if he wouldn't be able to come with me.'

'And is travelling alone something you want? Wouldn't you rather travel with someone you're crazy about, someone you could have great adventures with? Someone who inspires you?'

I don't reply, because that feeling, an energy, is beginning to burst through me, like a butterfly breaking free of its cocoon.

'I can't tell you what to do, Beatrice. But I can reiterate some advice. The heart wants what it wants. Don't be afraid of that, regardless of timing.'

And Leo's heart wants me.

'Didn't you tell Lizzie – now is the time to take risks, to dare to dream?'

I nod.

Aunt Jane reaches out and takes my hand. 'You must heed your own advice, Bea. And for what it's worth, I believe *the one* does exist. Surely Tom and I are evidence of that. Don't do what I did, don't let him go. If you

306

do, you run the risk of missing many years of happiness.'

It's then that the feeling takes over, and my thoughts are crystal clear. I've been hanging on to the familiar, the comfortable, too afraid of making the same mistake as my mother, to follow my heart. And before Aunt Jane can say anything else I'm running out of the graveyard and calling after Leo.

'Leo,' I shout, looking up and down the road.

Unable to see him I impulsively decide on the direction of the Tube station.

'Run, girl!' Aunt Jane calls from the church gate, causing me to smile gleefully, the wind on my face, literally racing to catch my dream.

'Excuse me,' I say, already breathless. Charles running after Carrie along the Southbank ready to declare his love to her flashes into my mind. 'Coming through!'

I'm not oblivious to the odd looks I'm getting but I don't care. All I care about is finding Leo and telling him, yes! Let's give things a go. Live life now!

By the time I get to the Tube I'm out of breath, I have a stitch in my side and there's no sign of Leo anywhere.

'You all right, love?' asks the station attendant.

I shake my head, unable to speak, a rising sensation in my throat that makes me think I might vomit.

'I was just looking for someone,' I eventually manage to say, turning in circles to find him. 'But I guess it's not meant to be.'

'What's not meant to be?'

At first I think it's the underground bloke again, my vision blurred from turning, but when I settle, and my

307

sight becomes clearer, I see exactly who it is. It's Leo.

'Leo . . .' I say, almost faint with relief – or perhaps just shortness of breath.

'Are you okay?' he asks.

I smile through my rapid breathing. 'I will be. Just . . . give me a minute.'

'Were you looking for me?' he asks, once my breath has returned to normal.

Gazing deep into his eyes I find myself saying, 'I think I've been looking for you all my life.' And I pray it doesn't sound as chronically cheesy as Andie MacDowell saying, 'Is it raining, I hadn't noticed.'

He raises his hand to my cheek and rubs it tenderly, staring intently into my eyes.

'For the first time in my life I realise I totally and utterly love one person, and it isn't Brit . . .'

'Is it the person standing opposite you now, not in the pouring rain?' I ask, half laughing, half crying.

'The truth is, Bea,' he says. 'I think I've loved you from the first second we met.'

Does he realise he's just quoted Charles to me?

'And I you.'

'So, will you come with me on tour? Travel for a bit, spend some time together. Be a bit spontaneous, like we both want to be, nothing and no one standing in our way?'

'I will,' I say, smiling broadly, having my very own Andie MacDowell, 'I do' moment. It's more impulsive than I would usually be, committing to Leo before I've broken the news to Simon, or handed in my notice, but there's something about Leo that makes me want to throw caution to the wind and live the life I'm capable of. 'But promise me one thing.'

'What?'

'No proposals. No talk of a wedding. Just you and me, without ties.'

'Deal,' he says, bending down until his lips are just fluttering against mine. 'Because, in the words of David Cassidy . . .'

And then he's kissing me, in a way that makes me never want to come up for air, and I know, at last, whether the timing is right or not, that I've definitely found 'the one'.

Acknowledgements

Writing this book was such a treat, one made possible by a squad of strong, skilled women, all of whom I admire greatly. To my agent, Juliet Pickering, thank you for always being my cheerleader, even when on maternity leave! To Hattie Grunewald, thank you for looking after me in Juliet's absence, you've been such a trooper.

At Orion I owe a huge thanks to Harriet Bourton. Thank you, Harriet, for all the opportunities you've brought my way over the last year. And, of course, to the mighty Olivia Barber, without whom this novel would not exist. Thank you, Olivia for your unbelievable commitment, general brilliance, encouragement and good humour – you're the best. To Justine Taylor, copy editor extraordinaire, it makes me feel safe just knowing you're there at the end of it all.

And at home, team Brown and Wood, for all you do, thank you.

One summer . . . One dream . . . One chance to make it happen.

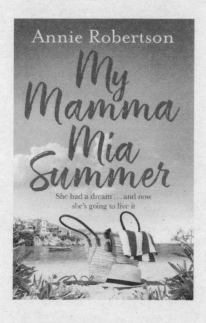

Laurel hasn't taken a risk her whole life. Now as summer dawns, she's going to do something that nobody expects of her. Laurel turns to her ABBA albums and her favourite film, *Mamma Mia!* She grabs her passport, dons her dungarees, and jets off to Skopelos for her own Meryl-inspired adventure ...

Laurel books into the faded but charming Villa Athena and befriends its eccentric owner. As she explores the island's famous sights, Laurel finds herself feeling strangely at home. So should she return to her life in London, or could this be where she truly belongs?

This summer dust off your passport, pack your best dancing shoes, and escape to Greece on your own Mamma Mia *adventure!*